↑UPLOAD

COLLIN TOBIN

Upload
A Red Adept Publishing Book

Red Adept Publishing, LLC
104 Bugenfield Court
Garner, NC 27529
http://RedAdeptPublishing.com/

First Print Edition: December 2012

DEDICATION

To my wife, Gina, for her love, support, and utter selflessness in allowing me to do this.

AUTHOR'S NOTE

I WANT TO ACKNOWLEDGE MY ENTIRE family for their ceaseless support throughout this exciting process. My wife, Gina, and my two daughters, Abby and Rachel, patiently suffered several nights and weekends of my absence or distraction, and I'm eternally grateful to them. Thanks to my brother, Kevin, and sister, Celina, for their very early support of very rough drafts. And finally to my father, who has always supported me in all that I've done, and to my mother, who's no longer with us, but of course knew and approved of this undertaking from the very beginning.

I've also reached out and found great support and feedback from my close friends Thor and Rob.

Along the way, I've met an incredible community of hard working and collaborative writers, and especially want to call out early beta readers and new friends: Katie, Cara, and Sharda. Lastly, I want to sincerely thank Lynn and her wonderful staff at Red Adept Publishing who helped me shape and mold this book into what it is today.

CHAPTER I

JAY

JAY COULD FEEL THE PIMPLE there, just below his right cheekbone. He studied the growth in his rearview mirror. *Jesus Christ, that pimple has aspirations.* He could even feel it with his tongue along the inner lining of his cheek. He could nearly bite down on it as if it were a jawbreaker he had mismanaged and somehow allowed to slip into the lining of his flesh.

His mother would have taken one look and rushed him to the dermatologist. His father wouldn't even notice. Dad no longer noticed a lot of things since Mom's death, like Jay returning home late into the early morning hours, cutting class, or even the occasional traces of cigarette smoke. No matter how much air freshener he sprayed, the smell he picked up at raves or parties still clung to his clothes. Jay stopped at a traffic light and was about to flick his apple core out the window when a lime-green VW Bug pulled up alongside his car. Two blond girls—shiny tops, candy-apple lip gloss, glittered, tanned faces—glanced over at him. They seemed a bit older. College-aged, he guessed. He was grateful his profile was his non-boil side. He tried to hold their gazes, but they turned away with prim smiles.

Jay took one more bite of his apple just as the light turned green. The VW jumped ahead, and he tossed the apple core through the dissipating cloud of their exhaust smoke and into the roadside ditch. He wasn't out cruising for chicks anyway. He was after something at least as interesting, maybe even more so.

He glanced over at the passenger seat. A Garmin Nüvi GPS lay to the right of his laptop. Between them, an apparatus of circuit boards and multicolored wires strung the two together. The mass of equipment chattered as he worked his car around a rotary to head back down VFW Parkway. He needed to go west to finish his nightly scouring for open or hackable Wi-Fi hot spots.

For the past few nights, he'd experimented and explored closer to Boston, and he had noticed a trend—a strange uptick of wireless signals the equipment had failed to properly recognize. He and his computer-genius friend, Bennie, had altered the detection logic to weed out those special signals and identify them.

As he passed what looked to be a darkened sports field complex in Cambridge, the laptop beeped three times. *A hit!* He immediately pulled over into the breakdown lane. He glanced at the dashboard clock: 9:25. He had promised to meet Bennie by ten o'clock. He looked back at the laptop. The signal was weak, but strong enough for the detection scripts to reroute the GPS and calculate a route along the park to get him as close to the signal as possible.

Jay cruised slowly along the perimeter of the park. He turned into a gravel parking lot, made his way to the far corner, and parked alongside the dim shape of a single-story beige building—the closest the GPS could get him to the source of the signal. He cut the engine and turned again toward the laptop. He executed a series of scripts to see if he could isolate the wireless signal. Seconds later, the report came back, raining white text down the black screen.

He studied the output. The connection had almost no download capability beyond one-half kilobyte per second, well below anything useful and nothing he would want to report to fellow wardrivers. But the upload speed was through the roof. With a caress of his fingers across the keyboard, he attempted to detect the content type of the upload.

As he worked, he mumbled, "No text..." Tap-tap-tap. "No images..." Tap. Lip bite. Tap-tap-tap. "Video?" He tried to peek into the uploaded stream, but the buffer length was too short.

Holy shit! Live video. He wouldn't be able to view the live stream without knowing more. With quick keystrokes, he siphoned the stream's bytes to his hard drive, saving a two-megabyte chunk. He then ran the stored output through a series of video decoders on his laptop. In under a minute, a video player popped up in a ready state. The status bar at the bottom of the frame noted twenty-one seconds of video in the queue.

The car engine ticked as it cooled. He clicked play. Large solid blocks of black, gray, and white skated across the laptop screen. No sound accompanied the video. As he moved his finger across the touchpad to close the player, a large amorphous mass leapt across the screen. Spots appeared in the upper left corner of the frame like irregularly placed pinholes or blown pixels, except for one distinctly straight line of three dots descending at an angle. *Orion's Belt? They were stars. Why would someone point a low-resolution camera at the sky?*

The car became warmer from the equipment. He cracked his window without taking his eyes from the screen. The video blurred again, and long black lines occupied a full third of the right half of the screen. The images looked like dark silhouettes of grass blades in front of a dull hint of some kind of skewed grid, as if the several segments of video were stitched together incorrectly, creating a diamond-shaped pattern.

3

Chain-link fence. Just beyond the chain-link fence, the nose of Jay's poorly hidden car peeked out.

A terrified scream cut through the darkness.

He jerked in his seat. *What the hell?*

He slapped his laptop shut and reflexively reached toward the ignition, but stopped before turning the key. His old car took at least three attempts to start, and he didn't want to be noticed. But how could he consider leaving? He couldn't bear to imagine his mother being in similar distress when she died, her calls going unheard—or worse, actually heard, but unanswered.

He punched the button on the glove compartment and grabbed his mini-camcorder, which he kept handy to include either video clips or still shots of the Wi-Fi spots. Dropping the camera into the front pouch of his windbreaker, he slipped out of his car. Crouched, he gently pushed the car door closed with his right shoulder. He moved up to the front quarter panel, trailing his fingertips along the engine-warmed steel.

He peered into the dark. All clear. He darted in the general direction of two single-story cinder block buildings opposite a pair of tennis courts, which were separated by a narrow, grassy gully. His legs felt weak with excitement. He stayed low as he moved toward the buildings, keeping an eye on the outer windscreens of the tennis courts, where the wireless signal seemed to originate. One structure was a closed-up snack stand, and the other looked to be a sports equipment shed. He slipped into the dark shadows of the narrow alley between them and listened, but all he heard was the pulse of his own heartbeat in his ears.

Then, he heard the voice again. Female. She made a sound that meant to be a scream, high-pitched, but stifled. It had come from the area between the tennis courts. A grunt followed—male—then a curse from the same male. Another high-pitched scream was smothered.

With his vision adjusted to the dark, he could discern a bit more of the drainage ditch between the courts. The screams seemed to have come from the ditch—the same ditch where his equipment had detected the wireless signal. He inched forward, keeping his back against the snack stand wall, not daring to leave the safety of the alleyway. He picked his way through the torn vestiges of candy wrappers, red-and-white-striped popcorn boxes, and Styrofoam cups. From his new vantage point, he peered past a set of light poles and into the ditch.

He quieted his breathing and did his best to ignore the smell of thickly sweet decomposition from the dumpster behind him. The muffled screams came less frequently and seemed weaker. He pulled out his camcorder and powered it on, cringing as it announced itself with a resonating ding. Adrenaline pumped through his body, making him feel light and energized. His hands shook as he unfolded the viewfinder on the side of the camera.

This is some major shit. He needed to act. Something horrible was happening, and he *had* to intervene. He had never so much as broken up a childhood fight. What was he supposed to do, face a murderer? A rapist? He thought of his mother and her brutal end, but shook his head to dispel the image.

No sign of a weapon of any sort. He could just rush the assailant and scare him off that way. Just as he braced himself to sprint toward the gully and scream at the top of his lungs, he spotted something to his left.

What he thought at first to be the passing lights of traffic in the distance slowly grew until the glow was a bright star in the corner of his eye. He turned and saw a dark vehicle charging across a nearby baseball diamond at breakneck speed. When the car flew over the pitcher's mound, the headlights lurched briefly, illuminating the alleyway to daylight clarity and spotlighting the lower half of Jay's body. He jumped back and shot another glance into the gully.

No movement.

The advancing vehicle looked to be a van, by its boxy

shape. The engine raced again, and the car went into an out-of-control skid. The vehicle crashed broadside into the fence at the far end of the courts. The chain-link absorbed the blow and reverberated with a metallic clatter. Visible from the side, the vehicle was not a van, Jay realized, but one of the newer-model Dodge wagons.

A dark shape popped up from the drainage ditch. The woman screamed, and the shape crouched again. Like a terminated connection, the scream cut off again.

Jay brought up his camera. The form stood again, then ran past the courts, toward the distant sports fields. The shape hurdled a squat fence, then disappeared into a shallow copse of dark trees.

Jay turned his camera to the Dodge. The driver's side of the car was blocked by buckled chain-link fence. Two men shouting in a thick foreign tongue spilled out of the passenger side. Both raced in Jay's direction. Backing deeper into the shadows, he banged his head on the lip of the dumpster at the back of the alley. Seconds later, the two men skidded to a stop at the mouth of the alley, only twenty feet away.

Hands shaking, Jay zoomed in with the camera. Both men wore dark jogging suits and held pistols. The shorter one also had a cigarette-pack-sized silver device with a bright-white screen that lit up his rough-hewn face. The guy turned and pointed toward the tennis courts. They ran to the dark crevasse.

The men crouched and whispered urgently. Long seconds passed.

Jay fought the urge to climb onto the dumpster and over the back wall to get to his car and haul ass. He couldn't be sure of much, but he was positive the men would soon search the immediate area. He had to get out of there.

With a hand on the side of the dumpster, he readied himself for an emergency exit. The men stood again and peered around. Both maintained a back-to-back posture as the tall one pulled out a cell phone.

A signature Nextel chirp was followed by the caller's indiscernible voice.

The tall one responded, "Nyet. I get it now." *Chirp.*

More chatter from the caller.

The tall one spoke next. Although the voices were still too muffled to understand, Jay noticed how the man's English came out deliberately, each word a heavy block hoisted into position.

To steady the camera, Jay knelt and rested against the cool cinder block wall. With the lens zoomed-in to the camera's full ability, he fingered on the night-vision filter. His hands still shook, but the video stabilizer compensated.

On the screen, the two men, as clear as if the darkness were merely a green dusk on an alien planet, crouched over a woman's body. Her torso was bare, with her shirt pulled up and her shorts down around her hips. Jay swallowed hard and looked at her face. She couldn't have been much older than he was.

The shorter man roughly pulled the shirt back into place, then touched her neck. *Is he checking for a pulse?* The tall one unzipped his jacket, slipped his hand inside, and came out with the same silver device Jay had spotted earlier. The moon glare glanced off the object and temporarily blinded Jay through the light-sensitive camera lens.

Afraid they would broaden their search area, Jay laid his camcorder on the dumpster and quietly hoisted himself onto the lid. Ready to launch himself over the wall, he looked back at the men. If they saw him, he would have the slight advantage of being over the wall before they gave chase.

The whoop of a siren lashed across the complex, and both men turned toward it. Red and blue strobe lights momentarily tinted their faces.

"Govno!" the taller one yelled.

The man shoved the device into the dead woman's face. A long second later, the device beeped. Seemingly satisfied, the men sprinted in the direction of their car.

Jay scrambled up the wall between the buildings and stood on his toes. Just above the flat roof of the adjoining building, he could see two police cars racing into the field from the entrance on the far side of the complex. He stuffed the camera into the front pouch of his jacket, launched himself over the wall, and ran toward his car.

CHAPTER 2

SATURDAY, 10:10 PM

BENNIE

BENNIE PUNCHED HIS STEERING WHEEL. He dreaded having to get out and knock, with the very likely prospect of coming eye-to-eye, or eye-to-waist really, with Jay's father. But no way was he going to let anything stop him from going to the rave, especially not after the humiliating hour he had spent in the Gap that afternoon. He had been trying to pick out a pair of junior-sized leather pants as a female store associate stalked him, refolding the same V-neck shirts over and over again while Bennie wheeled his chair through the racks of the kids' section.

"Can I help you?" she had finally asked, a tight smile on her lips.

He pointed at the faux-leather pants in his lap. "Not unless you're willing to help me try these on."

Even without trying on the pants, he had done well. He looked down and ran a hand down the slippery material covering his thigh. He rocked those pants. He looked up to study Jay's house again and sighed. Lights blazed from every room on the bottom floor. What the hell was going on in there?

"Screw it." He gulped the last of his Red Bull and tossed the empty can into the back of the van, where the middle row had been removed to make room for his wheelchair.

When he had received the modified van two years ago as a gift from his parents, he had challenged himself to see how fast he could exit from it. Twenty-four seconds was his record: four seconds to get out of his driver's seat and into his chair, five seconds to position his chair by the door, nine seconds for the sliding door to open and the ramp to unfold, and a final six seconds to roll down the ramp. But that was nothing when compared to the normal person's casual gesture of slipping out the door and slamming it behind them in three seconds.

Bennie's anger at Jay was tempered by the thought of how his friend would deliberately slow his exit from the passenger side, pretending to be busy with the seat belt, patting his jacket for his wallet, and fumbling for the door handle. If Jay was late, he probably had a good reason.

Bennie climbed out of the driver's seat and into his wheelchair. He operated the side door and ramp, and when the whirring of the hydraulics stopped, he trundled down to the pavement. He glanced at his watch. *A reasonable thirty seconds.* He worked the joystick of his wheelchair and headed toward the homemade ramp Jay's father had built to make their side deck accessible to Bennie.

Jay dreaded going to raves, using the excuse that he feared for Bennie's safety because Bennie crowd-surfed and got batted and bounced around like a beach ball at a baseball game. Any injury was worth the thrill, Bennie thought. Some wheelchair-bound people dreamed of running along the shore at sunrise, skipping rope, or bouncing a child on their knee. Bennie didn't have to dream. He had a friend who was willing to hoist him into a throng of mindless, drugged-out, energized ravers and then chase him down when he got tossed aside like so much river flotsam.

Take me to one rave a month. Was that too much to ask?

But of course, he didn't want to pressure Jay or do anything to push him away. Life, he knew, would naturally do that. With senior year on Jay's horizon, and college afterward, everything was in place to separate Jay and Bennie, probably, he feared, for life.

Bennie pushed the doorbell and waited. Before Jay's dad had gone all zombie-like after the death of Jay's mom, Bennie would have worried about ringing the doorbell so late. But Mr. Brooks had been occupying a different plane of existence for the last year. He had lost all capacity to grok complex abstract concepts such as space and time. Curfew had become a thing of the past for Jay.

No answer.

He leaned forward in his chair to press the doorbell once more, but the inner door swung open, startling him. Mr. Brooks stepped up to the screen door as if in challenge. His eyes darted to the left and right above Bennie's head as he scanned the street.

His focus seemed to settle on Bennie's van, then looked down. "Benjamin." His eyes were sunken like twin meteorites buried in the gray craters of his eye sockets. They jumped around wildly and began scanning the street again. "Where's Jay?"

Reluctant to raise any alarms, Bennie faked a laugh. "You know what, Mr. Brooks? I think we just crossed wires. I thought we were meeting here. Jay probably thought we were meeting at my place. I bet he's sitting out in front of my house."

Jay's father turned and looked back into the house. "I can call. Want me to call your house?"

Bennie flicked his chair control and edged forward. He craned his neck and looked past Mr. Brooks. He could see the entire kitchen, some of the dining room over the breakfast bar, part of the hallway, a glimpse of Jay's bedroom, and a slice of the family room in the distance. In the family room, a large pyramid of miscellaneous household objects took up

11

most of the floor, like a piece of modern art. As far as Bennie could see, every wall in the house was stripped bare. "No, no. Don't bother. I'll just head over to my house and catch him there. My mom's sleeping already, I think. I wouldn't want to wake her up."

Mr. Brooks nodded and started to close the door.

"Hey. Doing some art stuff?" Bennie asked.

"What?" Mr. Brooks turned back to the house. "Oh, no. Just, uh, just painting."

Bennie sniffed. Not a whiff of paint. "Well, don't worry about Jay tonight, and the... um, fumes. He's gonna spend the night over at my place, if that's okay?"

"More than okay. Bye, Bennie."

The door closed, but Jay's father just stood there, as if unplugged, still visible through the transparent white curtain and glazed glass of the door's window. Bennie pretended not to notice and worked his wheelchair around, back down the ramp. Mr. Brooks remained motionless in his peripheral vision. Bennie's scalp tingled.

Back inside the van, Bennie risked one more glimpse at the kitchen window. Mr. Brooks was still there, watching.

Bennie shifted the van into drive and muttered, "Freak."

CHAPTER 3

SATURDAY, 10:21 PM

STURGEON

STURGEON—NICKNAMED FOR HIS FISH-LIKE, LIPLESS, downturned mouth and the way his eyelids completely disappeared into his head when opened—sat at his desk, staring at the silhouette of his face in the dark screen of his laptop. His right knee bounced impatiently. He satisfied his agitation with the knowledge that the rest of his team could feel the floor tremors he was sending across the office like seismic activity before an earthquake.

Finally, the tall one bounded through the door with the shorter one in tow. Big and small. Sturgeon, being German himself, had the Russians teach him the words, and in lieu of their names, he called them as such: Bolshoy and Malenky.

"So did you get it?" Sturgeon leaned back in his chair. He tensed his brow without blinking to create the illusion of a nictating lens. He had practiced the expression in the mirror and enjoyed its effect on people.

Bolshoy dug in his pocket, pulled out the Hermes device, and placed it on the desk blotter. "Yes. We get it, but had rush. Police come."

Malenky, lethal only when behind a keyboard, stepped closer to the desk. "We'll need to call in for cover on this one."

Sturgeon picked up his smartphone and scrolled down his long list of medical contacts. He pressed a finger on a contact name. As the phone rang, he made a shooing gesture to the two Russians, who appeared relieved to exit his office.

After two rings, he heard, "Sir?"

Sturgeon connected the device to his laptop via USB cable. "Get down to Mount Auburn. Have one coming in you need to take care of. Sending you the specifics now." He hung up.

Another death. That made three this month. Not too bad, but he despised the risk of exposure. He hated chaos, events that required his attention, which pulled him up, as if he'd been baited, to drift closer to the surface. The heightened risk of exposure made him feel lightheaded and out of his element. He bounced his knee harder, sending shock waves out of his office, hoping they were strong enough to loosen everyone's bowels. He pulled out his desk drawer and grabbed a bottle of caffeine pills. He shook out three and crunched them in his mouth without water. He turned off the lights with a small remote and sighed in the temperature-controlled darkness, picturing himself gently drifting back to the bottom of the ocean, not to sleep, but to rest. He needed to gather his energy and ready himself to resurface again with a single swish of his strong tail.

When his head began to sizzle with a caffeinated buzz, he woke up his laptop with a shake of the mouse. The bright screen cast a frigid aqua-blue light across his desk. He double-clicked on a video player and selected one of his favorites.

The scene opened from the viewpoint of a motorcycle rider looking down at the swishing road. The chrome sides of the bike glinted as the rider darted through highway traffic. The driver worked the motorcycle like a needle pulling some invisible thread as he stitched into the air, lane to lane, at a hundred sixty feet per second. The cyclist looked back. Three police cruisers rushed him from behind, jockeying for position against a knot of panicked and confused drivers. The cruisers eased up, but quickly roared forward again, finding a fissure between the confused glut of vehicles.

The motorcycle appeared to hit another gear as the video frame bounced and the landscape skated by at a faster clip. Sturgeon sat forward in his chair, his breath growing heavy.

What were once mere colored dots on the horizon soon became full-sized vehicles slamming on their brakes and yielding to the motorcycle. The bike eased past each, turning the drivers and their vehicles into mere smears of color. The cyclist leaned left and crossed three lanes, cutting off a teen girl in the middle lane. *Deliberately,* Sturgeon thought.

The biker glanced back to see the girl fumble with her phone, then grab the wheel and wrench it, over-correcting her vehicle directly into the highway divider. The car and the traffic behind it disappeared momentarily in a cloud of dust and debris. A handful of cars miraculously skated through the chaos.

Looking ahead, the cyclist raced toward a slow-moving camper in the middle lane. The large vehicle jerked left instead of right and promptly crushed a red Mini Cooper against the guardrail like an empty soda can. The motorcyclist glanced back again. Two cruisers rushed in from behind him.

The cyclist looked down at his black-gloved hand as he cranked his wrist. The camera view lashed up and down as the bike broke free yet again with whiplash acceleration. Soon, a long empty stretch of highway beckoned. Sturgeon smiled at the mirage of escape. The crest of the next gentle swell of road stirred liquid in the rising heat waves. The cyclist glanced in the side mirror. The police strobes were shrinking from view.

The driver glanced down. The odometer clicked past forty-seven miles. The man seemed to be studying his inky, silhouetted reflection in the digital speedometer glass, which climbed steadily past 160 mph and settled at 170 mph. He leaned forward and hugged his chest against the gas tank.

The video vibrated, making Sturgeon feel a bit nauseous. But at 180, the vibrations ceased, and the motorcyclist seemed to have reached a new plane of existence, appearing to levitate above the road.

The motorcyclist ventured another quick look behind him and found nothing but empty, conquered highway. The man turned forward again, surely unrushed and confident in his escape, as a fatal curve materialized out of nowhere. In a fraction of a second, the motorcycle slammed into the Jersey barrier, ejecting the rider to sail straight through the air. For a few seconds, the guy appeared to have mastered flight.

Sturgeon's knee stopped bouncing as he devoted every available neuron to absorbing the final moment. He watched as the cyclist hit the oncoming grill of an eighteen-wheeler. He licked his lips, paused the video, advanced it a frame, rewound another frame, and forward again, like a cruel, yet playful god.

CHAPTER 4

SATURDAY, 10:49 PM

JAY

JAY STOMPED ON THE TAURUS'S brakes in front of Bennie's house and cringed at the unintentional squeal of tires. He leaned over the passenger seat and checked the house, a two-story Gable Front that had seen better days, its façade given a sickly pallor from the streetlights. *No lights or movement upstairs. Good.* He looked in his rearview mirror— no police cars behind him. *Even better.*

He gathered his laptop and backpack, exited the car, and ran up the front steps. Bennie couldn't possibly insist on going to the rave after Jay showed him what he'd captured on the laptop and recorded on his camcorder. He slipped inside the door, which was always unlocked, and rested for a moment in the foyer. His heart muscle felt paper thin and ready to burst.

Breathing deeply and evenly, he tiptoed down the hallway to the basement door, then made his way down the stairs. The ever-present hum of an HVAC system vibrated in the darkness, betraying the presence of Bennie's state-of-the-art computer lab, which occupied nearly half of the available space. He paused there. Each time he made his way down to Bennie's basement, he marveled at what his friend had been able to do by cashing in his college funds. With only the slightest of poorly kept promises to at least complete his GED, he had been able to parlay his parents' college savings into *this*.

He let himself into the lab, which was kept nearly as dark as the rest of the basement. He spotted Bennie's form silhouetted in the darkness by the large LCD monitor. A neon-pink pamphlet advertising that night's rave in Hadley lay beside his friend's elbow.

"Hey," Jay said.

No response. *Oh, boy.* Bennie didn't take missing raves lightly. Jay looked around the familiar room as he waited out the silent treatment. In stark contrast to the rest of the old house, the windowless computer lab was as immaculate as a Biosafety Level 4 lab at the CDC. An industrial-quality filtration and cooling system hummed in the corner, ensuring that the rack servers breathed air healthier than any human could expect. An impressive array of servers took up the entire right-hand wall, and Jay was fortunate enough to host his wireless hot spot website there. The recessed lighting in the drop ceiling was dimmed to an almost moonlight quality, barely illuminating the outlines of other personal computers and related equipment, which stretched along three large card tables like a battalion of hibernating robots. White Bose RoomMate speakers mounted in the ceiling corners quietly conspired with each other in the musical codes of downtempo-dub. With the exception of Bennie's wheelchair, the room was conspicuously absent of seating, save for one Aeron chair Bennie had purchased for Jay, the only sanctioned visitor to the lab.

Jay slid into the chair and rolled up beside Bennie. He laid his laptop, flash drive, and camcorder in front of his silent friend.

Bennie grunted. "What's this?"

"I think I just witnessed a murder."

Bennie's eyes filled the lenses of his glasses. "Say what?"

"A *murder*! I'm telling you, I was just trolling around, trying to locate those weird signals we talked about the other night, and I ended up in a park. There was a woman there being beat up, robbed, raped... Heck, I don't really know. Take a look at the flash drive. I intercepted a signal and recorded it somehow."

Bennie blinked. "Well, call the police, stupid."

"They already showed up."

Bennie shook his head and smirked. "Dude, seriously?"

"Just look, man." Jay pushed the flash drive and camcorder to bump into Bennie's keyboard.

Squinting skeptically, Bennie grabbed the flash drive and hooked it up to his laptop. He examined his own running programs on the display and sat back in his chair. "Whoa." His fingers danced along his split keyboard.

Jay crossed his arms. He could feel his heart still racing under the palm of his right hand. As hard as it was, he knew enough to be silent while Bennie worked. He tried calming his nerves by constructing a small pyramid of five empty energy drink cans while Bennie transferred the data from Jay's flash drive to the workstation.

Jay knew Bennie would initially resist playing the video outright. As with everything he did, Bennie would insist on approaching it delicately and thoroughly, like a scientist confronted with a sampling of a new, exotic virus. Jay envisioned each of Bennie's thought iterations like the musical loops floating about the room, redundant on the surface, but on deeper inspection, they cleverly modified themselves, mutating, improving, and mutely changing in one random aspect until something clicked, something worked, and the sound became new.

Jay inhaled and felt the antiseptically clean air penetrate his lungs, making each alveolus a bulging purse of oxygen-rich treasure, unhindered by dust and debris. He wondered

19

if computer labs were the last few places where one could experience the quality of the first Edenic 1.0 version of the Earth's atmosphere.

He watched over Bennie's shoulder as his friend continued to study the live video feed file, attempting to determine the standard, compression, encoding type, and other characteristics, like frame-rate, bit rate, sound frequency, and general quality.

"Huh. This stuff seems pretty good quality, considering it was from a mobile source and uploaded right over a wireless network," Bennie said. More to himself, Jay guessed.

Bennie had recently developed the nervous habit of stroking the right arm of his thick glasses. He said he liked the feel of the manufacturer's embossed logo. *Temple massaging for geeks,* Jay thought. It looked to be a comforting gesture, like a child caressing a special section of his blanket. Jay thought Bennie might nearly rub off the entire logo that night.

"Didn't have time for the rave tonight, but you had time for extended wardriving?" Bennie asked.

Jay shrugged. "Come on. Leave it alone, huh? Look what I found. And this is some serious shit. Maybe we can find something out that the police didn't."

While Bennie waited to transfer files, Jay fingered the rave pamphlet cleverly disguised as a lost-dog poster. He recalled the previous rave when he had carried Bennie through a thick forest toward a glowing barn with Bennie's head bobbing on his shoulder. Jay remembered the smell of herbal oil that constantly emanated from his friend as a result of frequent physical therapy sessions. Once, Bennie had even let Jay administer one of the Botox injections he took in each leg to alleviate the rare, but extremely painful, spasms in his legs.

Bennie had been quite pleased with himself when he cracked the code local ravers employed to advertise their next event, cleverly implanted throughout the entire state in plain view. He had proven his hunch by collecting a sampling of all the lost-dog posters in town for weeks and matching them against rave busts published in the local police logs. The colors of the flyers were a code in and of themselves. Orange meant Friday night, pink, Saturday night, and green, Sunday night. An array of other colors represented the rest of the week. Because of Jay's school, he and Bennie were only interested in the weekend events. Bennie had found the latest flyer nailed defiantly to a telephone pole directly outside of the local police station.

$700 reward. That was code for the cover charge, after moving the decimal twice to the left. *Please contact us at xxx-xxx-xxxx.* The last five digits of the phone number were the zip code of the town. *Answers to 'Postie.'* The name of the missing animal, minus the endearing "-ie" or "y" suffix, was the street name—Post Road. *Sex: Male.* Girls dance free, but boys pay. *Email contact: 1020boy@yahoo.com.* Embedded house number, usually that of an abandoned warehouse or farmhouse. *Age:10.* Start time.

Bennie snatched the flyer and flipped it onto the computer table. "So let me get this straight. You were in a wide open field—not near a Starbucks, McDonald's, or Tasty Town?"

Jay shook his head.

"Come on, you must have been by a Dunkin' Donuts. You wouldn't have been in Massachusetts otherwise." Bennie returned to his monitor, which displayed a set of file properties he had exported and piped into a tab-delimited text file. He nosed the cursor down the lines of output, leading it through several random-looking characters like a bloodhound through underbrush. He jammed his *down* arrow through the file as his impatience grew.

Jay had never seen Bennie so completely stonewalled on a problem. He couldn't tell exactly what it was his friend wanted to see, but he spotted a lot of "NULL" and "UNDEFINED VALUE" entries in the file. Jay lifted the shiny black pyramid of cans, walked across the floor, and unceremoniously dropped them into an empty computer monitor box with a loud clatter. Frustrated by Bennie's deliberate slowness, he returned to his chair. "Look at the screen capture of my map. I cross-referenced it with Google maps. There *is* a Dunkin' Donuts a mile south. You know their wireless signal isn't *that* strong."

"Well, this doesn't make any sense, then." Bennie pushed away from the desk and let his wheelchair roll back to bump against the second row of computers behind him. Jay held his tongue, knowing his friend's routine, and Bennie reluctantly rolled back to the workstation with a grunt.

Bennie's condition was called "advanced spastic diplegia." Bennie had told Jay that he hadn't tried walking in three years, and the last time had only been two steps with great effort. Bennie had described the motion as a cross-legged "scissor gait."

Jay had privately researched the condition online and watched a video of a boy demonstrating the motion—a crouched, twisted, marionette-like scamper. The boy's face in the video had been red with strain as he lurched down a sidewalk as if his ankles were bound by invisible chains, all the while carrying a great, invisible weight on his shoulders.

Even in a sitting position in his wheelchair, Bennie's fashionable attire, typically along the lines of faded jeans, a slightly askew trucker cap, and a black retro-grunge T-shirt, was forced into physical contortions never demonstrated by any mannequin. No fashion designer planned ahead for how the clothes became misshapen and misrepresented on Bennie's body as he struggled across the room via army crawl to move to a beanbag chair, the desk, or his bed. Of course, the physical handicap hadn't affected Bennie's mental drive and cognitive abilities. In fact, Jay guessed the opposite.

He stood and turned to the door. "I gotta take a piss." He ascended the basement stairs two at a time and paused at the top to listen, reassuring himself with the sound of Bennie's clicking keyboard. Jay ignored the first floor bathroom and continued up to the second floor. He tiptoed past Bennie's parents' bedroom and on toward Bennie's older sister's bedroom.

Stepping into the room, he filled his lungs with Chloe's current favorite perfume, Burberry London. He had figured out its name by methodically working down the line of perfumes on her vanity and matching them to her smell, which he carefully stored in his brain on the safest, highest, most esteemed shelf in the vaults of his memory. Everything in the room, no matter how many times he visited, remained excitingly foreign and exotic to him.

With her away to college, he had unlimited access to her bedroom, like getting a Speed Pass at the local amusement park. Everything had roughly remained in place since the summer, except for the ghost-like rectangles on the walls representing the posters and framed prints she'd taken to decorate her dorm room.

In a perverse version of *Goldilocks and the Three Bears*, he had already touched and considered most everything in the room. He only had maybe two minutes during each visit before he was too unnerved by the prospect of Bennie becoming suspicious, their mother waking up, or their father returning early from work.

He had already run his fingers through her entire closet, buried his head in each drawer of her bureau, and flipped through each of her books to look for a telltale note in the margins that would afford him any insight into her psyche. He had also scanned her high school term papers, studied her CDs and DVDs, and once found a collection of erotic short stories beneath her mattress. But his favorite activity was to lie on her four-poster bed.

He crawled beneath the open bedroom window, the lace curtains reaching out to him on the incoming breeze, and climbed onto her bed. He lay on his back and turned his head to smell her pillow sham. Stretching his arms and legs, he luxuriated within the same intimate medium she used to dream, to wonder, and to worry. He thought about her safety at college and wondered if she liked to jog late at night; he

23

imagined dark figures slinking between trees, following her. He shook off the image and turned onto his side.

He imagined he could still feel her body heat, perhaps some leftover cosmic fragment. Her golden tassels from graduation hung from the corner bedpost. He touched their silken threads, imagining it was her hair he touched as she hovered above him, sitting on his lap, the fullness and thickness of her mane cascading around his own head like a privacy curtain.

After a minute, he rose with a sigh, smoothed over her down comforter, and rejoined Bennie in the basement. In that short interval, Bennie had abandoned the video file and started scrolling through thumbnail picture galleries submitted by a webmaster for one of the several nude model websites he hosted.

Jay's own website, also hosted by Bennie, was slowly dying as more and more free wireless hot spots were being offered. Jay would have to kill the site soon, since sales had dropped and didn't look to be returning. Still, it had been a clever idea: a subscription-based mash-up website using Google's mapping API, free web hosting from Bennie, and his own helpful tips, updates, and warnings, such as SSID (Service Set Identifier) name changes or whether the owner monitored the access logs. Each hot spot he found was graphically reflected on the site, overlaid on a satellite map by a pulsing, light-blue orb with a diminishing circular gradient of color indicating the relative signal strength of each spot. The wireless hot spots bloomed and withered on his map like a live garden of irises, and he did his best to keep his data up-to-date and relevant, carefully cultivating new growth and judiciously pruning spots by those who either moved or wised up and secured their wireless network.

Jay looked over at Bennie. Unlike most people who merely needed to look up and to the left to concentrate or synthesize thoughts, Bennie's brain was wired such that he had to gaze into the forms of nude women to focus his thoughts and concentrate. Bennie viewed those images in such bulk and with such rapidity that Jay couldn't even focus on any one in particular. The overall effect was as if Bennie were merely studying a photographic series of desertscapes. Each nude was a breathtaking snapshot of a barren, beautiful desert where the sand ranged in color from a sensuous fallow brown to an innocent, lighter buff, the soft, light down along their limbs and below each navel like so much sparkling quartz. Each contour, all pristine and untrammeled, was lovingly rubbed smooth with the infinite calm and patience of the desert wind but for the occasional glimpse of desert brush creeping low and demurely from the corner of the frame. Jay had intuited early on in their friendship that Bennie wasn't viewing the pictures with passionate longing, but instead, with sadness.

Jay rapped a knuckle on the table. "Come on, dude. Play it already."

"Sure, but don't ask me to trust it. I'm going to play it in a virtual image, so if anything goes bad, it'll be self-contained." Bennie rolled down to another terminal and launched a virtual machine, essentially a representation of an entire operating system running inside the protected instance of a single running process. If anything horrible went wrong, Bennie could just kill the process without threatening to compromise the host machine or his network.

"It played fine on my laptop," Jay informed him.

Bennie huffed. "Well, *that* was pretty naïve." He launched the video file and dragged the virtual operating system screen onto a much larger thirty-inch wall-mounted monitor. "The video is optimized for four twenty-five by three twenty, but I'll expand it so we can see it. It'll degrade the quality a bit. Let's watch the entire thing first and maybe work through it frame by frame after."

On the screen, the quickly pivoting camera angle frantically swept between the star-riddled night sky and the chain-link fence of the tennis courts.

"No sound." Bennie turned to Jay. "Did you hear anything? Did this guy say anything?"

"No. But the guys that came later did. They had Russian accents, I think." Jay stood beside Bennie and pointed at the screen. "That black shape that blocks the entire view right here... I think that's the guy attacking her."

"How's she getting this? This is like maybe a video earpiece or necklace or something? Damn, I could use this for Mnemosyne."

The dark shape soon obscured almost the entire frame. The video shook violently and then suddenly jerked to the left, as if a tripod had been swept out from beneath it. Soon, the picture faded out, like an old television set shutting down, narrowing to a single point of light, and then showing nothing. Although Jay's laptop was still attempting to capture more, the video stream had been cut off, and Jay had recorded another three minutes of empty video in the time it took him to sneak back to his car.

"And then your camcorder?" Bennie shut down the virtual operating system and popped the digital video camera's memory card into his laptop. He played the clip. "Jesus, man, why's the picture bouncing around so much?"

The greenish hue of the night-vision-enabled video looked like a news broadcast feed from Iraq. The camera jerked from the crime scene toward the sound of a high-pitched V8 engine asked to do more than it was meant to do. The approaching vehicle's headlights jumped up and down, giving the impression of a wild four-legged animal in pursuit of its prey. The scene played out exactly as Jay remembered: the crashing of the dark-colored car against the chain-link fence, the assailant fleeing, the men groping the body, retrieving something from the woman, and then leaving the scene when the police arrived.

"Hmm," Bennie said. "She does seem dead. That's messed up, dude."

The clip ended in a blue screen and then displayed an

entangled couple kissing each other on a moonlit beach.

Bennie moaned. "You taped over my memories? You idiot!"

"Well, stop borrowing my camcorder, and this won't happen."

For the past three years, Bennie had undertaken an unsettling hobby, code named "Mnemosyne." Jay had trouble remembering how to pronounce it, to Bennie's never-ending frustration. *Something close to Na-moz-any,* he thought.

When Bennie wasn't programming and hacking, he videotaped unsuspecting couples during such precious moments as cuddling together on a local ferry, splitting a bottle of wine at an outdoor café in the North End, sharing a secret kiss in a dark corner of the Boston Aquarium, or walking hand-in-hand down the beach in Martha's Vineyard. He had rigged the front section of his laptop bag to accommodate a camcorder from the inside, enabling a view to the outside world through a small aperture, and he controlled the camera with a remote control. With the video evidence in hand, Bennie would employ his best hacking skills to determine who the couple was and, ultimately, where they lived. He catalogued the information, along with their Social Security numbers, in a database and updated it for accuracy's sake every few months—in case the people relocated, changed names, or died. His master plan was to anonymously sell the video memories to the same people in five years' time. Bennie's justification was that the couple hadn't had the luxury of documenting the moment themselves, so why couldn't he enjoy a small fee for reviving the memory for them? Jay had to admit it was a disturbing, but fantastic idea. Bennie would have an endless supply of video memories to sell, with new ones ripening on the vine each year like precious fruit.

He never learned how much Bennie intended to charge for the videos, but he imagined it would be a bargaining scenario in each situation. Jay wouldn't have minded retrieving a few extra memories from the time when his family had been whole.

Bennie moved the video file to an editing station, loaded

27

it into the software, and began to work the scrub control slowly back a few frames, then forward a couple. He worked back one more frame, pausing at the moment the shorter man passed his hands over the woman's face. Bennie inched the scanner ahead slightly and zoomed at the same time, focusing on a silvery flash of metal.

Bennie pointed at the screen. "What do you think that was?"

"Turn the volume up and play it again," Jay suggested.

Bennie did so, and Jay heard a beep over the rush of traffic in the background.

"What'd they just do?" Bennie asked.

"Dunno. I never got a good look at her. I jumped the wall and peeled out of that parking lot as soon as the police got there."

"So these guys, did they know the woman?"

Jay shrugged. "No idea. But I was thinking... check the police logs, see if a report's been made public yet."

Bennie punched in the local newspaper's website for Cambridge and pulled up the public police logs. The spotlighted piece read:

Mass. Woman—Suspected Homicide

Cambridge—Charlotte E. Faye, 71 East Main Street, was found dead late Saturday night at Jefferson Park.

The victim was thought to have been out jogging when she was attacked, police say. It was later determined by authorities that she was strangled. An ongoing investigation will be conducted by the Boston Police Department. If anyone has any information regarding the incident, they are asked to contact the authorities.

Bennie reloaded the wirelessly captured video and watched it again to the end. The stars, the fence, the dark shape, the fade to black.

"And that's when the video feed itself cuts off," Jay said. "As if it were all planned, like there was a second accomplice filming somehow."

"You mean like a snuff film?"

"Yeah."

"Mmmm—no." Bennie shook his head. "That doesn't add up. I mean, the point of view is from the woman. Was she holding the camera? Maybe this was some rape fantasy gone bad? Maybe the guy got too rough, hurt her, or couldn't stop."

"Yeah, but the Russians were somehow already coming for them. They already knew something bad was going on."

Bennie muted the music, turned on a rear projection television in the back corner of the room, and began scrolling through on-demand movie selections. "Leave me with all this for tonight, okay? This all makes shit sense, but there's a thread or two I want to tug on for a bit. Something about this timing. I need to think for a while."

Jay clapped Bennie on one skinny shoulder. "By the way, are you actually wearing leather pants?"

"Go screw yourself."

Jay headed for the door, but stopped when Bennie said, "Oh, hey. Your dad? Acting much stranger than normal."

CHAPTER 5

SATURDAY, 11:51 PM

BENNIE

BENNIE PAUSED AND LISTENED AS Jay mounted the basement stairs and left by the front door. He strummed his fingers on his split keyboard without actually pressing the keys.

A murder.

He performed a quick search online for stats in the Boston area. A colored map displayed violent crimes in differing shades of blue, like a slow-to-heal bruise extending north to south from Revere to Dedham and west to east from VFW Parkway to Morrissey Boulevard. Odds were if Jay was trolling that area on a regular basis, he would have ultimately run into something of the sort, no doubt, just as any police car would while rolling through the same high-crime area.

Jay wasn't one to pull practical jokes, but the video sure had the complete makings of one. There was nothing he hated more than being duped. The whole scenario deserved a healthy dose of his usual skepticism. After all, Jay *did* just get out of going to the rave with him. And the camcorder video of the two men crouched over the woman could have been copied out of any B-grade spy thriller. But on the flip side, he had never seen Jay's hands shake as they had when his friend first entered the lab. *Hard to fake that.*

Whatever the reason, Bennie hated being dragged out of his routine. He was ashamed of his selfishness, but he had plans and had already built up his anticipation: come back from the rave around one or two, spend a couple of rewarding and productive hours with his Mnemosyne project, and crash until the next afternoon.

He switched inputs on the widescreen from satellite television to his project server. He expanded a nested tree of computer folders, turning their plus symbols into minus symbols as more and more folders unlatched themselves like grapes dropping from a steadily clipped arbor vine. These little computer interactions were what soothed him, giving order and predictability to his world. Inside the folder of his latest video acquisitions, he circled his mouse pointer over the individual files. He imagined he was the pointer, body-surfing the crowd of Ecstasy-infused ravers, feeling the many-handed beast grope for him amid the humid rush of their shouts and screams and the crazed sensation of a fully dark room under strobe light, as if the room were in constant shock of itself.

He double-clicked on one of the video files. The display turned dark and then bright again as the camcorder came out of his coat and he positioned it above the line of heads in front of him. He had covered every blinking indicator light on the exterior of the camera with black electrical tape so as not to attract undue attention. The camera eventually found its object and zoomed in. Without knowing he had been filming in a movie theater, someone could probably misinterpret the subject of the video as two dark cells in the final stages of mitosis, one twist short of complete division.

But it was, in fact, the exact opposite: a young couple kissing, instead of separating. They seemed to want to consume each other and become one. In his lab, Bennie let

31

himself go completely slack, forcing an out-of-body experience as he floated into the young man's silhouette. He imagined the plush of her soft lips, her warm, sweet breath, the tickle of her hair on his cheek, and the soft trace of her fingers down his jawline.

Like a quiet, self-contained explosion, an aftershock of goose bumps raced down his arms. He had the same reaction at the raves each time he felt even the slightest touch of a stranger, male or female. The crowd pushed and pulled him, usually with violent force, but he didn't care. The feel of all those hands and their squeezing, scratching hunger didn't matter because new hands awaited him and grabbed for him, pulled at his limbs and hair, and tore at his clothes. He would die happy if he were drawn and quartered on the spot.

The kissing couple came up for air and then tilted their heads together, forming a tired- and content-looking archway, pretending to watch a movie they surely cared nothing about. Bennie had let the camera linger on the couple, anticipating the nostalgia they would feel in viewing the scene again, years down the road. If he were the guy, he would treasure *this* moment the most. Not the kissing and the groping, but the companionable silence and the familiar intimacy of two bodies hovering together in that tight, loving, all-accepting orbit. Yes. His heart ached for that—to be in the path of someone's adoring glow.

But they would never receive the video—it was lost to them forever. A blinding bright light filled the screen. An usher's flashlight. "Hey, you! What're you doing there!"

All heads had turned toward the handicapped boy in the back row. Bennie had been unceremoniously ejected from the theater and banned from the entire multiplex forever under the assumption he had been attempting to create a bootleg copy of the movie on the screen. So that particular video was his to keep.

He would have typically left the auditorium minutes ahead of the movie's ending and lingered in the lobby. Nobody ever looked at him for long. Who wanted to be caught staring at the kid in the wheelchair? Very exploitable. He could follow someone down a dark alley, and out of a weird sense of decency, the person still wouldn't dare look at him. He would have followed the couple out to their car, noted the license plate number, filed it away, and sent an anonymous offer in five years. But that one would remain orphaned in Mnemosyne forever.

He switched off the screen, and the room became dark but for the cheery pulse of green, red, and orange lights from his lab equipment. His own mini-rave. *Sucks.* What was worse, instead of complete silence, something more horrible filled the room. The sound, understandably ever-present in the lab, was a low-level monotone chatter: the crunching, munching sound of hard drives reading and writing data, like the sound of time itself being nibbled away at its edges.

Bennie blinked and swallowed, refusing to pass a sleeve across his eyes. *Enough of this self-pitying bullshit.* He remotely turned the dimmers to full and flooded the room with optimistic white light. With earbuds shoved deep in his ears and rave-house music blaring, he took his anger out on Jay's curious video feed.

CHAPTER 6

SATURDAY, 11:50 PM

STURGEON

STURGEON'S SECURE CHAT WINDOW POPPED up with a message from his lead programmer, Stephanie. *File's ready when you want it.*

Send it, he typed back.

He grabbed the arms of his chair and pushed back with a grimace, crushing the tension out of his spine. The pops and cracks tickled the base of his throat.

He looked around. No notes adorned his walls. No photos of friends or family members smiled back at him. His work space was pristine, untraceable to him, with the exception of his briefcase and laptop. It was crucial, he had been instructed, that he kept his work consolidated and easily transportable at a moment's notice.

22% transferred.

Sturgeon's on-site three-person staff, each member desperate in his or her own way, understood that their employment could end at any minute. But they remained undeterred, happy enough with the day-to-day promise of work and the imaginary payout he had promised at the end of the project.

Even his lead programmer, an attractive coed with short blond hair, wasn't privy to all the technical elements of the operation. He could tell after the first few weeks of her employ that she was less than thrilled by the nature of her work. Her main duties were to ensure that the grid of communications remained healthy and continuous and to keep tabs on one particular individual using all of her skills and the full arsenal of pirated government spyware Sturgeon had stolen during his earlier partnership with the DOD. He had convinced her that she was working in conjunction with the US government to monitor a former CIA agent on house arrest who was attempting to hack his way back into sensitive project files. She met that news with a blank stare, as she did most exchanges. She likely didn't believe him, but was routinely doing as she was told.

48% transferred.

His two Russian programmers knew a bit more regarding the design and nature of the project. They had to by virtue of the job requirements. He had rummaged through the online want-ad listings some nine months ago and stumbled upon a site listing for-hire Russian workers. Each offered a wide spectrum of professional services in exchange for counterfeit visa sponsorship. The agreements typically required the initial fee of illegally transporting them to the US, and most on the list were ready and willing to do nearly anything to ensure such passage.

He had posted his needs to the forum and received over a dozen hits the next day. The programmers who contacted him forwarded their discouraging resumes—unpunctuated, unformatted, raw text files full of defunct programming skills in languages like ADA acquired from made-up universities from untraceable Russian provinces. A similar experience followed in his separate, surreal search for killers for hire. The language barrier had been so thick and impossible that Sturgeon had the unassailable fear that in the utter confusion, in some fatal translation error, he would ultimately hire one of these foreign thugs who would happily travel five thousand miles only to arrive and kill Sturgeon himself.

63% transferred.

Sturgeon opened a new window on his laptop and pulled up a live view of his team, all of whom understood they were to work every minute while Sturgeon was in the office and didn't leave until he did.

Both Russians sat at the same card table as the lead programmer. Malenky was compiling new code received from the Mumbai team. Bolshoy, a life-sized killing totem awaiting Sturgeon's next command, slept in his chair, his arms crossed on his chest. Occasionally, one digit or another on his massive hands twitched just as a dog's paws would twitch during a nap. He probably dreamed of scooping out some victim's eyeballs.

Before Sturgeon found the Russians, he had hired the young woman, a desperate UMass computer science grad out of work since her matriculation the previous spring. Only a week after she had started, he had received the call from the big Russian.

"You post need for Russian programmer?" Bolshoy's trilled "r" in the word *Russian* was forceful and impressive sounding, like a turbine engine sucking in a foreign object and spitting it out through its impellers.

"Quite. Very senior programmers," Sturgeon answered and began running through the technical prerequisites of the job.

Bolshoy cut him off mid-sentence. "And I see similar post from you in different forum for bodyguard? If I and cousin do both, you hire? You pay more, yes?"

Bolshoy and Malenky turned out to be St. Petersburg-born Russians—Malenky was a bona fide programmer specializing in cutting-edge video technology, and Bolshoy was a bona fide cold-blooded killer equipped with a cozy array of violent skills. As Sturgeon learned later, Bolshoy had acquired those skills just as any American kid would learn to swim or ride a bicycle. At the slightest provocation, or with enough monetary incentive, Bolshoy could most certainly send a bullet through someone's cranium just as fast as his cousin Malenky could set a breakpoint in a debugging session.

100% transferred.

Sturgeon unwound his headphones and glanced at the surveillance feed of his workers once more. Stephanie hunched over her workstation, working slightly more frantically than usual. Like most intense programmers, she cursed and punched at her keyboard in disgust as she worked. Feet upon his desk and a Mountain Dew at his right elbow, Malenky had pulled away from his terminal to leaf through a GSM Security manual. His brow was a tightly stacked cord of concentration.

A small pressure-sensitive device, compliments of the US government, approximately the size of a warming plate for a coffee mug, was plugged into one of Sturgeon's USB ports. He pressed his palm to it. A red strip scanned up, then down, and the borders of the device glowed green, allowing him to open the video file.

The device conveniently bypassed the process of entering the encryption keys manually. Only two entities could view the raw video: those with the encryption key and Sturgeon. Although Malenky knew it was video data, he was required to manipulate the video blindly, massaging it as a black box of ones and zeroes, never having the luxury of viewing the full composite parts.

Sturgeon pressed play. The scene, as always, was from first-person perspective. A young, barely pubescent girl nonchalantly unbuckled a chunky belt that held up her neon-green glittery skirt, which unceremoniously slid down to her ankles. In the dim light of what looked to be a hotel room—indicated by the blazing mid-day sun trying its best to peek around the thick curtains—Sturgeon could hardly discern her young, boyish hips in silhouette.

On his screen, a graphical user interface wrapped the video with a plethora of information on display. The video had arrived yesterday. The time stamp reported it to have been initiated at 11:12 a.m. and terminated twenty minutes later, with some blackout spots in between.

Naughty Mr. Gerraty, the personal assistant to Massachusetts's own Senator Pearson, was back at it. And inexplicably, Gerraty would not pay. No matter how much Sturgeon threatened him, he refused. *He must be insane,* Sturgeon concluded. And that was why Sturgeon had to make him pay the ultimate price.

He watched the video once at normal speed and then again at double-time. He exported the video to MPEG format, re-encoding it into a format specifically marked to have originated from a slim new Sony Handycam that would be covertly placed in Gerraty's possession.

The encoder's progress bar slowly crept past 15 percent as it converted the video file.

Malenky had stolen a proprietary filter that gave the impression the video was shot by handheld camcorder, imbuing it with jitters, shakes, and unsteadiness the human eye had learned to identify as amateur videography. Additionally, he was able to develop an overlay that effectively imitated the signature details of a number of popular digital camcorders: date and time stamp, time elapsed, etc. In a final, especially nice touch, he was even able to artificially introduced blurs and resharpening effects. The only problem was the subjects of the movies never acted as one would be expected to while being taped, but that was a small nuance that so far had gone undetected.

Once the video was exported, he burned it to a writeable mini-DVD. "Bolshoy," he said in a quiet, conversational tone.

The Russian was at his door in seconds. Sturgeon handed him the DVD, neatly wrapped in glossy black paper and affixed with a gold label with one word printed on the front: *Prostitution.* He gave Bolshoy careful instructions for planting the video and the camcorder in Gerraty's vehicle and what to do with the prostitute.

Bolshoy slapped the top of Malenky's bald head on his way past, and they both shouldered on their leather jackets before heading out the door. They always kept their weapons in their oily black Dodge Magnum, so as not to raise suspicion with their coworker.

Sturgeon leaned back in his chair, lacing his hands behind his head. *A job well done.* Although he was unable to make money from that particular target, the frame-up still provided him some measure of relief. He could feel the pressure boiler of his anxiety back off ever so slightly, releasing in the smallest of degrees, enough to prevent a self-destructive explosion.

He would get his money back. Oh, yes. He would get more. *Much* more.

Stephanie approached his open office door. "Mr. Sturgeon?" She nervously hugged her arms around her chest, not quite able to meet his eyes.

Her fear only served to anger him and chill his icy nature further. "Yes? What is it, Stephanie?"

"We have a problem?"

She had that annoying habit, true to form of her generation, of ending her statements interrogatively, each upward inquiring lilt like a wedge working its way beneath his sanity, one pseudo-question at a time.

He leaned forward in his chair, his insides twitching like an awakened, uncoiling snake. "Continue."

"Cell tower seven—the one from the other night where Bolshoy and Malenky went? Our system detected a—I can't be sure. Someone skimmed one of the uploads. I think."

He waited in silence, his cue for her to continue.

"Not a network error. Not a software error, I think."

Sturgeon's spinning mind analyzed whether the local police at the murder scene had intuited something Bolshoy and Malenky had overlooked. Had something been left behind? Had Malenky and Bolshoy been spotted by some other security camera they hadn't seen? Was there an eyewitness? There was that exposure again, that sensation of being drawn up to the surface. He wasn't sure, but thought he could feel his insides expanding, as if from a noxious gas. The bends. He was literally going to explode. He felt it everywhere, in his head, in his joints, his heart, and his intestines, each ballooning out and growing dangerously thin from internal pressure.

The dumb ruble heads were getting antsy lately, and he didn't want to further their discontent. They would likely tear out their removable disk drives and jump out the window onto the sharp holly bushes and gravel at the first sign their cover was blown. He didn't want to panic them.

Stephanie stammered, "N-Not one of Bolshoy's n-n-null pointers. Someone siphoned *video*."

CHAPTER 7

SUNDAY, 12:10 AM

JAY

JAY DROVE HOME AT A slow pace, each turn of the wheel adding to his growing dread of seeing his father. Most houses were dark, as daybreak was still several hours away. The cool night was still and hung about the neighborhood languorously. But the coming day could be sensed, like a vaudeville performer in between acts, quietly sitting and smoking in front of his dark mirror, sipping at his bourbon and rechecking his makeup.

Suddenly, a bottled water truck overtook Jay and trundled past.

The vehicle evoked an ominous quality, as if it were an actual vehicle of death, trolling up and down the neighborhood streets to snag the poor souls who had passed in the night. Jay imagined the captured souls kept cool and in plastic bottles for their ultimate delivery. The truck turned the corner, its brake lights burning a flash of brimstone red.

At the top of Crescent Hill, the jaundiced eye of his father's attic-level dormer window gazed toward the expanse of the rest of the dark, sleeping town. Jay pulled the car into the garage and cut the engine. He stared at the doorway to the kitchen, feeling immediately claustrophobic. Just him and Dad. Who was he kidding? With Dad so distant, if Jay were being honest with himself, it was really just him. With Mom gone and their scant extended family scattered throughout the Midwest, life had felt incredibly lonely for the last year. By contrast, even Jay's dim memories of childhood felt fuller in some way. Jay remembered always having someone around when he was younger, some neighborhood boy or close classmate, no doubt due to his mother's careful arranging. Not that he expected his current friendships to be forged through his parents, but he was certainly putting all his eggs in one basket with Bennie.

Ever since his mom's death, his relationship with his father had become nothing short of intolerable. Their formerly easygoing, joking, trusting relationship had deteriorated and left behind an odd, dry precipitate that easily slipped through Jay's fingers. Nearly all of his father's verbal exchanges had become monosyllabic utterances, as if he were unnerved by Jay's presence or by what he might say to Jay, or Jay to him.

Each conversation at breakfast and dinner was roughly fashioned of the same stilted material, as if his father had transformed into some awkward, ill-equipped babysitter who was trying to follow instructions written in another language.

His father would enter from offstage to interact with him as little as possible—a bit character in a complex play.

"Done with breakfast?" his father had asked that morning.

"Yep." Jay studied his father, trying to discern something from his expression that would even hint at explaining the awkward behavior and his seeming abhorrence of his own son.

"Got your homework done?"

"Yep."

"Right, right. Well, I'll be upstairs if you need me." And his father had left.

He would still hug Jay, too hard it seemed, and that only served to confuse Jay further. Jay tried to ease the awkwardness by not pushing the point too far and making the possible mistake of confronting his father about what the hell had happened between them. Jay just rolled with it, acting as if their relationship were everything it had ever been, hoping his father's grief, or whatever it was, would dissipate and they could rebuild their relationship. Jay couldn't help but feel his father was perhaps blaming him in some way for the loss of his mother, even though that didn't really make sense.

He slipped out of the car, but couldn't quite bring himself to go inside. He sat atop the three steps that connected the garage to the kitchen. Twirling the car keys, he remembered coming home from school that dreaded afternoon.

His father had been sitting in the quiet living room, looking slumped and beaten. His eyes appeared as if dual augers had worked on them for hours, roughly attempting to bore out the painful loss through his eye sockets.

Several attempts to speak were thwarted, mere squeaks, but not entire words. "Mom's gone, Jay," Dad had finally said. "She's..." His father raised trembling hands, then dropped them. "Gone."

Stunned, Jay remained standing in the doorway with his backpack over one arm. He grasped the newel post for support. In several disjointed fragments, Jay's father explained that his mother had apparently been car-bombed in the Financial District downtown.

For that afternoon, Jay had affixed himself to the television in his bedroom, watching the news as if it were his only connection to his mother. Her coverage had taken up hours and hours of airtime on the news channels. The most common photo each broadcast used had been from her FBI Academy graduation ceremony. In the picture, her slim patriotic hand was raised in the air for the swearing in, and she wore her conservative black suit with her long blond hair pulled back in a severe bun.

But like dissipating smoke signals, the coverage dwindled,

her face only showing up on occasion during daily news summaries and an initial re-spike in coverage when a new lead pointed to a local terror cell in Boston, but which proved to be false. After two weeks, she disappeared from coverage entirely.

Jay knew his mother had been working with a new private security firm as FBI liaison in conjunction with the Department of Defense. Jay had always thought that if she were ever hurt, it would be spearheading a siege on some survivalist compound or becoming the premature wake-up call to some blissfully sleeping sleeper cell with the roaring crash of a twenty-five-pound door ram. It turned out he was right. That was exactly, horrifyingly in line with how his mother had lived, or at least died.

Jay scrubbed forward through those scenes as Bennie had through the video in the lab. Recalling his memories and playing them back in real time or slower caused too much pain. But each time he evoked the memory of receiving the news of his mother's death, he had to see it through to completion, despite the anguish, as if he had to end the video once it was begun at a certain key frame, bothered that he was missing something.

He forwarded past the wake, his viewing of her small, lonely urn on a cherrywood pedestal, the shocking cold of the urn's metal against his lips. The sensation forced tears from him as if they were all connected to the same razor wire that was being yanked out of him, death's plumber snaking out his insides for the gnarly clot of his soul. He recalled images from later in the dark reception room: accepting the greasy kisses of elderly, overweight relatives, the suffocating hugs that failed to realize he already wasn't breathing, the prompt summer rain at the funeral, and the birds, who hadn't received the unfortunate news in time to prevent their gaiety, chirping through the dark pine forest that backed the cemetery.

The last weekend in April of the previous year, his mother

had awakened him, trying to revive a long-lost tradition: going to yard sales. His parents used to go all the time before having Jay, he had learned. And when his father's interest had waned, his mother enlisted Jay as her bargain-hunting buddy. However, Jay had slowly grown tired of the outings, just as his father had.

So he had been surprised to be awakened by his mother shaking him that late April morning, with a marked-up classified ad and Metro-West map in hand, pleading with him to go along. "Come on, Jef-Jay. Come with your mom," she said. Jef-Jay was a family joke. Not terribly often, but enough times that Jay noticed, each parent had accidentally called him Jeffrey, apparently the first name they had chosen for him—his grandfather's name. So they would call him Jef-Jay as a term of endearment.

Grunting, Jay flipped away from his mother to face the wall, seeing if she would give up or at least offer a better argument for pulling him out of bed barely after dawn on a Saturday morning.

"Jay, I need you. Please. We'll go to that Thai place you like on Route 9."

Jay turned over and gave her a tired, blind smile.

She kissed his cheek. "I'll be in the car."

They stopped at Dunkin' Donuts and got some coffee and muffins. The mixture of the warm sun glare settling on his lap like a faithful dog, the caffeine boost, the sugar coursing through his system, and James Taylor cooing through the six speakers in his mother's Ford Escort soothed him.

Jay had the duty of navigating. To his disappointment, his mother had already traced their route with a grease pencil on a piece of transparency film taped on top of the map so as not to mark up the book. That was supposed to be *his* job. The sites of all the sales were numbered according to the order of their visit.

These tended to be multi-family efforts that cornered the market on stuffed animals, racks of clothes that smelled as if they had done duty as floor liners in horse stalls for a year, scratched glassware that would have been rejected even by a recycling facility, stained and sticky plastic toys that were often broken, and board games with ripped cardboard cases. Entire shelves were generally full of dusty *Reader's Digest* volumes and Charles Dickens's complete works.

After the ninth such sale, Jay asked, "Mom, why are we looking at all this junk? What are you looking for?"

His mother turned to him, her mouth taut as if she were indeed looking for something and not finding it or fearing she was going to miss it. She shook her head and bit her lip. "Just trying some new places, Jay. Mixing it up a bit, you know?"

They did buy some items—a pair of gently used gardening gloves, a hot-air popcorn popper, a brass clock that at one time rotated brass balls as part of its timekeeping mechanism, but surely couldn't any more, a difficult-looking novel by Nabokov, a paperback collection of one of the *MAD* artists, Al Jaffee, and an all-in-one screwdriver kit for his father—which rolled around in paper bags in the back.

Her warm brown eyes were pinched in the corners, and Jay noticed the strain in her forearms and knuckles as she gripped the wheel. "I just want to be with you." A forced smile creased her face. She turned to him. "So, where to next?"

Jay sighed, consulted her transparency, and re-taped it so the overlay lined up.

Toward evening, they finally returned home. She stopped so quickly in the driveway, her miscellaneous bags of used junk slid off the backseat and clattered to the floor. She appeared not to have noticed. "Tell your father I have to go into work tonight."

She was always strong when the situation called for it, but Jay couldn't help but see a barely perceptible wet glint on her lower lids. "Okay, Mom."

"I love you, Jay." Her voice trembled slightly.

"Love you, too," he said, making the tone of it sound

unnatural, to indicate to her that he knew something was wrong, but it was her call to explain screwing up his Saturday in such an absurd way. He closed the road atlas and started to hand it back to her. She squeezed both eyes shut and wordlessly pushed it back into his chest so hard that the cover and several first pages crumpled in the process. He raised his eyebrows, and with deliberate slowness to show his confusion, he slid the map into his backpack. He grabbed the bags from the backseat and shut both car doors.

The car leapt in reverse, the front nose's undercarriage scraping on the lip at the end of the raised driveway. The engine roared as she took off down the street. A silver Range Rover narrowly avoided hitting her broadside as she yanked the car onto the road that would spill her back onto Route 9. The Range Rover's horn blared, and the woman inside gestured wildly.

That was the last time he had seen his mother alive.

Jay pocketed the car keys and lifted his head from his bent knees. He inhaled the comforting, familiar smells of the garage, stood, and let out a sigh. When he walked into the dark kitchen, another, stronger smell hit him—fresh paint.

Acting much stranger than normal.

The kitchen appliances, cabinets, and small breakfast nook appeared to have been waiting up for him, in a slightly propped-up state, but had at one point lost hope, patience, or both, then slipped into a gray-blue slumber. He noted several of the wall hangings were missing, and much of the furniture was draped with drop cloths. His father was painting—*everything*. It was a complete mess. His mother would never have allowed such chaos and disorder. She would have methodically tackled one section at a time and used her own advice: clean as you go.

He warmed up some Cheez Whiz to a molten temperature and poured it over a plate of Tostitos. He pulled away a bedsheet that covered the breakfast bar, sat down, and munched away, letting his thoughts wander.

"Jay."

He jumped and turned to see the dark silhouette of his father in the hallway, backlit by the light in the foyer. "Dad."

"Couldn't sleep?"

Jay didn't know whether he should be relieved he hadn't been caught staying out so late or depressed that his father hadn't noticed. "Yeah, just got hungry." He poked at the congealed plate of pseudo-cheese, as thick as Silly Putty since it had cooled.

His father flicked on the small chandelier lamp over the breakfast nook. The illumination barely made a difference in the room and merely spotlighted a bowl of rotting bananas. Jay looked at Dad in the new light.

Of late, his father had been letting his beard grow for four and five days at a time before shaving it. A smear of black paint marked his forehead, the black half of the yin-yang symbol missing its white twin. Jay had noticed black was his father's latest medium for the last year, in dress, mood, and pigment. His fingernails and the rims of his cuticles were forever blackened to some degree, so much so that Jay wondered if people mistook him for a mechanic.

Dad gently squeezed Jay's shoulder on the way to the fridge.

"You painting the downstairs?" Jay asked.

Stooped and nearly engulfed in the Frigidaire's white light, Dad looked like an old man quietly surmising the beginning of his personal afterlife. "Ah, yeah. Slow start, though." He pointed at the crisper drawer where he kept his beer. "Want one? We still got some O'Doul's."

His mother would drink O'Doul's at parties and get-togethers, so she wouldn't feel so left out, but could still be raring to go at the chirp of her beeper at her waist.

Jay lifted his can of Pepsi and shook his head. He got up and dumped the plate of nachos, now amalgamated into one. He looked at the empty wall above the trash bin. "Where'd you put the clock?"

His dad's head popped up from the depths of the refrigerator. "I'll have it all back in a few days."

Jay nodded.

His father stuck his head back in the refrigerator. "Oh, by the way, I knocked over the computer and broke the monitor. You'll want to stay on your laptop until I can replace it." He pulled out a bottle of beer, popped the cap, and slugged half of it down.

"Hey, Dad?"

"Hmm?"

"When can I see what you've been working on?"

His father let out a quiet beer burp and patted his stomach. "Right now, if you like."

Jay followed his dad upstairs and then up the wooden ladder to the attic. For early spring in New England, the attic was still a tolerable temperature, as long as the sole window was propped open. His father's official painting studio, a converted guest bedroom on the first floor, still remained intact, but was largely untouched since Jay's mom had died. His father only ever went there when he had to retrieve a particular brush, putty knife, or cleaning tool.

His makeshift attic studio looked more like a hideout. The family's accrued treasures and memories were carelessly swept into the crook of one end as if by bulldozer and were covered loosely with paint-strewn bedsheets. A single bulb hung from the apex of the ceiling. Old rusty nails jutted out from the rafters at odd angles, put there by previous owners for whatever reason—to hang old jackets, army bags, cross-country skis, or themselves. Similarly, the floor was as treacherous as it had ever been—a loose patchwork of cast-aside particleboard, linoleum, rug samples, and plywood. That left plenty of room for the occasional misstep to send someone plummeting to the second floor.

Jay approached the easel-mounted three-by-three-inch canvas. Oh, he had hoped for so much more—some portraits of his mother or nice seascapes of the Cape, or even some oddball controversial art piece. He stepped toward the canvas to pretend the artwork was complex enough to deserve more than a passing glance. What looked at first to be an amorphous puff of smoke was on closer inspection revealed to be several carefully placed dots.

He wanted to offer some encouragement, but he was at a loss for words. Instead, he could feel his cheeks filling with hot shame blood. "Pointillism."

"That's right." His father picked up his black-smeared palette. His thumb poked through and wiggled, like a blind newborn organism sniffing out danger and sustenance.

"But what is it?"

His father gripped Jay's bicep tightly. "It's what it is and what it isn't. Do you see that?" Dad paused and turned his head as he did to garner extra attention, the light from the single bulb striking each of his deep-blue eyes. He pulled Jay close, then pushed away again.

Jay shook his head.

"You will. I'm going to work a bit longer."

"Dad, I think I'm going to skip tomorrow. I don't feel so good."

His father nodded and twitched his brush against the canvas.

Jay numbly climbed back down the attic ladder. In his bedroom, he unknotted his sneakers and fell onto his bed, still clothed. Sleep had become a dreaded, dark, and anxious time. His resistance weakened at night, as if he could no longer uphold the straining pulleys of his sorrow. And they squealed unsympathetically, the ropes slipping through his relaxing hands, lowering the great cold boulder of his mother's absence on his chest.

In the last year of his mother's life, on the occasion Jay suffered a sleepless night, he would inevitably find her downstairs. The entire first floor would be dark but for the glow coming from the family study, where she would be working feverishly at her computer. The computer screen would cast her face with a blue-white morbidity. She typically worked those nights with a polarized privacy screen that would Velcro onto the face of the monitor for security reasons imposed by the FBI for at-home work. She nevertheless welcomed Jay's company and would often fix them a late-night snack of fried bologna sandwiches, carrots and veggie dip, or nachos, if Jay had his way.

Granted, those weren't the treasured days of old when they would split a bag of microwave popcorn while watching the latest A&E movie of the week or take their books out into the breezeway to read in comfortable silence, but those midnight sessions had still been togetherness. Mother and son hunched over their respective monitors, she on the larger computer, and he on his laptop. They would work in an understood silence, sharing the occasional smile between rapid keystrokes, the disk head of his mother's workstation similarly munching on the snack of its own hard drive.

He got the sense her latest work was either something extremely difficult, or perhaps, by the fleeting, scared look that would cloud her features like a passing shadow, she was in over her head. He hoped it was the former. Her pupils would sometimes be large and predatory, not taking in even his general shape, it seemed. After brief recognition in her eyes that he was neither an advantage toward reaching her goal, nor an obstacle, she just saw through him.

Dad, a painter by trade who had to accommodate those same moods himself, said Mom was merely "in the zone," and that Jay should generally back off. Those possessed, almost blind stares of concentration chilled Jay, but they were worth enduring to spend the time with her.

Jay stirred in bed, finding a more comfortable position. He spent most hours before sleep fending off the self-destructive delusion that his mother wasn't gone. He was struggling with the denial stage of grief, he guessed, despite having seen a photo of the wreckage on television. Her car had been obliterated so completely that all that was left was a large black, skeletal hand, a claw of singed metal, fingers spread upward, palming within it somewhere the charred remains of his mother. At his core, he could not accept the truth of her death, but he chipped away at it every night.

He pried off his left shoe with his right as his thoughts circled around what a farce his life had become without his mother—out cruising every night for wireless hot spots, flunking his classes, his father spending weeks painting canvases that would look the same if they were used as filtration screens in a sewage treatment plant.

His brain mechanically flipped through images of the day, much like Bennie through his nude galleries—the murder scene at Jefferson Park, wireless routers, Bennie's inquisitive blinking cursor cutting through the thick, hostile bamboo of a text file, the uniquely captured video from the perspective of the female victim, his own camcorder video, his father's absurd paintings. Each image was ground to a pulp in the churn of his mind, until select fragments floated to the top. A synchronicity lay among some of these elements, waiting to be brought together.

Just as he toed his right shoe to remove it, he fell fast asleep.

CHAPTER 8

SUNDAY, 11:10 AM

BENNIE

AFTER HIS PHYSICAL THERAPY APPOINTMENT, Bennie napped. He awoke refreshed, but briefly confused by the bright-red digital numbers of the alarm clock as if his mind had awakened without preloading its complete set of software libraries. The digital cyphers of each number connected with a twist as he stared. Like chain-link fence.

Suddenly, the rush of the last forty-eight hours came back to him like a magician spewing forth his full deck of cards into the air. But one card remained in his white-gloved hand, stiff with expectant applause. It was the calm, steady, red flash of something else, something he couldn't yet place.

He grabbed his phone and dialed.

Jay answered immediately. "Yo."

"Can you meet me this afternoon? I want to go to that park and look around."

"Sure. But how about tonight instead? Like after seven. It'll be better if it's dark when we snoop around. It *is* a fresh homicide scene."

Bennie snoozed, rising and falling in and out of

consciousness as if upon the swell of an active ocean, the vague impression of the sun's rays changing positions in his room like a restless attendant. Toward dinner, he awoke again. He wolfed down a heated-up can of ravioli, downed a diet soda, and burped so hard it burned his sinuses.

A half hour later, he pulled into the same lot Jay said he had peeled out of the previous night. He parked alongside Jay's Taurus. Bennie got in his chair, rolled to the back of the van, then opened the side door. He straightened the brim of his trucker hat and deliberately paused long enough for Jay to read: "A good word for today is *legs*. Spread the word." Jay just shook his head.

Bennie looked around as the wheelchair ramp lowered. A smattering of other cars littered the parking lot. Just beyond, the tennis court lights blazed. A college-aged couple in their twenties patted the ball back and forth on one of the middle courts, their laughter and sneaker-slaps echoing across the parking lot.

The ramp hit the gravel with a *whump*. Bennie glanced again at the young woman playing tennis. *Sweet Jesus.* As with every time he saw a beautiful woman, he felt a heavy graveness transform his face, a funereal expression of mourning—the loss of yet another opportunity. He struggled to break his stare. "So take me to the spot."

Jay gripped his chair and pushed him over the gravel in the general direction of the courts. The chair rolled easier on the grass. Jay guided them in between the first two tennis courts. The wheelchair listed, and Jay corrected their course as they rolled along the edge of the drainage ditch.

Bennie studied the ground. The grass looked beaten down and muddied, likely more from the police and ambulance personnel than from the actual crime scene. Jay got down on all fours and swept his hand through the longish grass as if soothing a large beast back to sleep. The harsh brightness of the tennis lights created a strong contrast of light and dark everywhere. Individual blades of grass cut deep fissures of black shadow into the ground, making a thorough visual scan nearly impossible.

"What are you hoping to find?" Bennie asked.

Jay continued to rub and stroke the grass in larger circles. "I don't know. Those two guys wanted something badly enough that they took it off a dead woman. Maybe I can find a piece of it, or maybe they dropped something." He found a bottle cap and threw it over his shoulder. "Any chance you can access the autopsy?"

"Doubtful." Bennie turned to watch the girl rush the net to retrieve a drop shot. He shifted in his wheelchair and scanned the edges of the field. His fingers blindly groped in his chair bag, and he pulled out a Wi-Fi locator device. He flipped a switch on the side and held it up. "Nada. No signal. Not anymore, anyway."

Jay stood and brushed off his knees. "How could so much information have been transmitted? Right from this spot?"

Suddenly, a ringtone of MC Hammer's *U Can't Touch This* chirped from the courts. The young woman removed a slim black phone from the sweat-shiny cleft of her chest.

As she pressed her phone to answer, a switch flipped in Bennie's head. Jay moved behind the chair and started to push, but Bennie held the wheel.

"What?" Jay asked.

Bennie straightened his arm and pointed behind him. He watched Jay's eyes follow his finger toward the skyline, scanning just above the pine trees in the distance. Bennie turned in his chair to look at what he had noticed all along, but had given no significance. A small red light from a nearby cell tower signaled, coolly alerting them of its presence like a video game cheat-code that had kindly surfaced itself for Bennie, who was hopelessly stuck on a particular level.

Jay smacked his forehead.

"What if the signal was piggybacking on the cell tower?" Bennie asked.

They scrambled back to the van, with Jay doing most of

the scrambling. Bennie hit the gas before Jay could buckle his seat belt. They cut across the parking lot and got back onto the main thoroughfare.

Jay pointed. "Go along there."

On the opposite end of the forest that skirted the athletic complex, Bennie pulled alongside an ancient cemetery. The askew, rotting tombstones looked like an ancient skull's broken-off lower jaw, partially buried and overgrown with turf. He leaned over and grabbed a flashlight out of the glove compartment.

In a rush, Bennie had Jay carry him out and put him into his chair. Jay pushed the chair across the street, through the cemetery, and finally into a nearby copse of trees, where a uniform carpet of orange-gold needles eased the way. As they mounted the hill, Bennie looked back, feeling paranoid for the first time. He could barely see the van through the trees that had rushed in behind them, agents of the forest quietly blocking all exits.

As they approached, he spied the tip of the cell tower poking through the tall firs like the North Star, leading them deeper into the forest. Yet the gap between themselves and the tower never appeared to decrease. Traffic on the road was hushed, buffered by the natural sound barriers of the trees and underbrush.

Jay stopped and leaned an arm on Bennie's chair to catch his breath. Darkness had descended with extreme abruptness.

"Come on, dude. Your vagina hurt?"

Jay grunted and resumed pushing. "Gimme some light at least."

Bennie switched on the flashlight. The beam was immediately swallowed up at the edges by the ravenous dark, but Jay seemed okay with it. Bennie looked up at the tall canopy of dark branches and slightly lighter sky. The dampening effect of the trees made him feel small and vulnerable, like a lonely deep-sea mini-sub miles beneath the safe surface.

They finally made it to the base of the tower, only to find a convenient utility road approaching the same tower from the other side.

CHAPTER 9

SUNDAY, 1:57 AM

BOLSHOY

AFTER PLANTING THE **DVD** IN the subject's car, Bolshoy had no trouble finding the girl. She was back out on the street, wandering through the North End, cautiously picking her way through the natural urban obstacle course set by the homeless, the drunks, and those oblivious, repulsive four-legged beasts, otherwise known as "couples," on their way to their next bar hop.

The young prostitute looked like a little girl at a dress-up party who had lost her way and fallen through a trapdoor, straight to the bottom stratum of human existence. Her neon-green skirt flashed in the dark like a fishing lure working its way through the murky depths of the city.

He pulled over to the sidewalk so Malenky could lean out his window and chat her up. After a quick exchange, she slid into the backseat. He grimaced with disgust at her shiny outfit. Its gaudiness reminded him of Western excess, something never tolerated in his mother country.

He was barely able to meet her eyes in the rearview mirror as she unsnapped and snapped her purse, applied lip gloss, and picked at her thickly caked lashes. Her broad Asiatic eyelids drooped with affected calm as she powdered her face.

She would be a fun distraction from the dullness of his recent work. The missions had become tiresome with the unsurprising sameness of the routine: dropping off DVDs in mailboxes, on welcome mats, in cars, and in jacket pockets in coatrooms. He and Malenky were nobody's couriers, nobody's mailmen, not with their skills.

But work became more interesting the times he had to return to people when they didn't pay. He would first tail them for part of the day, maybe nudge their car on the turnpike during their commute. Once they arrived home, happy to be alive, he would park his car outside of their home the next night, revving the engine on occasion to ensure he was seen. Then, things got interesting.

It was all about escalation. If they still refused to pay, he would pull into their driveway and squat there. No one ever dared to call the police; every single one of the extorted knew the price of doing that: instant exposure. Videos did not lie. He had to hand it to Sturgeon. Credit was due there. But that didn't make him like the man.

The little black packages were attacks of conscience made tangible, a palpable menace, and Bolshoy was an extension of that same deadly regret. Sadly, most of the blackmailed would eventually fold, submit, and pay, and he and Malenky would be called off and sicced on the next victim.

He had not yet been given the chance to escalate to the next tier of harassment—the execution of family pets. He could only hope that day would soon come. All the same, he was becoming intensely impatient, feeling like a dog with no bite. He needed to *kill* to feel alive, and the need was not being satisfied by his employment with Sturgeon.

The real grunt work came from finding ways to retrieve the device from those occasional subjects who had died with the implant intact. The system was astute enough to capture, at least partially, all of those deaths. He and Malenky would get a name and a GPS coordinate. Then, they would improvise from there, orienteering for dead bodies. Some devices could not be retrieved in time, but that was okay, as those deaths were generally extremely violent and disfiguring—high-speed car crashes, industrial accidents, and falls from great heights. Threat of exposure to the program was of no great concern there. The last thing a medical examiner would notice among a still-vibrating pile of human bone, gristle, and tissue would be a tiny device hardly discernible to the naked eye.

He accelerated through the yellow light, turning right onto 91 North, toward the target motel. The powerful Hemi V8 engine vibrated beneath him. He rolled and cracked his neck and slowly began to transform himself in his mind to the thing he hated most—the scourge of modern history: the cowardly, retreating Russian soldier. The black leather sleeve of his jacket became the combed gray wool of Czar Nicholas II's disloyal soldiers. The fine accoutrements of the dashboard turned into the blocky controls of a Russian tank—though he knew those were not made until Nicholas II was overthrown. And the never-ending patches of construction around Boston were imagined as the several looted and destroyed land-owning estates of Nicholas's loyalist elite. His entire persona changed as he straightened his posture and flexed his jaw. He became angular, exact, and purposeful in all of his actions. He was a well-trained soldier, turning the steering wheel robotically in a calculated, point-guard fashion, driving with mathematical precision. The GPS murmured quietly in the background as if engaged in an intimate conversation.

His phone buzzed, and he flipped it open to find a text message from Sturgeon. He kept the device low and out of sight of the prostitute in the backseat.

steal the key to room 18
toss bed strip girl strangle
and then get back quick
have a problem with cell tower

He slipped his phone back into his jacket and pulled

into the motel parking lot. Malenky walked toward the front office while Bolshoy waited outside of the locked motel room with the girl. Bolshoy watched through the lobby window as Malenky distracted and flustered the motel clerk with intentionally thick and threatening Russian-English phrases. While the clerk was bullied out from behind his counter, Malenky palmed the necessary key with a simple sleight-of-hand maneuver.

Bolshoy remained rigid. Ramrod posture. He was an entry guard protecting his grandfather's estate. The girl sidled up beside him, slipped her tiny hand up the front of his shirt, and rubbed his stomach. She jerked her hand back, surprised, as if it had been pricked. He smiled. She was surely shocked at the hardness of his stomach, like rubbing one's hand across the cold, slick, unforgiving surface of a cobblestone street.

She slipped her small hand under his shirt again and cooed in unconvincing approval. She was over a foot shorter than his six-four frame. He shifted his stance and could feel the cold barrel of his Makarov pistol snuffling its nose down the crack of his hind quarters.

Malenky came down the walk with the room key dangling from his finger. Bolshoy checked for the picture in his pocket, but instead touched a piece of glass—his special weapon.

He had found it in the ruins of their family's abandoned Russian estate. After comparing old pictures to the overgrown forest, he measured with careful steps the full scale of the different rooms, the massive library, and his grandmother's sitting room. A few octagonal pieces of colored glass had lain strewn about a particular section of forest floor. He remembered the colored window from family pictures that had led to his grandmother's butterfly garden. The cousins had divided the pieces of glass as keepsakes.

He kept all but one of his pieces carefully wrapped in a steamer trunk by the foot of his bed. He carried one exceptionally beautiful lime-green, sickle-shaped, ironically enough, shard in a protective sheath at his side at all times.

The case consisted of two pieces of rough leather sewn together, meant to prevent any fracture of the glass. One end of the glass was wrapped in duct tape as a handle. The shard was capable of slipping across a throat with a whisper while severing both arteries.

He dug farther in his inner jacket pocket and finally located the laminated picture of his grandfather's estate taken by his grandmother from a hot-air balloon at her sixtieth-birthday celebration. His heart swelled with pride, then with anger for such loss. His blood pressure rose, causing the veins below his eye sockets to pump so hard they tickled his face. The protective laminate was cool to the touch, but as he trailed his fingers blindly along it, he imagined he could see through his fingers, see the skyline and the plush, sun-warmed linden leaves. His fingers detected distant warmth, residual heat from those impossibly bright and shiny Russian summers in the countryside, still trapped in the picture, each color and contour of the scene captured like a well-preserved fossil.

Malenky tossed him the room key and returned to the car, settling back in the passenger seat with a dog-eared reference book for video game developers.

Bolshoy unlocked the motel room door and shoved the girl inside.

"Hey!" She rubbed her bicep, puffing out her highly glossed lips.

He leapt upon her in an instant and ripped off her clothing like a bear skinning a salmon.

She stooped to recover her scraps of clothing, but he grabbed her and threw her toward the bed. Her body sailed over it to crash into the headboard. A gaudy painting of a Cape Cod sunset fell behind the bed, as if protecting itself. He jumped onto the bed and kicked away the pillows, comforters, and sheets before falling on the crumpled girl. Her panties ripped off with a swipe of his thumb.

He felt her attempt to loosen muscles, to relent, to facilitate. Path of least resistance. He could see her reasoning. She would let him get it over with, then be on her way. She stared without seeing, her black eyes filmed over with detachment.

"Hold this." He handed her the laminated photo of his grandfather's estate.

She took it. His hands slipped toward her warm throat. He resisted the urge to bring out his glass sickle. Those were not Sturgeon's instructions.

"Look at trees. Look at silver undersides of the leaves. You can see path of breeze through trees, no?" He seemed to be able to wrap his grip one and a half times around her small throat. "Do not drop picture. Look!" He moved her small chin with his wrist to focus her stare toward the picture. She must stare at it, even as she thrashed and convulsed and her eyes bulged.

She threw the picture down, which maddened him further. With both hands around her neck, he squeezed.

He squeezed and squeezed as he would a tube of dried glue. He watched her closely, nose to nose. Her ocular capillaries burst like small, slow fireworks. A pity she had thrown down the picture. She could have regarded the last peaceful place on earth he had ever known, a place he could never return to, but that he offered to all his victims. She could have departed the world with at least that.

On his way back to the office, his fingers rolled over the nubs of the leather steering wheel, remembering her slim, fragile neck and her tiny vertebrae that had popped in his clenched fist.

CHAPTER 10

SUNDAY, 7:40 PM

JAY

JAY LOOKED AT THE GENTLY sloped road they had somehow missed. "Well, shit."

Bennie laughed. "I doubt we could have gotten on that road. It's probably chained off and more protected than the cemetery." Bennie instructed Jay on what to look for as far as standard equipment on a cell tower. "You're going to have to make it close to the top to see any of the key equipment. Mostly, on this style tower, if you see more than two dishes, something's been modified."

"I won't be able to see anything," Jay complained. From his vantage point, the cell tower may well have been the very axis the Earth was turning upon, hinged deep into space by some large, slowly grinding gear. "If any men in black come, you take care of them."

Jay hopped over the four-foot chain-link fence that surrounded the tower, then jumped up and over a small wooden, padlocked bin huddling against the structure. At the base of the tower, he took a deep breath and started the long climb up the spine. Immediately, the action evoked dim memories of his childhood passion for tree climbing. The ascendance was an odd reversal of swimming, the temperature cooling instead of warming as he rose. With every step, an unnerving and invigorating sense of agoraphobia flooded his senses, dizzying him. A self-protective alarm increased in internal decibels as he rose.

His fingers and hands quickly bled their warmth on each cold steel bar he touched. Dimly discernible sections of red and white spray-paint passed as he climbed. The tower emitted a steady drumming buzz, as if it were a large mutant insect that could barely contain its excitement as the dumb prey took measured, careful steps into its glistening, gaping maw.

Jay guessed the tower to be about one hundred feet in height. He stopped roughly ten feet from the top. Wrapping his arms around the ladder, he fixed his feet more firmly and twisted around to investigate. The fir trees acted as ineffective guardians, leaning in at each breeze to monitor Jay's work, their dark limbs making impotent attempts to pull him down. The buzz was louder, as if, like the mixed colors of the spectrum made black, the sum of human voices and cell phone conversations had blended to create the droning hum.

Jay thought he could almost discern the slight curvature of the earth. Car lights swirled through the neighboring streets like tardy stars hurriedly arranging themselves in the firmament above. He took in one last three-hundred-sixty-degree view to file away the panorama in his mind, then concentrated on the task at hand.

At shoulder-height, two dishes were affixed to the upper portion of the tower. Both faced in opposite directions like long-shackled dungeon prisoners who had nothing else to say to each other. But he found no third dish, no third apparatus of any kind. Although afraid of touching an electrically live or hot piece of equipment at the top of the tower, Jay was still compelled to feel around for any abnormalities. Nothing had been in the grass. And it looked like nothing was on the tower either.

Wouldn't it really top things off if he missed a rung on the climb down? Gravity would pull him to her breast in her hasty love, not recognizing the hard earth in between Jay and herself. *Splat!* He carefully disengaged his right arm and began to run his hand up and down the tower. Metal bracings, rivets, overlapping brackets... His fingers encountered a braided tangle of wire and cable.

Effectively blinded but for moonlit shadows, he closed his thumb and forefinger around one of the wires and traced it up, expecting to reach the back of the right-side dish that eavesdropped on conversations to the west, toward the athletic complex. His finger snagged on what felt like a roach clip, then he felt a warm plastic box inches beyond. He grasped the box and gently turned it over while respecting the precarious tension of the wires and clips. A small green light pulsed at its base. He let the box go and trailed his fingers farther up, finding another intercepting clip and then the normal wire of the dish. He couldn't follow the wire all of the way to the back of the dish, but he was sure it terminated there.

He felt on the opposite side, but didn't find an identical box leading to the second dish. He cupped his hand around his mouth. "Hey, Bennie!"

"What?"

"I think I found something—a box. It doesn't look right. It's new. It doesn't belong. What do I do?"

"How big is it?"

"I don't know. Like a video cassette?"

"What's a video cassette?" Bennie never missed an opportunity to display his techno-snobbery. "Is it attached to anything?"

"Yeah, two tiny clips and plugs on either end."

"Listen, grab it. Those wires aren't electrical. They're like phone wires."

Jay considered that. "Then how is it powered?"

"Good point," Bennie admitted.

"Fucking A, Bennie!"

"Are the clips rubberized?"

"Yeah."

"Then if you stay on the clips while you disengage it, you'll be fine. And don't drop it!"

Jay took a deep breath and pinched the bottom clip, hoping the tension of the top clip would hold and the box wouldn't fall ninety feet to land on Bennie's head. The bottom clip dutifully released. Reaching with his left hand through the ladder so as not to give up his full grip, he unhooked the top clip and was able to pull the box free. It cooled in his hands almost immediately. A lot of throughput. He slipped the box into his jacket, zippered the coat to his throat, then tucked the tails into his pants before starting his descent.

Bennie called, "You just cut off about a thousand people's calls, dude. You better boogie us out of here."

Once on safe ground, Jay wasted no time in pushing Bennie back through the forest. The flashlight bounced wildly, and any unforeseen stump or root would have sent both of them flying. Each additional second spent getting Bennie installed in the driver's seat of the van pressed down on Jay's lungs until he felt he couldn't breathe.

Bennie pulled out his cell phone. "Zero bars! You rock, dude! What the hell did you just do?"

Good question, Jay thought, getting back into his own car. He also wondered what little ocean of secrets might be in the box, a technological conch shell awaiting Bennie's inquisitive digital ear.

CHAPTER II

SUNDAY, 8:20 PM

BENNIE

BENNIE RAPPED ON HIS MOTHER'S door. "Mom? You awake?" He heard a rustling, then the creak of a box spring.

"Bennie? Just a minute."

He leaned forward in the lightweight wheelchair they kept upstairs for his occasional use and cupped an ear. More rustling and what sounded like a gasp.

"Come in, sweetie."

The doorways downstairs had been widened for his wheelchair, but the ones upstairs hadn't been. He pushed open the door and wheeled up to the threshold until his arm rests butted the outer frame. He clucked his tongue. His own mother wasn't handicapped accessible. "Why's it smell like clove cigarettes and roses in here?"

She was still in her nightgown, likely had been all day, he guessed, sitting in bed with a paperback facedown on her lap. She wore her familiar frown, borne of worry, guilt, and love. "Oh, Bennie. You caught me red-handed. A mother's allowed her little indulgence once in a while."

"Don't worry. I won't tell on you. But you better hide that can of Glade."

"I'll do that." She flipped back the comforter, exposing her pale, stubbled legs, and wiggled her feet into her slippers. Her expression tightened as she walked to the doorway. She rested her hands on his shoulders and stared into his eyes. He had forgotten how piercing those gray eyes could be, a soldered gray, hard and insistent. "Honey, are you all right?"

"Jeez, Mom. Yeah, I'm fine."

"You don't look fine. You look tired."

He backed his chair away and broke off her stare. Five more seconds of looking into her eyes, and he would have succumbed. Like a Trojan Horse virus, she would have gotten well inside his head, and he would confess all: Jay's video, the dead jogger, and disrupting cell phone activity for a large part of Cambridge.

He scratched at a small coffee stain on the arm of his chair. "I'm totally fine. I just wanted to tell you I'm headed to Jay's tonight."

"Your sister's home."

"What? For the day?"

She shook her head.

"Why?"

"We'll talk later. You have fun at Jay's. *Safe* fun. I want you staying in. No carousing around, or I'll put some kind of GPS tracker on your van."

Bennie smirked. "You know what GPS is? I'm impressed. So, what's it stand for?"

She looked up toward the ceiling and gave it a full ten seconds of thought. "Geriatric Pole-vaulting Service?"

He raised an eyebrow.

"No? How about Gonadal Positioning Service?"

Bennie barked a laugh. "Close enough. Night, Mom."

CHAPTER 12

PETER K. HAMORI, MD

DOCTOR HAMORI, STILL TIRED FROM a relatively pointless eyelid surgery for some rich old bird, threw off his coat and collapsed in his chair. He let out a satisfied grunt as he worked off each of his shoes and cracked the small knuckles of each toe. Stretching his full frame, he sighed and rested his feet on the edge of his leather-topped desk. A large pile of patient files stared back at him, but he refused to meet its gaze.

As was his custom, he pointed a slim silver remote toward the far wall. Gently, Tchaikovsky's "Garland Waltz" ebbed its way throughout the room, calming his nerves with each new cleansing wave from the orchestra. He employed another remote to open the outer curtains, but left the inner silk curtains in place, imbuing the office building with a misty, dreamlike quality. Despite temporarily ignoring the dictation files, he sensed them there. They insisted upon themselves in his peripheral vision, a uniform manila mountain of folders with bright stickers signifying the first three letters of each patient's name.

He set his watch and drifted into a much-needed forty-five-minute power nap.

When he awoke to the digital beep, the pile of dictation remained, unmoved, demanding. He decided he would check his mail before plunging into the dreaded task. Besides, the mail was a much smaller pile.

In a rapid flip through the contents, he stopped briefly at a letter from a hot little sales rep who had visited last week. She was pushing some new collagen facial filler on the verge of being approved by the FDA. He grunted. She was self-aware enough to use her looks to forward her sales. A full-color portrait sat snug in the lower left corner of her envelope. He made a mental note to follow up on that.

When he moved to place the rest of the mail back on his desk, a slim package fell into his lap. The parcel was tightly wrapped in shiny black plastic. He flipped it over. No postage. No address. A simple gold label affixed. *SEDATION. What the hell?*

He looped his thumb around and ripped open the wrapping. Inside was a clear plastic case holding a mini-DVD. He considered waiting until morning and having one of the front desk girls scan it for viruses. The office was empty but for himself and the nighttime cleaning staff. He could hear the muffled sounds of cleaning carts rolling through the offices and the workers occasionally scolding each other in hushed, urgent Portuguese.

No, he couldn't risk handing the DVD to anyone else before seeing it first. With a trembling hand, he slipped it into his computer's tray. His screen desktop—a snapshot of himself, his wife, and his two boys on a stone beach in the French Riviera—was replaced by blackness, then video.

The video showed one of his female rhinoplasty patients; she was completely nude. His jaw dropped as he grabbed his mouse and brought up the video controls. The lower-right display revealed sixty minutes of video lay ahead.

He watched in horror as full-color video displayed all of his sins—sins he assumed to be known by him alone, a hermetically sealed secret held between himself, the unconscious women, and his ever-precious supply of nitrous.

There was redheaded Miss Tummy-Tuck, her pale, lightly

freckled stomach like a pool of warm lanolin. Young, sweet, and supple Miss Liposuction was followed by a slightly less pleasant tryst with Miss Sclerotherapy, although he had to admit that she did have some fantastically shaped legs, once he had worked wonders on her spider veins.

In shock and disbelief, he let the video play while he continued to smash his surgical headgear. Tryst after tryst mocked him. A virtual courtroom of violated patients was molested. At the end, a super-imposed note appeared in the upper-right corner:

As you can see, you are being watched. We have everything we need to destroy your life and your family. You have one thing you need to do, and if you do it well, we will destroy the evidence you have just viewed. Secure 100,000 US currency and transfer from your account to our numbered account by way of the secure link below. Work completely alone on this. When you have the money ready, click the active link below, and we will relinquish all original files to you.

Click Here >

He moused over the link, which revealed an unregistered website with no domain name, just an IP address. He hammered the fragments of headgear again with the bookend, gouging and ruining the leather desk cover.

Where the hell is it?

CHAPTER 13

SUNDAY, 8:21 PM

JAY

JAY STOOD IN THE **WELCH'S** parlor and listened to the steady whine of Bennie's rail chair as it ascended the stairs. The first floor was quiet and dark, but for the soothing respiration of the floor vent. Bennie had taken his rail chair up to the second floor to talk to his mother. Jay was surprised the chair worked. The device was a favorite target of Chloe's. In the aftermath of an especially heated argument, she would jam the chair rails with Tuff Stuff foam, throw the circuit devoted to it, or even leave the upstairs button depressed with a broom jammed against the opposite wall.

From what Jay had witnessed, Bennie's mother did little to referee the sibling rivalry. She rarely left her bedroom. She also tended to sleep all day, then stay up nights to smoke, read, and shuffle about her bedroom. Jay wondered if she suffered from some sort of depression. Bennie's father, who worked the third shift as security dispatch at one of the local community colleges, was hardly ever at home because he tended to pick up extra shifts.

Jay strolled around the small, but cozy room. An

overstuffed green sofa stood against the wall to the right. A three-paned bay window looked out over the dark front yard. To the left of the window, a large and ornate old-fashioned radio occupied most of the far wall. A gold-framed mirror hung above it, reflecting Jay's image like an accusation, as if letting him know he, too, was being watched, and further snooping would be duly noted and reported.

In the corner of the opposite wall, the cold fireplace presented a scattered array of family pictures, varying in size, shape, frame, and even bearing. He had seen these before, but had never had the opportunity to study them closely. Jay stepped closer to the mantel. Pictures of Bennie occupied the middle of the collection, like the pistil of a flower surrounded by the outward-facing, protective petals of the rest of his family.

He snapped on a standing lamp near the sofa and returned to the pictures. With the sole exception of Chloe, no immediate or extended family member was especially photogenic. The series of pictures gave the impression that the sum of all life's threats, pitfalls, and disappointments assembled together and presented itself into a fearsome form to that family. Some intimidating force steadily haunted them. The portraits of the cornered faces remained unorganized, hesitant, and trapped by something too strong to oppose. All were clearly resolved to protect Bennie to the last, but ultimately perish together, in devoted solidarity to the group.

Jay studied the pictures of Chloe. He was intrigued to see her progress from saggy diapers to toddling around in puffy pleated jeans, then later in her "tweener" years, approaching puberty, already showing hints of her long legs in leotards and glittery dance pants. In later photos, he could spot only the slightest trace of the awkwardness of puberty still evident in her comically long legs, short torso, and permed hair.

He moved on to the more recent vacation photos from last summer. They must have been taken during the early August trip when the family had gone to Hyannis, staying in the cheapest possible motels on the main strip. The family appeared a bit more brazen and healthy in those pictures, self-confident before the backdrop of the sun and crisply breaking waves, a warm bronze-tipped feather brush generously swept over their shining, open foreheads.

To Jay's regret, Chloe had worn a one-piece swimsuit, but he could still trace out the scalloped curve of her waist, her smooth stomach beneath the ocean-wet black Lycra, and the slightest hint of swell below her navel. He studied the soft teardrop of her well-formed upper abdominals, farther up to her fragile, bird-like upper arms. Even her natural standing pose was alluring, with her right knee bent slightly forward and canted inwardly to her left. Her hip was cocked, showing more outer thigh, a crescent hint of her apple-shaped—

"You want me to sign it, or what?"

Jay whirled around.

An unreadable expression on her face, Chloe stood in the doorway, well out of the range of the lamp's purview. She leaned on the jamb with her arms folded across her chest. She wore a short tee and roomy plaid lounging pants. The same knee jutted forward and swayed in an almost admonishing side-to-side motion.

Jay's face flooded with hot blood, as if his body were attempting to slow the hormonal fire raging in his hypothalamus. "Oh. Hi, Chloe. I didn't think the spring semester was over."

"It's not."

Jay waited, but she offered no explanation. He pointed at the picture. "That was, ah... That was when you went to..."

"Hyannis." Her eyes sparked, even while half-lidded.

"Yeah, Bennie invited me, but..."

Bennie had invited Jay as a way to help him with the recent loss of his mother and "to meet some babes." Bennie had spent the entire week before the trip with two mauve five-pound dumbbells, doing his "Curls for Girls" regimen. The invite had been a no-win situation for Jay. He couldn't go

75

because of how inappropriate he would have felt having fun in the midst of his mourning. Even if he had gone, Jay wouldn't have wanted to ogle other girls on the beach, especially with Chloe sitting on the same blanket.

She shuffled into the room in scuffed ballet shoes, stood in front of Jay, and placed two light fingers on his crossed arms. "Hey." She paused for a long moment. "I never got to say sorry about your mother. That was a horrible, horrible thing. She was so nice, so beautiful."

She was nearly an inch shorter than Jay. Her gaze up into his eyes turned his knees into quivering liquid globes. "I..." His voice cracked. *Oh, no.* With horror, he realized Chloe's face had begun to shimmer. The room began to swell and sway, and finally blur. He was about to cry.

Perhaps in a rush to help avoid him the embarrassment, Chloe stepped closer and embraced him. She slipped her arms under his and around him, then lifted her chin so he could conveniently bury his at her neckline. Her touch, the warm human contact, was like a ripcord that had been pulled loose in the tightly packed feelings he'd been carrying on his back.

His chest ratcheted twice, and his tears fell on her neck, matting her hair slightly and dampening her clavicle. He gently pushed her away, at once grateful and mortified. Despite his embarrassment, he didn't fail to register the clean smell of her skin and the swell of her breasts under her T-shirt.

"Can you tell Bennie I'll be outside?" he croaked, his head drowned in phlegm and his nose stinging of saline. He walked, seeing nothing but carpet, then threshold, wood floor, threshold, porch floor, deck. Out by the van, he let his hitching breath work itself out like an old engine that refused to stop.

Eventually, Bennie came outside, and Chloe followed, lugging two overnight bags for him. Bennie's smile faded when he looked at Jay.

Chloe kept her eyes downcast and her actions brief and economical. She gave Bennie a quick peck on the cheek and glanced up at Jay with an abbreviated smile. "See you."

She waved as they backed out of the driveway. Jay nodded back and managed a half-smile to Chloe as Bennie gunned the engine and made his way toward Jay's house over the sleeping and deserted midnight roads.

Jay hadn't bothered to ask his father if Bennie could spend the night. Dad hardly seemed to care lately and would figure it out in the morning when he saw the van in the driveway.

CHAPTER 14

SUNDAY, 10:34 PM

BENNIE

BENNIE WORKED HIS WAY THROUGH the veteran level of *Call of Duty 4* while Jay sat on the bed with the black box they had retrieved. Bennie's lips felt already chapped as he worked his tongue around the perimeter of his mouth, a side effect of fully concentrating. Jay had propped him up in the gaming chair with decorative pillows from his parents' bedroom so he wouldn't fall over. Despite the sound of the game, Bennie could still hear Jay's father's heavy pacing across the bedroom ceiling in the attic, but he didn't mention it. He was sure Jay heard the same.

Jay flipped the device around like a Rubik's cube, but with no pivoting mechanism. "So, how do we figure out what this box does?"

"Probably need to crack it open. I brought my Dremel. We can slice into it without hurting the components." Bennie took out two oblivious Nazi guards, only to be thrashed to death by a couple of German shepherds. "Damn!" He faked throwing the controller at the television. "Whatever it is, it's overriding the entire cell tower. But it's a serial process. Cell calls are still going through. We saw that hot chick answer her phone, right?" Resurrected in the game, he baited the dogs, dispatched them, then took out the guards. Red mists of blood exploded through the backs of their heads.

"So you think the tower was somehow hijacked to receive video signal?"

A third guard jumped him from behind and bayoneted him to death. "God*damnit!*"

"Hey, how many deaths did you get? Gimmee." Jay hopped off the bed and traded the black box for the controller.

Bennie traced his fingers along the disconnected wire dangling from the box. "Fiber-optic, high-intensity wire." He rapped on the hard rubber casing. He could get in there, no problem. "Forget the Dremel. Throw me a knife."

Jay grabbed a Swiss Army knife off the top of his dresser. He handed it over, and Bennie began carefully working at the rubber.

"Careful, dude," Jay warned, taking a step back.

"Whaddya think, it's gonna explode?" Remembering Jay's mother, he immediately regretted the joke. He carved into the rubber seam along the edge. Peeling back the top half, he could see an adhesive had been used between the rubber outer coating and the inner plastic, making progress difficult. He methodically peeled it off like the skin of some forbidden fruit, curling the black hide away from the box while he turned it against the knife. "Some kind of protective layer. Weatherproofing, maybe."

Reassured it wasn't booby-trapped, Jay sat next to Bennie.

Once Bennie freed the box from its outer shell, he found a thin layer of red foam. He peeled it off with his fingers. Something caught his eye. He held the box up to the brighter light of the television, the screen showing the Load/Save Game menu.

"Property of MD Defense Systems and the US Department of Defense." He tossed the box to Jay and then pitched forward onto the floor to army crawl toward the computer desk.

"Jesus, don't do that, Ben." Jay put the device aside, stomped over, and hoisted Bennie into his wheelchair in the corner of the room.

Getting that kind of help embarrassed Bennie, but he let it go. Jay pushed him up to the desk, then hit the lights and flopped onto his bed. Bennie searched the web, his quiet keystrokes soon backed by the sound of Jay's gentle snoring.

CHAPTER 15

KEITH HAMMOND

KEITH WATCHED AS THE TELEVISION screen blinked blue, then an amateur-looking video displayed a view of a highway overpass with cars silently streaming below. A sneakered foot entered the frame, sliding its way toward the edge of the sidewalk on the bridge, nudging shards of shattered brick into the stream of traffic. He experienced the same shock as he had when accidentally catching his reflection in a storefront window. For a moment, he didn't understand, but then he recognized his shoe.

He leapt toward the DVD player and jabbed at the pause button. As much as he could identify his own hand, he knew his own right sneaker—worn down to dirty canvas at the toe, the same flap of loose rubber that had peeled away from the sole. He fast-forwarded past several clips, all of him on bridges across the state, covering at least a year's worth of mischief. He looked at the black wrapping paper in his hands and read it again: *ASSAULT WITH A DEADLY WEAPON*.

He rewound again. There he was, last winter, experimenting with pebbles. He nudged one, two, then several over the side of the bridge with the toe of his boot. In the next clip, he rooted out fist-sized rocks from a wooded area near his target, stuffing three or four in each pocket. On the bridge, he made contact with a windshield of a Volkswagen Bug on his fourth try. The car swerved and spun a one-eighty in the grass of the median. He remembered noting that the Volkswagen's center of gravity was too low and that he needed something like an SUV.

There he was again, getting smarter, camouflaged in gray slacks and a gray bomber jacket, invisible among the bridge's metallic-gray supports, trusses, and superstructure, nudging convenient pieces of crumbled sidewalk over the side and into traffic.

The final clip was from last week, with the cinder block. He still remembered carrying the huge block in his backpack. It had been heavy and dug into his shoulder blades, yet felt so good, so right. He watched the traffic whoosh northbound up Route 495 like a fast-moving river. Whatever far-seeing camera had been on him had seen *everything*. The camera spotted the same tan SUV he had picked out as a target from roughly a half-mile away. There he was, just as he remembered, dropping the black backpack to the ground, unzipping it, and pulling out the block. There was his same smooth, casual motion as he hefted the block halfway up the tall side rails to rest briefly on the middle rail.

Keith shook his head and grasped the television with both hands, ready to tear it off the wall. The view zoomed in on his fingertips as he gave the large block one last, gentle push to send it thirty-something feet down to smash almost perfectly into the SUV's front windshield. The lens seemed to follow him as he rushed to the other side of the bridge to watch the truck swerve, catch on its two side wheels, and flip once, twice, three times before catapulting the driver out the side window.

A message popped up on the screen:

You are quite the little bridge troll, Keith. Consider us the Billy Goats Gruff. As you can see, you are being watched. We have everything we need to destroy your life and your family. You have one thing you need to do, and if you do it well, we will destroy the evidence you have just viewed. Secure 100,000

82

US currency and transfer from your account to our numbered account via the secure link below. Work completely alone on this. When you have the money ready, click the link below, and we will relinquish all original files to you.

Click Here >

CHAPTER 16

MONDAY, 9:21 AM

JAY

JAY AWOKE TO THE ALMOST-FORGOTTEN morning smell of bacon, eggs, and coffee. He opened his right eye and, for a quick second, believed he had gone blind. He couldn't see anything but white, no matter how wide he opened his eyelids. Left eye. Still white. He raised his hand to rub at his eye socket, and he brushed a waxed paper bag. He turned it around.

"I got you and Bennie some breakfast. Where is he?" Dad was sitting on the bed, leaning against the headboard.

Jay rubbed his eyes and looked around. *Good question. No Bennie.* His sleeping bag was an empty rectangle on the rug at the foot of the bed. He turned to look out the window. The van was gone. "Dunno."

Jay sat up against his headboard and opened the bag. There were two bacon, egg, and cheese sandwiches inside, and two medium cups of coffee stood on his desk. He might not be blind, but he was surely seeing things. "Dad?"

His father regarded him with his typically somber, remote expression, but there was something new—a spark of engagement in the eyes and a slight indentation in his cheek that was reminiscent of the father he used to know.

The light in the room was brutally honest on his father's face. His normally thick dark hair was greasy and thinner, segmented into thatches that exposed pale white scalp. His patchy beard looked especially haggard. His eyes, although sparkling a bit more, were hazy and overworked. Since his father had buried himself in his painting, they hadn't done a single thing together.

The last time he even remembered them enjoying each other's company was the spring of the previous year, just before his mom's death. They had been cleaning out the gutters, pulling clumps of decomposed muddy leaves and moss and dropping them into an aluminum barrel on the ground. When the heavy clump of decomposed matter landed in the barrel, a resounding boom echoed across the backyard and into the trees, which they both agreed sounded like the revolutionary war cannons they used in the reenactments in Concord each year. With each hit, his father had yelled from the roof, "Give me liberty or give me death!"

His father spoke, interrupting the reverie. "I finished my series last night, Jef-Jay."

Jay pulled himself up farther. "Can I see it?"

He placed a heavy hand on Jay's chest. "No, not yet. But you will." He paused for a moment as if wanting to elaborate, but then appeared to change his mind. "I left the address on the butcher block. It's in Cambridge tonight, at seven. I want you there."

Jay's phone began to vibrate, steadily working its way toward the cliff's edge of his end table. He silenced it.

"Be there, Jef-Jay. Tonight at seven. I left the address for you. It's a performance art piece of sorts."

"Okay, Dad," Jay replied, but his father had already left the room.

The phone buzzed again, and he flipped it open. "Ben? That you?"

85

The person on the other line sounded breathless, and he could hear rustling bags, a car horn, and the roar of an engine.

"Yeah, screw you too!"

"Bennie, where'd you go?"

"Jay, you have to skip school today. Meet me at the cell tower park. Base of the tower. And I mean *haul ass*. I have an idea, but I don't know how much time we have."

"I'm there, dude." He snapped shut his phone, wolfed down his sandwich and coffee, threw on a T-shirt and jeans, and raced out to his car. He left his street, wheels squealing, and nearly clipped an oncoming car. He waved in apology to the blank black windows of a Dodge Magnum.

He met Bennie in the parking lot, the breakfast sandwich somersaulting in his nervous stomach. Bennie had Jay follow his van back out of the sports complex and toward the far end of a self-service gas station. Once there, Jay hopped out of his car and jogged to Bennie's van.

The van's front seat was covered in plastic bags from a nearby electronics store, along with his toolkit, a portable rotating saw, a soldering kit, two A/C adapters, and a drill. The smell of heated metal and burned plastic permeated the interior. Even behind his nicotine-colored lenses, Bennie's bright eyes shone. He was jazzed.

"Take this." Bennie handed him the black box.

It felt heavier. He studied it closer. He could barely discern a thin seam along the component's casing where Bennie had cracked it open through its center, lengthwise, and later resealed it. He traced his fingertip along the seam. Still warm.

As Jay pushed Bennie back across the street and toward the sports complex, Bennie explained the plan, his high voice a vibrato over the rough terrain.

"So, I didn't find much last night on the defense contractor we found on the box, 'MD Defense.' But I found a cached yellow pages link to MD Software Solutions in Cambridge. But I couldn't find any other record of it. We can check on that later. But it hit me that whatever this box is doing to intercept cell traffic and whoever is doing it—the government, terrorists, some hacker, whoever—we have the opportunity to take full control of this chokepoint. Any traffic coming in, we'll intercept and hand off. I arrayed ten one-gig USB devices into a portable drive. The stream of data will get split and written there, and a duplicate stream of it will still be relayed—without too much delay, I hope—so whoever's doing this doesn't notice I've hacked in, and neither will the cell customers. If I had more time—watch the roots here." Bennie pointed ahead and continued, "Maybe I could have relayed it back to my servers, but this'll have to do. So I don't have a great idea of how much input is streaming through this tower, and it's kind of a blind process. It'll be writing every kind of communication, so the splitting of the signals will stop as soon as the drive is full. It might fill up in an hour or in two days. I have no idea."

Jay pushed him up the last hill, and the full broad base of the cell tower became visible. Thankfully, no one was there. Bennie warned him that their escapade from the night before had probably disrupted cell service, and they had to be on the lookout for any added interest in the area. That morning, Bennie had searched online for reported outages on cell carrier message forums and outage maps. Cambridge still seemed clear, for the moment.

"I attached a cheap wireless router into the device, so when we want to download the contents of the drive and clean it out for the next batch, we just have to come within eighty feet or so and pull it down from my—branch, Jay, branch!—from my laptop."

Jay backed Bennie into a thick bramble so that he was hardly visible from the base of the cell tower.

"Take these." Bennie handed Jay a small pair of miniature silver binoculars. "I'll be the lookout below, but it wouldn't hurt if you looked around a bit yourself as you get higher."

"How many coffees you have this morning?" Jay asked.

"What? Just one..."

"Yeah, one carafe."

Climbing the tower once again, Jay felt the morning sun warm his back and arms. But the tower itself had maintained the night chill, and its rungs were so cold they burned his palms and fingers. Against the cloudless light-blue sky, he could see the black cable idly swaying in the cool forest breeze near the top of the cell tower. The frozen black face and slit vertical eyes of the connector regarded him like a hanged man's blameful expression. It appeared untouched since he had disconnected it the previous night.

Nearly halfway up the tower, where the neighboring fir trees crowded the structure the most, he paused to catch his breath. He looked down to see Bennie give an anxious thumbs-up from a nearby hill, where the thick bush obscured his chair.

With the rigged-up interception device pulling on the shoulder straps of his backpack, he quickened his pace. The height filled him with a sense of vertigo, reminding him again of climbing trees as a boy, when he would pretend the sap in his hands was a Spiderman-like secretion to improve his grip. He remembered the thrill of finally arriving at the tops of the tallest trees in the local forest, the way the limbs and trunk became thin and rubbery and swayed back and forth in the thin breeze. For some reason, he felt even less safe on the tower.

He calculated maybe thirty more steps to go before he'd be at the point where he could plug the device back in and get the hell out of there. How did he ever think this was a good idea? Or even a worthwhile one? What good could come of it? He was still a minor. At least that was something in his defense when the FCC descended upon them with the full weight of their prosecutorial abilities. His intestines felt like a cornered, claustrophobic serpent that had just realized there was no exit and had begun to wind its way into a self-destructive knot.

His hands had become stiff and painful. He could no

longer feel the texture of the paint-flaked, rusty ladder rungs and could only perceive that his grip was occupied by some blank mass.

He looked up. The cord hanging above his head was an animate limb of the tower, reaching down to help him. High above most of the trees, he could see clearly. Neighboring businesses, a school, and the rooftops of surrounding neighborhoods surfaced like a lost drowned city resurrecting itself from the rolling green waves of the trees.

"Hey, fuck face!"

He looked down. From the bushes, Bennie pointed an exaggerated finger toward the dirt-packed service road that linked the cell tower to the town-owned utility road. Jay grabbed the small binoculars hanging around his neck and directed his magnified gaze to the entrance. The chain lay curled across the road, the padlock shining a small bright flash of warning. Twin contrails of recently stirred dust were settling on the road and falling in a synchronized dance along the path.

"Shit."

A utility truck pulled up to the end of the path, and a man in a crisp white shirt, blue jeans, work boots, and red suspenders lumbered out of the driver's door. He reached back into the cab, pulled out a work belt, and clipped it around his hips. His face was obscured by a white hard hat. He unclipped a pair of work gloves from his belt and fitted them on as he strode toward the tower.

The geometry of their imperfect plan, between himself, Bennie, the cell tower, and the threat of exposure from the service road, became painfully obvious to Jay in that instant. Bennie was on the opposite end of where a service repair person would arrive. Jay looked back at Bennie, whose grim face was a sheet of white, his large glasses slipping down his face as he pulled at his wheels to embed himself farther into the bushes.

Jay waved wildly at Bennie, not daring to speak, but

Bennie's petrified stare would not disengage from the approaching repairman. Bennie worked his way deeper into the bush and then suddenly, as if finally winning a fierce tug-of-war, broke free from the bush's tangled grasp and plummeted down the opposite side of the hill. His eyeglasses popped off his nose, but were saved by the flexible strap that held them on his neck.

Jay watched as Bennie's bouncing head disappeared from view. To his credit, Bennie didn't make a sound as he sped backward down the hill. Dread scenarios appeared before Jay. The stiff arm of a waiting tree. A rock wall. One of those rusted iron fence posts they'd avoided on their way up the hill.

The repairman, still calmly unaware, opened the padlocked wooden box at the base of the tower and rummaged around inside it. Jay hugged the tower's ladder, trying his best to become one with the structure, but he knew that wouldn't cut it. The man would make his way up the ladder, without question, and anything Jay did would only delay the inevitable. He had no way down.

The man finished his rummaging and moved to the base of the tower. He paused to speak into his radio.

Jay looked up again. *No escape there, either.* The top of the tower terminated in a single point, like an artist's first lesson in diminishing perspective, around which curved a crow's nest.

Would it be so bad if he let himself be caught? It wasn't like the guy knew his name. Maybe the repairman would dismiss him as just another lost youth caught making a dumb decision to climb a local cell tower on a dare. How bad would the fallout be? No. That wasn't an option. He couldn't let the guy catch him red-handed, turn him over to police, and have the police involve him in some investigation.

Could he jump the guy? In watching action movies, Jay always believed he would have poor luck in any effort to "partially" injure someone like a true action hero could— knocking out the bad guy with a quick karate chop to the scapulae or an energetic, but controlled rap on the head with a sap or pipe. He knew with his luck, he would no doubt kill the person on the spot and manage to injure himself in the process.

He held his breath and waited. The cold tingle from his hands and forearms raced up his entire body, as if the top of his skull had popped off and his body were filled to the brim with liquid nitrogen, freezing his body and petrifying it down to the last nerve.

Bennie still hadn't resurfaced. If he was okay, he was surely crawling, but toward Jay or back toward the van was anyone's guess.

The repairman planted his foot on the first rung and raised his hand and head simultaneously to reach up for the next. Their eyes met.

The man's relaxed, half-lidded eyes widened in surprise, as if making visual room for the enormity of the moment. His expression hardened, his brow forming an angry knot of grizzle. "Hey!"

Before the man made another move, Jay scrambled to the outer skeleton of the tower, away from the safety and convenience of the ladder. An unexpected warm breeze drifted from the open field and curled in at the base of the tower. The air seemed to push at Jay's back like a rescuer reassuring the jumper that it was okay.

But he couldn't jump. How would he even land? He envisioned his femurs popping loose from their sockets and driving themselves through his torso, killing him instantly and simultaneously forming a crude, self-supporting headstone on the spot. Could he jump and land flat into the pine needles and grass? He wasn't sure if he could clear the tower's cement base.

With no other option, he climbed higher on the outside of the tower to give himself more distance from the man and to ensure he didn't land like a burst water balloon on the cement below if he did decide to jump.

The man resumed his ascent. At every step, Jay would check and find the man looking up at him as they both climbed. The man was older, almost grandfatherly. Even from his height, Jay could see shaking jowls and the wrinkled, rosy-red back of the guy's neck.

The man looked up again, his mouth a grim slit. His red cheeks worked in and out like a hard-working bellows.

Jay readied himself for the inevitably embarrassing and awkward struggle. The man would grab at his feet, perhaps rip off a shoe, possibly unhook his claw hammer from his belt and swing it at him.

The man looked up again, perhaps to speak because his mouth opened. But no words came. All Jay could hear was the breezy white noise at the tops of the trees.

A spot at the base of the man's throat bloomed wider like a black flower. A fine pink mist coated the lower rungs of the ladder. The man's furry white eyebrows arched and froze like a seagull readying for flight. He crumpled and tumbled back down the short distance to the concrete, his boot awkwardly catching on a rung and turning his body as he fell. He hit the ground like a sack of groceries, his utility hat popping off and rolling a short distance before settling.

Jay jerked the binoculars up to his face. A black Dodge Magnum sat crouched on the access road, shiningly evil, like a witch doctor's black magic token carved of hardened tar resin. The car seemed familiar, but he couldn't quite put his finger on why. The doors were open, and the vehicle looked unoccupied. Two men jogged toward the cell tower, one of them tucking a long-nosed handgun into his jacket.

Jay immediately recognized the two Russian men from the previous night. *Had to be them.* He slipped back inside the protective frame of the tower and onto the ladder, quickly covering the remaining distance to the disconnected cord like a spider monkey, hoping the thicker tangle of infrastructure would obscure him. He ripped the black box from his backpack and plugged in the stubborn connectors.

His fingertip accidentally touched the active prong of one end while forcing the connection, sending a shock like the tail end of a cracking whip to explode in the center of his heart. He lost his grip on the ladder and groped blindly for it.

Once steady, he moved back to the exterior of the tower. Without giving himself time to reconsider, he one-footed a crossbeam on the tower's outer frame and leapt into the air, arms pinwheeling, eyes squeezed shut, aiming for the nearest tree, hoping at least one of its arms would save him.

The first sign of impact was like a right cross to his cheek. He opened his eyes to the blurred sight of the trunk of a tree.

The tree he had chosen was covered in sharply pointed branches. His right leg found no purchase, but his left knee had lodged into the crook of a larger branch. He hugged the circumference of the tree like a ziptie ratcheted to the tightest notch. Only when he attempted to adjust the position of his left leg did he realize a sharp nub had poked through the loose fabric of his jeans and just missed the soft tendon on the inside of his left knee. He yanked his knee free.

His head rang like an aluminum baseball bat pinging off a poorly hit fastball. He forgot for a moment why he had jumped. He looked down. The only signs of his escape were bark fragments floating to the forest floor.

The blow to his cheek spread as if the tree trunk, exposed for so long to the cell tower, emitted high-frequency wavelengths of pain. He held still for a moment. Out of the corner of his eye, he could see one of the men, the taller one, climbing the tower two rungs at a time. In no time, the guy was at Jay's equivalent height on the tree.

Below, the short bald one grunted and cursed, pulling the repairman by his ankles toward the service road. The tall one continued to climb, and in record time, he reached the point from which Jay had jumped. The man held the box in his massive hand, turning it, investigating it. His eyes followed the connecting wires to the top of the tower where they met the dishes near the top. He shrugged, let the box go, and began his descent. Jay blew out a lungful of air he had been holding as an ant fearlessly crawled across his face.

Back on the ground, the tall one gathered handfuls of pine needles and dirt and ground it into the cement base where blood had spattered. He rubbed a handkerchief from his pocket over the bloodied bottom rungs, then jogged to join his friend.

He looked down again to see Baldy loading the dead repairman into the back of the Magnum. Baldy tossed a set of keys to the tall one, who jumped into the cab of the utility truck. They pulled away in a broiling cloud of dust.

Jay worked his way down the tree in a barely controlled slide. He dropped the last ten feet onto his tailbone. He scrambled to his feet and limped to where Bennie had been.

Bennie was nowhere to be seen. A disturbed trail of leaves, torn moss, and broken branches terminated at the lip of an active culvert, but he found no chair and no Bennie. Jay slid down the hill over the moss, needles, and leaves. Downstream, what he initially took to be a discarded shopping cart was the mangled wheelchair lying fifty yards from the mouth of the culvert. He tried to remember what Bennie was wearing so he could at least spot the color of his clothing, but his overloaded mind wouldn't allow the request through—a denial of service attack on his brain.

"Bennie!" Jay screamed.

CHAPTER 17

MONDAY, 10:49 AM

BENNIE

BENNIE HEARD JAY'S SHOUT, BUT was unable to unclench his jaw in time to answer. The pain was excruciating. Suddenly, a phrase he had heard and never quite understood came to him: *exquisite pain.* That was exactly it.

An echo, like a second Jay at the other end of the forest, called again.

A minute passed as Bennie hovered his hands around the broken leg bone he didn't dare touch. The pale blur of Jay's head poked into the mouth of the tunnel. Bennie felt for his glasses. *Gone.* Jay seemed to hesitate at the mouth of the tunnel.

Bennie shifted slightly to wave, and a long knife of pain impaled his very core. He worried that when he crawled in as far as he could he had possibly done even greater damage. Jay started to walk in the opposite direction, downstream toward Bennie's wheelchair. *He can't see me.*

Bennie turned away from the bloody mash of his leg and found he could barely work his jaw free enough to speak. "Help. Over here."

Jay turned back.

Bennie shifted his chest toward Jay, but his hips remained twisted and away, toward the dark depths of the tunnel. "Here," he repeated.

Jay worked his way through the shallow stream, tripping and slipping over the slick stones. He arrived in a clumsy splash. "Are you hurt?" Jay moved a probing hand along Bennie's back, hip, both knees.

"I'm janked."

Jay splashed in the shallow water and came up with Bennie's glasses. The lenses were luckily undamaged.

"Scratch-free." Bennie beamed.

With his vision back, even in the dimness of the tunnel, he could see a red abrasion across Jay's cheek that looked painful. He pointed at it.

Jay shook his head. "It's nothing. Let's see what you got." He reached down to pull at Bennie's pant cuff. Bennie involuntarily pulled back, and Jay hissed. What looked like the broken stalk of a young bamboo shoot jutted out of the front of his leg at a thirty-degree angle, midway between his knee and ankle.

"Goddamn it, Ben." Jay pulled his windbreaker from his backpack. He loosely tied the sleeves around Bennie's leg.

"How bad is the pain?"

Bennie hissed. "I've been zero-dayed, dude. I don't think I can handle it."

"Hey! Where's your thing? Your syringe? Can we use that until we get you to the hospital?"

"Yeah, I guess maybe. But don't leave me."

Bennie accepted Jay's cupped hand of water from the stream. The cold water felt good and bracing. After a minute, he could feel his heart finally slowing and his breath becoming more regular. Possibly afraid to come near his injured leg, Jay dragged him by the armpits the short distance out of the deeper water, through small mounds of creek silt, twigs, leaves, and litter. Electric arcs of pain shot up his leg, but

UPLOAD

he bit off the urge to whimper. Instead, he concentrated on breathing and pretending everything outside of his lungs was not his and, therefore, could cause him no pain. It helped. He leaned his head against the curved wall of the tunnel when he heard a soft plop by the opening.

We're dead meat.

Although aware he should be more concerned that they had been found, he couldn't summon sufficient fear. No fight. No flight. Nothing seemed worse than the pain that singed his leg like a constantly applied branding iron. How'd they find them? He looked downstream. His chair lay downstream on its side, half-submerged, one wheel gently turning in the current, the bright silver spokes slicing at rays of sun. A trickle of pine needles spilled over from above, followed by one, then another tumbling pine cone.

Jay scrambled to his feet to run deeper into the tunnel, and then stopped, as if just remembering Bennie. *Go*, Bennie thought. *Go without me.*

But instead, Jay scrambled back and shielded Bennie's body with his own. *What would that get him? Two more seconds of life maybe.* Bennie closed his eyes, accepting whatever was to come. He listened to the burbling brook.

Surely, Jay's mother was waiting for them on the other side of some invisible barrier. She'd soon reach through, grab their hands, and lead them to a place where he didn't need his chair. Their wounds would wash away like a makeup artist's cheap trick, the mystery of her death and all deaths instantly unraveling as she pointed out the obvious trapdoor, the deceit, the trick of the knot, untangling it to its absurdly simple solution.

He squeezed his eyes tighter and waited for the silent bullet to cleave his skull, re-anoint his forehead with the kiss of unholy gun oil from the smoothly rotating jacket, and open the natural seam of his sagittal plane like a plump nut.

"Jay? Bennie?"

He opened his eyes.

Chloe's upside-down face hung from the top of the tunnel. "Chloe!" Jay shouted.

She disappeared and then reappeared from the side of the tunnel.

Warm relief flooded over him as his sister forged up the stream. He wanted to shout, cry, and clap. But all he could manage was a lazy smile.

She ran toward them through the shin-deep water, her eyes wide in shock. "What the hell is going on? Those men. They just... they just killed that repairman. Who are they? Are they looking for you?"

Jay shook his head. She had too many questions he didn't know the answers to yet. "What are you doing here?"

"I followed you guys. I knew something was wrong by the way you two were acting all secretive. I tailed you here and hung back in the woods while you climbed the tower. I was going to stop you when the repairman showed up." She looked at Jay, as if he were the older one. "Are you both insane?"

Without waiting for a response, she turned and crouched beside her brother. She started to untie Jay's makeshift tourniquet. "Oh!" She covered her mouth.

The whiteness of the bone shocked Bennie once again. Appearing to glow in its pureness, the teeth of the splintered bone exposed pulpy marrow and fragments of torn flesh.

Chloe turned and heaved. Then, she pulled out her cell phone. "I'm calling for an ambulance. The police. Those men could come back."

Jay snatched the phone.

"What the hell are you doing?" she asked. "Look at him!"

"We gotta go," Bennie said. A steady chill had begun to climb up from his legs.

Jay held her phone behind his back. "Listen, Chloe, Bennie and I are in the middle of some serious shit that we haven't totally figured out yet. Just give me at least the walk to the car to think before we call anyone yet." He cautiously held out the phone. "Okay?"

"You mean this wasn't just a stupid accident?" she asked.

"No, no. It was. But what we were doing at the time wasn't."

The leg pain surged again. "We saw a man get shot just now. Killed. Capped. Right by the cell tower."

Chloe furrowed her brow. "What? Where are you going?"

Jay stopped at the opening of the culvert. "I'll be back. A minute, I swear. Bennie, fill Chloe in with as much as you can."

Bennie summarized the events from Saturday night to present: the murdered jogger, the captured video, and finally, their sabotaging of the cell tower transmission.

Chloe shook her head. "And whose stupid idea was it to mess with private property and climb a cell tower *a second time*?"

"Both of ours," Bennie said.

Chloe screwed her formidable gaze into Bennie. It felt a lot like his mother's stare.

Jay returned with the slighter, temporary-use wheelchair and Bennie's backpack that contained the syringe used to control painful spasms for his spastic diplegia. He held out the syringe. "This should help, right?"

Bennie accepted the syringe and injected the Botox around the perimeter of the tear. He felt some immediate numbness, but pockets of pain also seemed to just move away and concentrate in other areas.

They made their way out of the forest with Chloe pushing the empty, damaged chair and Jay pushing Bennie in the spare one. The lighter chair seemed harder for Jay to manage, slowed by his limp and the deceptive shade that appeared and folded in on itself, hiding cleverly placed stones and roots.

The pain overcame him, and he could hold back no longer. He whimpered as quietly as possible. Soon, they were out of the cool damp shadows of the forest and in the expectant sun, drawing more than a few stares from passing traffic.

"You take your car back. Leave mine. I'll drive the van," Jay said.

To Bennie, the light and dark pockets of the forest seemed to have followed them to the van as he fell in and out of consciousness. The hushed phone conversation from the front seat between Jay and Chloe. The vague impression of questions being put to him by Jay. He couldn't hear much above the pain that seemed to shout into his ear. He began to welcome the darkness that kept returning. It pulled itself over him like a leaden blanket.

He came to suddenly and looked outside. How long had he been out? The car skidded to a stop. He took in a deep breath and lifted his head.

Jay was already out of the driver's side door and running to his house. Chloe slipped into the passenger side of the van and waited with him. She placed a cool hand on his arm. Bennie watched Jay run to the house and swing open the front door.

But he froze with only one foot inside. Instead of taking the stairs back down, he vaulted over the railing and slammed into the side of the van by Chloe's window. "We've been broken into."

"Where's your Dad? Is he okay?"

"I don't know. Do I go in?"

Chloe slid over into the driver's seat and shifted the van in reverse.

"Look, Jay. Come with us, and we'll call the police. I have to get Bennie to the hospital. He can't wait any longer."

"I can't leave. My dad could be in there. He could be hurt."

"Don't be an idiot, Jay. I can't sit and argue with you. Go to a neighbor's house and call the police. Don't go in there by yourself. Whoever broke in could still be inside. I'm taking Bennie to the hospital. My keys are under the seat."

Bennie sat forward to tell her no, he would stay with Jay. But the van lurched, the words escaped him, and the darkness returned.

CHAPTER 18

MONDAY, 11:19 AM

STURGEON

"**S**<small>IR?</small>" Sturgeon turned his chair to face Stephanie, but instead of stopping, he kept going. He continued to spin in circles, letting her image skate by in his vision with each revolution. *What tower had she said before? Seven.* He continued to spin. *Four. Five. Six.* On the seventh turn, he stopped and stared at her. He rarely spoke to her, and when he did, he slashed his words into her, envisioning each as a sharp flash of knife against her soft skin, each of her winces a crimson-marbled curd of yellow fat unfolding itself before him like a gruesome nighttime flower. Maybe when he was done there, that was exactly what he would do. No shooting. A nice, intimate cutting. Waves of vertigo, like brushstrokes over still-wet paint, blurred his thoughts.

He brandished his smile like a sickle. "Yes?"

She tried to maintain his gaze, but eventually lowered hers ever so slightly toward his sternum. "That tower. Cell tower seven. Where the interrupt was this weekend and the disconnect?"

The idiot actually paused for him to answer. "Yessss? Go on." He dug his nails into his palms, his tension temporarily relieved as the nails punctured half-moon slices into his skin. First the siphoned video, then this. Had they been compromised?

She scratched her head and looked back toward her workstation. "Well, it's back online. I didn't do anything to fix it."

He didn't like that at all. And he didn't trust cell towers magically coming back online. "Get them back here."

He could no longer take the pressure. He needed to sink low again, where he belonged. He ached for deep, dark anonymity. It was time to tighten up and gather all the loose ends.

CHAPTER 19

MONDAY, 11:35 AM

JAY

NO NEIGHBOR INVOLVEMENT, JAY DECIDED. He knew what would happen. One neighbor would hold him back while another had a look. No way. Nobody would stop him being first to help if his father was hurt. He steeled himself, not quite convinced he was making the right decision. Glass shards crunched beneath his feet as he entered his kitchen and looked around warily. The walls remained bare, and the same sheets and cans of paint were scattered throughout the house.

"Dad?"

No answer. All he heard was the hum of the refrigerator. He circled the downstairs and found each room the same—walls stripped bare, paint cans and bedsheets strewn throughout the house.

"Dad! You here?" He ran up the stairs two at a time and made quick work of searching through the upstairs bedrooms and closets.

He grasped the cord to the attic stairs, then froze. All that time his father spent in the attic, disconnected, silent, brooding, painting all those horrid black shapes—he pictured his father hanging from the rafter, a neat cord of clothesline rope around his neck, his face purple and bloated. But that didn't explain the broken door glass in the kitchen. Instead, maybe his father was still up there, being interrogated by the Russians looking for his son. He pictured the large one's huge hands around his father's neck, squeezing tighter and tighter.

Jay ripped down on the cord and ran up the stairs while they were still settling on the floor. Before his head even broke level with the attic floor, he knew he had it wrong. The attic was dark, still, and empty. He reached out and flipped the light switch set in the wall near the top of the ladder.

The only thing hanging from the rafters was the lightbulb. All of his father's canvases were gone, and his easel was folded and placed neatly in the corner. The greater bulk of the attic's contents was still pushed to the far corner of the room.

Jay's legs felt like a rope bridge whose supports had been cut simultaneously from both sides. He fell to his knees and stared at his thighs, feeling the weight of tears gather and drip down the bridge of his nose. He watched as the tears plopped onto his faded jeans and restored damp circles of new denim. An overwhelming desire came over him to just stay in the attic and let whatever happened happen. Bennie was in the hospital. Chloe was safe. His dad was gone, but what could he do about it? Yes. He would lay there in the attic and let the nastiness of the world just rotate around him and do with him as it liked.

He slumped onto his side to see how it felt—total resignation. A new kind of relief washed over him. Not the relief of a clear conscience or of doing something right, but a relief comparable to a resolute suicide. Not caring could feel *good*. He let the relief of giving up creep up his limbs and throughout his body like an advancing rigor mortis and pictured it moving a nerve fiber at a time.

He opened his eyes. How long had he been there? He cast

his gaze up to the ceiling, where he had been glad not to find his father, and spotted what looked at first like a wraith of black paint. Because of the structure of the rafters—the upright beams meeting together at the apex of the roof and the smaller eight-inch-long two-by-fours nailed into each upright at even intervals—the paint smears made no sense. Jay stood, wiping at his dusty knees, and circled back to the opened hatchway to the stairs. As he moved, keeping his eye on the ceiling, the smears began to reassemble like a clever movie studio's logo. His father wouldn't let him rest and was telling him as much.

RUN

He read it again, unable to pull the three simple letters into a word that had meaning.

RUN

When the word finally sank in, Jay stumbled across the room and lunged down the stairs. In the kitchen, he picked up the phone to call Chloe. Then, he had a new thought and punched redial to call the last number dialed.

"Edelberg Galleries. May I help you?" a woman answered.

Gallery? Crap. He had almost forgotten… his father's showing was that evening. "Oh, hi. Um… this is Jay Brooks, Stephen Brooks's son?"

"Yes, of course. We're looking forward to seeing your father tonight. We received his canvases by courier this afternoon. Do you know if he's left for the showing yet?"

Jay looked up at the bare wall for the kitchen clock, then checked his watch: 5:22. "Um… he said he might be late, um… due to a family emergency."

"Oh, I'm so sorry. Is everyone all right?"

"Yeah, um… we think. But I'd like to come and meet him when he gets there. Will that be okay?"

"Of course," she said. "We were hoping for a small introduction from him at the start of the evening and to have him on hand in the event of any questions or possible sales."

"He'll do his best to be there. Thank you."

Jay hung up and tried texting his father's phone. What was the name of the company Bennie had found on the device? He typed: *where r u? r u ok?* He sent the text, then hesitated. If his father had been kidnapped for what happened at the tower, would he have known about those guys beforehand? Did this tie into his dad's strangeness over the last year? The showing tonight? He sent another: *what is md software slns?*

He knew his father didn't always have his phone with him, but it was worth a shot. He then speed-dialed Bennie's cell.

Chloe answered, sounding out of breath. "Hey, Jay. We're pulling up to the ER just now. I've already called my parents."

"I'll be there."

"Don't. My parents are wired and asking all kinds of questions. I told them you two were being stupid idiots and joyriding together in Bennie's chair at the park. Once they get here, I'll meet you back at my house."

"Okay, fine. Chloe, I think whoever we messed with this week with the cell tower stuff knows who I am. My dad's missing."

"Are you sure he just didn't step out?"

"Not without his car. Plus, he left a message." Jay told her about the painted "RUN" in the attic. "I have to grab a bunch of stuff for Bennie, but I think it's best that both me and Bennie don't sleep where we're supposed to tonight. I know this sounds weird, but my dad made me promise to be at the art showing tonight at seven. I *have* to be there. I think there's something more to it that I'm not getting yet. Can you come with me?"

"Yeah, sure, but—"

He hung up and quickly gathered a change of clothes and his toothbrush. He ran to the bathroom and found a circular bandage in the bathroom closet to protect his raw cheek. He suddenly realized he may not be back home for a long time, or ever, and stopped for a second to consider what else he might need.

Hard drive.

The computer was turned off, and the monitor still hadn't been replaced. With no time for care, he ripped open the computer's plastic tower casing, popped out the hard drive, and threw it in his bag.

He jumped in Chloe's car and was at her house in minutes. He banged on the front door, and as soon as Chloe answered, he said, "Let's get all Bennie's stuff. We can talk in the car."

They gathered Bennie's laptop and all its accessories into a duffel bag and were on their way back to Cambridge.

"Aw, shit." Jay banged the steering wheel.

"What?" Chloe asked.

"Cambridge? Art gallery? Look what I'm wearing." He gestured at his bloody, dirty clothes. He looked at Chloe's capris and T-shirt. "Sorry, but that won't do, either."

She threw her hands in the air. "I wasn't thinking. You were in such a hurry."

"Okay, I can't go back to my house. I'm worried whoever took my dad will come back around again."

"Well, if you can't go home, and your dad is now gone, is it safe for my parents to go home? Shouldn't we warn them?"

Jay considered it and shook his head. He had to bluff to keep Chloe's head in the game. "They're clearly after me. I think Bennie's safe. You're safe. Your parents will be fine."

"Okay. Well, for the clothes, let's do what everyone else does when they need nice clothes and can't afford them."

Jay raised his eyebrows. "Steal them?"

"No. Rent them, silly. There's at least three rental places between here and Cambridge on Route 9."

Two miles down Route 9 East, Chloe guided him into a parking lot in front of a store that rented formal clothing.

"Great idea, Chloe. Let's hurry."

They split up with different attendants and were quickly measured for a tuxedo and a cocktail dress. In the bathroom, Jay stripped off his sewer-smelling clothes and cleaned his face in the sink. He wet his hair and hand-styled it. After putting on the tuxedo, he went out and waited for Chloe.

She exited the dressing room a few minutes later with the shoulder straps of a black dress sagging by her elbows. She held the front against her chest with a demure left hand. "Can you zip me?"

The sight of her delicate clavicles and the flushed pink swell at the base of her throat made Jay swallow hard. He envisioned pressing himself to her, making their chests, stomachs, and hipbones connect like electrical contacts. He turned her consoling hug from the other night into something else entirely in the brief second he gave himself to take in all of her before she spun around, sweeping her long brown hair to the side, exposing her neck like a willing vampire victim. The zipper had flipped and lodged itself in reverse on the inside of the dress, and Jay's resulting fumbling was both stirring and embarrassing.

Chloe paid with a Discover card reserved for college expenses, and they ran back out to the car. As Chloe worked on her makeup in the visor mirror, Jay called the gallery and got directions from the Mass Turnpike. Traffic was light, and he found a metered spot available on the same block as the gallery.

A trim college-aged Asian woman was handing out flyers at the door. Apparently, his father was only one of several burgeoning artists being premiered. His show didn't start until seven, so Jay and Chloe browsed the rest of the gallery in the meantime. His father's space was allocated to the far wall. On their way, Jay grabbed two glasses of champagne sailing by on a silver tray and handed one to Chloe.

"Now what?" she asked.

Jay checked his watch: 6:15 p.m. "I'm not entirely sure. My dad was very serious about my coming. He wouldn't take no for an answer."

"Do you see him anywhere?"

Jay scanned the room. "No."

His father's work was to be displayed along a bare wall, over twenty feet long. Hung from the face of the wall was another extruding wall just as long, but only three feet high. A placard on the far left of his father's blank wall read: "Stephen J. Brooks, Collection: It Is And It Isn't." Jay touched the wall. Just then, the recessed lights that spotlighted the wall went dark. Several shadowy shapes swarmed from some hidden offstage area.

Jay grabbed Chloe around the waist and started to pull her back. A dollop of her champagne plopped onto the floor.

"Jay, it's okay," Chloe reassured him and pointed at the wall.

The black shapes didn't advance toward Jay and Chloe, but clambered to the wall. Several patrons of the gallery turned from other exhibits and gathered behind Jay and Chloe. Each of the dark-clothed assistants carried two of his father's small canvases. They simultaneously withdrew rubber mallets from the pouches of their dark hoodies, held frames to the wall, and tapped once to fix them in place. After repeating the procedure with the second paintings, they returned behind the wall, as efficient and orderly as an insect hive. Each canvas employed the same pointillist method, representing recognizable shapes: a barn, a tree, and an eagle.

The lights came back on, illuminating the final canvas. The painting was the one his father had shown him in the attic, the shapeless one that didn't look like anything at all. To combat his wooziness and flush out the champagne, Jay flooded his system with carbonated water and nearly sent his brain into toxic shock, but still, the gallery continued to revolve slowly around him. The lights, the people, the exhibits... all developed a Gaussian blur. Even the distinct conversations blended, and concentrating on a single one became hard. He enjoyed Chloe's warm presence at his side as she laced her fingers into his, resting her temple on his shoulder as they strolled.

Hopeful that, despite everything, his dad might show, Jay asked Chloe to stay a few minutes longer. They studied a collection of photographs entitled *"Meani*al Labor," which contained close-up photographs of blue-collar workers throughout Boston—toll takers, construction workers, firefighters, policemen, postmen, janitors, and cashiers. Overlaid on each of the faces in angry red letters were the person's top five pet peeves against those they serviced.

The toll taker was an elderly black man. The resolution of the photo was such high-quality that the pores of his face appeared as tar-filled teardrops in his skin. His watery eyes were an otherwise-stunning rich brown, but the inner spokes of his iris were irregular and dirty yellow, like a suicidal star exploding in shame behind the eclipse of the pupil.

Over the almost microscopic inspection of his face, in stern block letters, the picture iterated over his customer pet peeves:

CUSTOMERS THAT WAIT UNTIL THEY GET TO ME TO GET THEIR CHANGE READY

DIRTY PENNIES

CLEAN PENNIES

ROLLS OF PENNIES

BROKEN DRIVER'S SIDE WINDOWS

Chloe sniffed, rubbing her cheek against Jay's shoulder. "What is it?"

"I'm worried about Bennie. He looked so scared. What happened today? What are you doing with him anyway? Are you using him?"

Jay turned to her, shocked. "Hey, slow down, Chloe. We're just a couple of guys who stumbled onto some serious, serious shit. Neither one of us knows what's really going on, but we have to find out. Whoever's behind this witnessed a murder and didn't come forward, and just today killed a man for intercepting whatever they're trying to do. As to why I'm friends with Bennie, I like him. I've never really had to explain it. No one's asked me to. Do I have to?"

"A cripple. An oversexed, bitter, basement-dwelling recluse."

"Listen, Chloe. I'm worried about my father. I'm also worried about myself and about Bennie. That's my top priority. Don't ask me to justify my friendship with your brother." His words all came out sterner than he had intended.

She wiped the back of her thumb across both cheekbones, careful not to smear her eyeliner. She nodded, lifted her shoulders for a beat, and let out a breath.

"Hang in there. We're almost out of here," he said.

Promptly at nine thirty p.m., his father's canvases were gathered and boxed. On the way out, Jay felt a heavy hand on his shoulder.

A balding man in a dark suit and light-blue cravat stood behind Jay, pleasantly smiling. He held a manila folder in his hand. "Mr. Brooks?"

"Yes, Jay Brooks. Stephen's son."

"Allow me to introduce myself. I'm Gerry Edelberg, owner of this gallery. We were so sorry your father couldn't make it to his own showing. We did receive a message from him earlier in the day to entrust you with his artwork if he didn't show for some reason." The man indicated for Jay to follow as he made his way behind the front gallery desk. He lifted two white cardboard boxes onto the countertop.

"Yes, thank you." Jay and Chloe each grabbed a box and headed back out to the parking lot, making a quick detour to finally retrieve Jay's car, which he was relieved hadn't been ticketed yet.

CHAPTER 20

MONDAY, 9:55 PM

BENNIE

BENNIE SNATCHED UP THE HOSPITAL phone beside his bed on the first ring. "Hello?"

"Hey, how ya doing?" Jay asked.

"I'm laid up. They reset the bone. Glad I was passed out for that part."

Jay laughed. "Well, I'm glad you're in good hands."

"So, what the *hell* happened today?"

Before Jay could respond, Chloe spoke up in the background.

"Hold on," Jay said. "I'm going to put you on speaker."

"Bennie, we're on the way," Chloe said.

"No rush, guys. Just bring my equipment."

"Got it right here," Chloe said.

"Hey," Jay said, "we went to my dad's gallery showing. He wasn't there. He was taken, I think. The house was broken into. He left a message for me in the attic. Someone's onto us somehow, and they've pinned it on my dad."

"What do you mean *taken*?" Bennie thought of how Mr. Brooks had looked Saturday night. *A hunted man.*

"Gone. His car's still in the garage."

"You mentioned a message. What'd it say?" Bennie asked.

"Run."

Silence fell over the line. A monitor to Bennie's left beeped, sounding at the moment like the music played on a quiz show while everyone groped for the correct answer. He shifted in his bed, sending a twinge of pain to his hip. "Listen, just get over here, and we'll figure this out."

Thirty minutes later, Jay and Chloe rushed into the room, filling it with welcome noise and movement. Bennie hadn't realized until then how lonely he'd been getting.

"Do you think your dad's okay?" Bennie asked.

Jay shrugged and looked away. His lower lids shined, brimming with tears. He ran a quick arm over his eyes and threw a gift shop bag onto the hospital bed.

Bennie dumped the contents onto the bed. *Fitness Magazine* and *Marie Claire.*

Jay cleared his throat. "We should have checked you into a nicer hospital that actually has Wi-Fi. I thought you could use these."

"Ha. We'll see about that," Bennie said as he accepted the duffel bag from Chloe.

He noticed Jay and Chloe staring at his leg, which had been raised in traction, but wasn't yet in a cast. Chloe touched the facial abrasions on his cheeks and forehead as if they were hot embers. She grimaced when she spotted the head wound high on his crown that had been shaved, stitched, and bandaged. She gave him a hug.

"How were Mom and Dad?" she asked.

"The usual mess, but they chilled. Finally." He unzipped and checked out the duffel bag: laptop, several illegal peripheral devices, cables, wires, antennae, a small tool kit, a hard drive enclosure, a portable DVD player, and a wireless mouse.

"That's all the stuff you wanted," Chloe said.

Jay threw what looked to be a plastic toy onto Bennie's

lap. "It's one of those geriatric claws. I thought you could use it."

Bennie picked it up. He turned it, squeezed the handle, and watched as the mechanical claw slowly closed and came together, completing an octagonal grasp. He read the large capital letters imprinted on its side. "The Gripper."

"A good tool for the elderly and infirm," Jay said. Chloe elbowed him in the ribs.

Bennie hung the claw from his bedside and made a mental note to get Jay back for that.

"And here." Jay handed him a box. "Our hard drive. I thought if they—whoever they are—think my dad's involved… I don't know, maybe they tried to contact him via computer or hacked in to snoop around? Maybe you can trace their steps? I don't know."

"Nice." Bennie started to fasten the hard drive into an enclosure that would allow him to attach a screen, monitor, and mouse. "They tell me I'm in for at least three days, so I've got the time."

"And…" Jay lifted two cardboard boxes onto the bed. "Here's my dad's artwork from tonight. I don't know what you can make of it. He called it 'It Is And It Isn't.'" He shrugged and pointed at the boxes. "But there's something there. Gotta be. My dad was really weird about me going to the showing. He insisted on it. So I think there's something, some message he couldn't get to me otherwise."

Bennie doubted it, but kept quiet. What would a painter know about embedding secret messages?

Jay rolled a portable table over Bennie's lap at an angle to avoid his raised leg. Bennie felt like a slowly assembled cyborg. He started to arrange his laptop, devices, and peripherals on the table as naturally as one would tie a shoe—or assemble a rifle.

"Why don't you guys hang out in the cafeteria? But keep your cell phones on."

CHAPTER 21

MONDAY, 4:02 PM

STURGEON

STURGEON DOUBLE-PARKED HIS 750i BMW outside of Bolshoy and Malenky's Cleveland Circle apartment. No goddamned way was he going to drive around for forty minutes looking for a spot. The traffic in Brookline had not quite hit maximum density, and if he made his visit quick enough, he could get back to the office unscathed and in full possession of his car. He crossed the sidewalk and without turning, in one smooth motion, expertly leaned into a passing jogger, hitting the guy low at the hips.

The jogger flipped and tumbled into the faux-brick face of the apartment building, settling in a lump on the sidewalk. His shiny, shaved legs scrambled for purchase. "What the hell?" He got to his feet.

Sturgeon lunged forward and stomped his foot, and the runner took off like a scared rabbit. That little action let off at least enough pressure so he could think clearly when he got upstairs.

An hour earlier, Sturgeon had received a call from Stephanie about Stephen Brooks.

"We have another problem now?" she said. "The house-arrest you have me watching? He made an Internet attempt on his computer, which I intercepted, and then he had a courier pick up some artwork at his house. When he signed the electronic invoice, he wrote some really weird crap about—"

"Send it to my device."

A small image appeared on his Blackberry. The script, condensed into the narrow window allowed by the signature capture device read:

Stephen Broo—help me I'm trapped in my house they killed my wife and there's no way out

He had to put a lid on this before the Leadership found out and got involved. He buzzed the apartment and was let in. He paused for a moment in the foyer to collect himself and accrue some level of control. He couldn't let Bolshoy or Malenky see him flustered. The Russians were like pit bulls; they would only respond to those they respected, and if that were ever compromised, they would have to be put down. He leaned against the mail slot counter, his hands idly sorting through the piles of misdirected mailings.

Stephen's previous attempts to contact the outside world had been a mere nuisance, dealt with by Sturgeon's voice-altered calls, then a persuasive visit from Bolshoy and Malenky. He had hoped the last two attempts would be Stephen Brooks's final tries. But he had been foolish to think Stephen would remain self-contained to the end.

Keeping Stephen under house arrest, per the directives from the Leadership, was proving to be an impossible task, especially while secretly trying to exploit the project for his own benefit. Gains for the year had been immediate. Once the program had been officially terminated, then secretly revived by some subcommittee or other, little oversight had been instituted. Therefore, Sturgeon was rarely disturbed, with the exception of the occasional contact from the Leadership to check his progress on capturing and cataloguing crimes in the video library. The program would consider the beta testing complete when at least twenty percent of the unsuspecting recipients had committed any level of crime and the evidence could be used in court.

Sturgeon already had that much, but he didn't let on to the Leadership. Fully three-quarters of the recipients had been catalogued engaging in all sorts of interesting, or at least highly suspect, activities. But Sturgeon wanted more video captures that could be fruitfully exploited for financial gain.

In the meanwhile, he dutifully submitted his reports to the DOD to show that he was making progress in "shutting down" the program and destroying all documents and data that might indicate the US government's involvement. If he could keep the program running for a few more weeks, he would have enough money to retire.

Sturgeon smoothed the wrinkled flyers and mailings that he had crumpled in his fists. He could feel the blood in his face slowly dissipating, like mercury in a cooling thermometer. When the flyers and envelopes were finally in neat, straight piles, he raised both fists and slammed them down. With a squeal of dislocating hinges, the entire counter crashed to his feet. *Screw calm.*

He climbed the four flights of stairs, knocked, and brushed by Malenky as soon as the door opened. "Where is he?"

Malenky led Sturgeon through a comically tiny, dingy-gray kitchen and into the living room.

Bolshoy sat on a black leather sofa, his barrel chest heaving as if he had just finished a workout. In one corner of the room, the Red Sox scrambled across the widescreen television in a game broadcast live from a mere four miles away. In the other corner sat the bound form of a man in a straight-backed wooden chair. He wore a candy-red beard of blood on his chin and cheeks.

Sturgeon walked over and stood in front of him. "Why, *helloooo,* Mr. Brooks."

CHAPTER 22

MONDAY, 11:58 PM

JAY

JAY ANSWERED HIS PHONE AS soon as it rang.

Without even a hello, Bennie asked, "Does your dad know binary?"

"Binary code? Like ones and zeros?"

Chloe sat across from Jay in the cafeteria, gripping a small cup of coffee.

"Yes, Jay. Like ones and zeroes. Can you just answer the question?"

"Well, yeah, he does. My mom bought him one of those geek binary clocks as a gag birthday gift. But he took it seriously and spent a week learning how to tell time by it."

"So he knows binary to numerals. But could he do the same with letters? Does he know enough?"

"I really don't know." Jay thought for a moment. "I think he bought one of those quick-reference guides, so maybe. Are you saying there really is a clue there? I mean, if there is, my dad's been working on that for, like, weeks. He would have started way before we screwed with the cell tower. Maybe it *isn't* me they're after."

"We'll find out in a sec." Bennie hung up.

Five minutes later, Bennie texted, telling them to come back to his room. When they got there, Bennie didn't look good, and Chloe's concerned reaction was clearly registered on her face. His skin had a diaphanous sheen in the harsh overhead fluorescent lighting, and the blue-green of his veins was discernible like a faded tattoo of a banyan tree.

Still, he energetically explained his breakthrough. "It was obvious that the only painting that could have any meaning was the one your dad wasn't able to make into a real shape or object." He lifted the painting that had caught Jay's eye at the gallery showing, the last one to be displayed. "And what did you say he called the series? *It Is And It Isn't*? What's another way to say that? Yes and no. True and false. *Ones and zeroes.*"

"Binary," Jay said.

Bennie nodded. "Your dad chose something he knew how to do, pointillist painting, and melded it with something he knew we, or at least *I*, would know. He chose a textured canvas and then either painted a dot or didn't. A dot is a one. No dot is zero. Look. It's repeated over and over." Bennie spun a yellow legal pad toward them, revealing a series of ones and zeroes:

0101001101110100011000010110111001101100011001010111100100100000010001110111001001100001011100101011100110110101110110110110001000000100010001100001011001110011000100111010101011100100111110010010000001000011011011110110111011101100110111001100101011000110111010001101001011000110111010101110100

"In this abstract looking painting, you've got a cleverly encoded name and place from your father." He flipped over a page and showed them his excited scrawl: *Stanley Grayson Danbury Connecticut.*

"I called the guy. He kept hanging up, then finally answered. I woke him up, and he was really bent at first. But I convinced him you needed to talk to him. I told him your dad was missing and his last message to you was Grayson's name. The guy insisted he would only meet in person, so you need to go there. He sounded kind of... I don't know, paranoid or something. Oh, and take your dad's netbook with you. I found a design schematic in your mom's folder I can't make sense of, but maybe this Grayson guy can."

As Jay grabbed one of the empty cardboard boxes to repack his father's artwork, he noticed a shipping invoice at the bottom. He immediately spotted the beginnings of his father's familiar signature. He plucked it out of the box.

"What is it?" Chloe asked, moving to stand beside him.

Jay pointed at the long signature printed out in fuzzy dot-matrix and running off the page:

Stephen Broo—help me I'm trapped in my house they

Jay and Chloe were on 84 South, ten miles from the Connecticut state line. Chloe pretended to call from the hospital to tell her parents she would be spending the night with Bennie and that after some errands, she would see them after lunch tomorrow back at the hospital. Jay had no one to call, but he did stop by an ATM so they could get a cash advance on Chloe's credit card. Chloe dozed, her head against the window, while Jay drove.

They arrived just after two in the morning, able to go straight to the address, thanks to the GPS. Jay studied the dark form of the house in the bright moonlight. The large log cabin was set deeply in the woods, at the end of a quarter-mile gravel path. The land sloped steeply away from the road, and the foundation and large beam supports that leveled the cabin were exposed in the front, making it all the more grand and impressive. A tired-looking green Toyota pickup sat in the circular gravel driveway, and a much older tractor rested by a shed in the back.

Chloe grabbed the tiny netbook Bennie had pre-loaded with a schematic he had found on the Brooks family hard drive, which Bennie had hoped he could identify.

They went to the side door, as Grayson had instructed, and Jay pressed the doorbell. Seconds later, a short man who was maybe five-three and in his late seventies or early eighties opened the door. His large brown eyes appeared to be swimming in iodine solution through his thick, sun-sensitive lenses. Jay jabbed Chloe, silently noting the similarities between his glasses and Bennie's. Chloe covered her mouth to suppress a giggle.

"You must be Jay and Chloe." When they nodded, he added, "Come in. We'll talk in my study."

"Sorry for stopping by in the middle of the night," Jay said.

Grayson turned and led them inside. "Bah. Old men never sleep." Despite his age, his stride was still purposeful, his posture a labored attempt at erectness. Everything in his house was a study of angles and order. All objects were dusted, polished, and in their place. The walls were carefully adorned with portraits of Grayson and his probable wife at miscellaneous ceremonies and tropical retreats, snapshots of other family members, probably his children and grandchildren, and some amateur photography of roses, presumably from his garden.

They passed a laundry room and two closed doors on the left and a bedroom on the right. The guy finally stopped at the end of the hallway. The old man's liver-spotted hand hovered carefully over a keypad on the wall, the longish yellow nail of his index finger slowly tapping out a key combination. Jay heard the click of a deadbolt releasing and glanced at Chloe. She raised her eyebrows.

"Come in, come in." The old man waved for them to go past him.

The study looked to be a converted master bedroom with a telltale walk-in closet and private bathroom attached to the far side. Grayson strode around a large desk and over to the single window. He turned the wooden shutters, closing them against the moonlight. A soft whirring sound and a hint of movement behind the slats suggested a plate of some sort descending, covering the entire aperture of the window. Jay glanced at Chloe again, and she shrugged.

"Have a seat," Grayson said, awkwardly turning his gaze from Chloe to Jay as if addressing a much larger audience.

Jay chose a seat in front of the desk. Chloe plopped in the chair beside him, then opened the slim netbook from her backpack and turned it on.

Grayson settled behind his desk and slid one trembling hand along a pristine blotter as if idly petting a treasured pet. "Your friend on the phone said something about an urgent meeting?" he asked, attempting a calm smile. "Persistent fella. I hung up on him at least a dozen times. I finally answered to yell at him. He said your father was missing, and somehow your dad had my name?"

"Yes, that's all we have, really. My dad's been missing since yesterday, and the last thing he shared with me was your name. He was very serious about me connecting with you."

Grayson shook his head.

Not knowing what else to say, Jay told him about the first intercepted communication between the woman and the cell tower at the park in Cambridge, about the Russian thugs, the device on the cell tower, his father ultimately going missing, and the only clue left behind being Grayson's name in a coded painting. "And I don't know if any of that stuff even matters. I mean, my dad was working on that painting a long time before the whole cell tower thing. But it all just seems too... I don't know, like too much of a coincidence."

"A painting, you say?" Grayson asked. "And why didn't he just give you my name if it was so urgent you get it?"

Jay shook his head. "I don't know. I... he must not have been able to somehow."

"And you say you captured a video transmission between a woman and a nearby cell tower?"

"That's right."

The old man paused a long while, holding his breath, and

finally let it burst out his nose. "For one, my research was discontinued thirty years ago." He shrugged, drummed his fingers, and glanced at the secured window for a time. "I should explain. I started my career in the Army as an MP. Volunteered before college. Eventually was stationed in Germany. My first assignment was to investigate war crimes, specifically crimes against civilians by our own soldiers, and fragging—soldier-on-soldier violence." Grayson fixed his gaze on a corner of the room where Jay was sure a silent film reel was playing in his mind.

"Over time, I had gotten a taste for this kind of work. I relished the idea of tracking down criminals. And criminal investigation is a special kind of challenge. When you think of it, it's the criminal that *gets* all the advantages. Murder, especially. Homicide cases are like a one-sided duel. The killer gets to pick the place. He gets to pick the weapon. And he gets to count his paces well before you even know you've been challenged." Grayson scowled, his furry eyebrows surfacing out of the shimmering reflective pool of his glasses.

"After the Army, I went to school at Harvard and double-majored in engineering and sociology. I graduated and resumed my passion for chasing violent criminals. I applied and was accepted to the FBI academy and thereafter joined the Boston FBI branch as a technical consultant to the Kidnapping and Missing Persons Division. This was before any hard or soft applied sciences were really seen as tools to a criminal investigation. There was no DNA analysis, no microscopic fiber retrievals, no criminal profiles. All we had were any pieces of hard evidence left on the scene, like a child's game of Clue, and a hell of a lot of investigative work to put it all together. Eventually, I grew tired of playing catch-up with these criminals. I needed to somehow inject myself earlier, where I could possibly help *prevent* crime, or at least witness the last few seconds of it. Gain an advantage finally." He paused. "Have either of you ever heard of phrenology?"

Chloe raised her hand a little, as if she were in a classroom.

"The study of human facial structure and correlating that to a propensity for crime."

Grayson smiled. "Smart kid. Yes. The research was quickly debunked, but the line of thinking appealed to me. At least someone was trying to take measure of how we can predict or prevent crime, possibly save people instead of merely trying to track down and prosecute the criminals after the fact. Especially for the child victims of these crimes. All these terrible acts done to kids—they were raped, abused, burned, tortured, and then discarded like so much trash. You don't know how bad it can get, how hard it is to see these broken children, the pain still on their faces."

Jay noticed tears gathering at the corners of Grayson's eyes.

"For those children to have realized that all of humanity had abandoned them at that last moment." He shook his head. "What must she think when she realizes there is no hope, no help? Just the day before, her greatest personal responsibility and burden was perhaps to tie her own shoe, and today, here is an animal doing God knows what to her. Now she has nothing. She has to face total abandonment, helplessness. She has to both conceive of for the first time and greet the true prospect of death in the next coming minutes, days, hours. Do you understand? All of human suffering, *all of human suffering,* is brought to bear upon this poor child. Every horrible, painful, unrighteous death throe is hers to experience, alone. Can you imagine how *alone* she feels? The protective golden bubble of youth smashed open to reveal... what? Nothing? Cold, irreverent space? That pain has no end? Human evil has no bounds?"

His hands had begun to shake, and his cheeks reddened. "Excuse me," he said and pulled out a handkerchief. He blew his nose unashamedly, three successive honks like a duck call. "Back to my story. In 1963, my wife and I lost our first daughter, Lily. She was six years old." He paused again, smoothing out the blotter paper that he had unintentionally gathered in his fist. "I'm sorry. I mean to speak generally, but inevitably, in the maze of my thoughts, I end up at the same place no matter where I start—with my poor Lily's death. Every year, my late wife and I would stay up for four days straight and try to imagine, empathize, replay what Lily must have gone through. The anniversary was just last week. An odd coincidence that you called now, perhaps."

The old man was quiet for a good minute, staring again at the same fixed point in the corner of the room. On his desk, a cherrywood antique clock fashioned as a horse and buggy ticked away patiently. The carriage driver slowly whipped a stiff gold switch, never quite reaching the stubborn horse's inanimate hindquarters.

"So I had been at the FBI for eleven years, and I pulled in all the resources available to me, legal and illegal, all favors, to root out my daughter's killer. We had blood typing at the time, and we did have a sample of this guy's blood from the scene, though it wasn't entirely necessary. The drifter had killed Lily in his own apartment, three miles from our home, and left her inside of his foldout sofa before fleeing the state. We knew who he was, and it was just a matter of time before we found him. Almost three years later, we did find him, several states away in Arkansas, picked up on attempted kidnapping of another girl. I flew directly there and was given ten minutes alone with him before he was duly processed and booked."

He slammed his fist on his desk, and Jay jumped in unison with everything on its surface.

"I stomped him like a cockroach." His eyes almost disappeared in his furious squint. The man's jaw muscles worked furiously. "You might not see it now, but I was strong then, a bear. I wrestled in college and lifted weights all my life. They say you see red in ultimate anger. I saw nothing but light and shadow. Truth and untruth. Crime and punishment. I pounded his nose into a red mash, then slammed his head into the steel toilet in the corner and raked it along the bars. Like I said, nothing but light and shadow, as if I had divided in two then, or at least Siamese twins, the beast inside me, all my anger, given as much rope as possible to do what I needed to do." He stabbed each syllable out onto the blotter with his thick forefinger.

Jay imagined the damage those hands had wrought, half-expecting to see traces of caked blood lining the old man's knuckles.

"I needed to feel some form of justice, revenge, and then the other side of me, the part that had to process all this, shut down, reduced everything to a sufferable blur." Grayson pulled a set of keys from his front pocket and worked them in his hand like Japanese meditation balls. "I was so close to snapping his neck, but then realized I was *enjoying* the pain he was in. I *liked* that he was being forced to understand the full measure of anger the world can have for someone who does such a thing. He will never be able to deny that. I had the back of his neck over the edge of the toilet..."

His eyes moved down to the left of the desk and the empty braided rug as if he were seeing the killer once more. "I was ready to stomp on his neck, you know, like I was trying to split a piece of cordwood, and then I looked into his pathetic, weepy eyes. Something clicked then, real subtle. I don't think I was fully aware at the time, but on reflection, when I looked into his bloodshot, near-dead eyes, they weren't full of horror, fear, or pain even. They were half-lidded in—acquiescence, I guess? I realized right then that *those* were the last eyes to see my daughter alive. And likewise, they were the last eyes my daughter had looked into. Until she passed out or died, the full extent of what had been done to her over those four days had been essentially recorded, but into a vessel that would not much longer be of this earth. That's when I thought of the 'Fight Data Recorder.'"

Grayson unlocked the bottom drawer of his desk and pulled out a mottled-brown accordion folder. He unwound the string from the clasp, flicked through the contents, and finally pulled out a set of papers. He unfolded several and smoothed them out on his desk. Chloe approached his desk, and Jay circled to the other side to look over Grayson's shoulder. The folding pattern of the drafting paper had permanently scored the drawing beyond repair, but the 3-D perspective of the device was still clear, complete with exact measurements, angles, and a legend describing its several components.

The old man used a finger to trace the smudged outlines of the drawing. "Granted, this is very rough and absurd, impractical even, but I was working on this on the sly, on my own time. I didn't have all the materials I would have liked."

The model was of a single lens secured to an almost featureless face by a thin strap, like those found on eye patches. The eyepiece looked like a foreshortened section of an antique telescope and had a depth of an inch or so. What looked like wires originated from the lens and snaked around the leather strap, finally parting around what would be the ear to a heavy battery pack and a second resistor-looking device.

"This is the first functioning Fight Data Recorder. The first human black box device, finally code-named ARGUS." Grayson slid the design aside to reveal another mechanical drawing beneath it. "And this is the receiver component. Battery-powered, it's used to activate the lens, a small low-res camera, really, and transmit about three minutes of grainy, nearly indecipherable images to this receiver. I had no solution for storing this, of course. Someone would have to be monitoring the receiver during the transmission."

Grayson seemed to be getting excited as the original passion for his work flared inside him. "Now I want you two to imagine something. Imagine all of the unsolved crimes you can—all the beatings, rapes, kidnappings, murders, domestic abuse, robberies, drunk driving, even the suicides. Remember all the headlines, all the news, and all the episodes, if you watched them, of *Cold Case Files*, *Unsolved Mysteries*, and *America's Most Wanted*. There are *thousands* every year. Think of the parents who have devoted half of their lives searching for runaway or kidnapped children, knowing they may not necessarily get their child back, but just determined to fulfill that small creature comfort—the need to *know*. What were her last moments like? Was it quick and painless? Was it an accident? Was she calling for me? With very few exceptions, all of these events could have been solved in real-time or better yet, prevented, if authorities could see what the victims were seeing during these crimes. Think of all of those unjustly killed people, all of that lost life, the crimes sitting unsolved for years, when all the while, the truth behind each of their deaths is curled up in their brain, Exhibit A, among perhaps the last gathering of their active neurons, but can never be retrieved. We've lost our last and only witness. *If only we could have seen through their eyes.*"

Grayson explained that the prototype was enough to interest the intelligence division of the FBI, and he had been given his own lab and a staff of six to pursue the practical application and development of the device. Both civilian and military applications presented themselves. The military interest wasn't his intent, but he had been passionate enough about it to see it through to fruition in whatever eventual form it may take.

Grayson flipped through successive models, more sophisticated in design and in draftsmanship as his program received more funding and interest. The optical lens became smaller and smaller. The leather strap disappeared, giving way to a bulky-looking pair of sunglasses, then eyeglasses. The power source, transmitter, and receiver got smaller and smaller with the advancement of battery cell technology and the microchip. The final design was a painful-looking contact lens Jay thought couldn't possibly be transparent enough to see through, with circuitry and wire leads that trailed along the temple and up the hairline to a small battery and transmitter clipped to the inside of the wearer's shirt.

"Were contact lenses invented by then?" Jay asked.

"Sure, in the forties even." Grayson sighed and walked over to a cabinet in the corner. He wheeled out a large film projector on a rolling cart and popped off the reel that was on there. He flipped on a switch to warm the lamp. "There remained several fundamental flaws. It was painful to wear, vision was impaired, and worst of all, it was *obvious*, so it couldn't be used in any clandestine way by the CIA or undercover FBI. I suppose it would have served as a good crime deterrent, but so would a whistle, for that matter. Some test subjects lost partial vision in their eye after more than a dozen field tests. The circuitry was cooking the retina."

He shrugged. "If you put it on ex-cons to monitor them, say, they could just rip it out, and at the time, each piece cost upwards of three hundred thousand dollars to build. Let me show you the last known application of the device, from over forty years ago, before it was no longer supported as a project. I think it was the most exciting, but most outlandish application." Grayson chuckled.

He moved back to the cabinet and pulled out a film reel, which he snapped onto the projector. Jay went over and dimmed the lights.

Cast against the white study wall behind the desk, a somewhat obstructed aerial coastal view presented itself. The picture was of such poor quality, it looked as if it might be snowing in the scene, but the green growth along the shore suggested summer temperatures. Along the beach, people were sunbathing, milling in the water, and strolling up and down the waterline. The view faced steadily ahead, but was constantly obstructed by a fluttering, grayish-brown mass, as if some part of the lens were obscured. Every minute or so, the picture would fade to complete black, but then revive itself again within seconds, as if rebooting. As the camera panned right, the beach disappeared, giving way to tall sea grass and shallower waters. From wherever the camera shot was coming from, Jay thought it was amazingly steady for being shot so long ago with no stabilizing software built into the camera.

Suddenly, the picture jerked up and then down. The

camera spun wildly and tumbled. The frame filled with what looked like rippling water, swirling as if being flushed down a toilet, an outward finger of sand and razor grass rotating around and around—and then blackness.

When the film reel emptied and fluttered, Grayson shut off the camera. "That, my young friends, was a bird, a Canadian goose to be exact, wearing the FDR. We constructed sixty receiver stations every fifty yards down a stretch of the Connecticut coast. Unfortunately, the goose got shot four hundred yards in. My team had failed to realize that hunting season had commenced that week."

He shrugged. "It seemed like a nice application. Take out the human element and use animals. You could be quite cruel to them then without worrying about prosecution, and it seemed like a great fit for servicing the US in the Cold War. We could capture and outfit a bunch of Russian pinko albatrosses, and the Cold War would have been over within a matter of months, not years. We never overcame the problem of the weak broadcast range and thus the need for several receivers. That would be impossible to do in Russia and highly impractical. In addition to that, spy planes had already emerged as a partial solution. To boot, human intelligence was still a far superior tool to what we were proposing. So they shut down the project. I got transferred out and worked my final three years behind a desk, mentoring junior agents in the kidnapping division, but my heart wasn't in it. We were back to the old cat-and-mouse, always-too-late model. I smuggled some of the research and design back to my house so I could still work on it."

Grayson gestured at the folder. "But my wife got the lung cancer in '85. She battled it for a good while. That took a lot of my energy, and afterward, all my drive. Oddly enough, about five years ago, I was asked to come back and consult for a week. Someone had been combing through closed projects and was intrigued by mine. They wondered about the efficacy and applicability of reviving such a project in the desperate midst of the Iraqi war. Perhaps they were thinking of outfitting soldiers with them. The Patriot Act had given the government such leeway with wiretaps, war tribunals, and the whole lot that they probably felt they might have enough money and rope to take the FDR a final step further and make it a reality. So I summarized for them where we had left off and what the technical and practical difficulties had been. They were somewhat dismissive and not very enthusiastic, despite having flown me in on their dime and putting me up at a pretty good hotel. They had noted over the phone that some documents were missing, so I gave them back the originals at the meeting, but I kept copies for myself. They apparently never realized this film was missing, though."

The man looked drained and in dire need of a nap. "So I'm surprised to hear any mention of this project after it was killed a second time. That young man—Bennie, was it?—mentioned on the phone that he found something on your home computer."

Chloe nodded. "Yes, Bennie. He's my brother." With a few quick taps on the keyboard, she pulled up the PDF schematic Bennie had supplied. She spun the laptop around so that the old man could see it.

Grayson slowly rose from his desk and slouched toward the netbook. He leaned forward, inspecting the display. The design was a cutaway of the human eye. In light gray pen, the several organic components of the eye—the pupil, cornea, iris, lens, and the ocular nerves—were finely detailed. In red, below the anterior chamber and just above the lens, a slim disk was embedded.

On a hunch, Jay pointed at the disk in the picture. "Click on that."

Chloe clicked on it, and a new full-color, 3-D design appeared. It looked like the inner component of the iris, the darker part that circled the pupil. Several semi-transparent leads projected out of the circle, like a many-pointed star, labeled *Signal Booster*. A red, vascular-looking tendril labeled

EPI detector came out of its back. Another clear tendril connected to a microscopic disk with a parenthetical label and arrow, *To tear duct*. Two clear films, like two overlaid contact lenses, were labeled *TEG(2x)*. They encased the tiny disk on both sides.

"*Holy...* it's my ARGUS!" Grayson's face collapsed, but his eyes remained on the screen. "Given what you've told me so far, I say that if you take this to the authorities, you'll be signing your own death certificates."

They bandied around some ideas, but didn't come up with anything new. "My mom's last assignment—she said it was surveillance related. This must be what she was working on."

Grayson apologized for not being able to help more. He said that since he wasn't involved in any recent incarnation of the project, he was as much of an outsider as they were. As he walked them out, the old man looked deeply troubled and drained, like a wax-bottle candy that had been sucked dry of its contents.

At the door, he grabbed Jay's elbow. "You tell me the minute you learn anything more. I know for a *fact* this project was shut down. Whoever has revived it is up to no good."

Once they were back on the road, Chloe called Bennie. She updated him on what they had learned from Grayson, mentioning "FDR" and "ARGUS."

A knee-jerk reaction to call his father passed over Jay like the shadow of a quickly moving cloud. He stopped himself from reaching for his cell phone. At the very least, his father's distracted demeanor lately made much more sense. An odd comfort. His father had surely been under the influence of some unseen force. The coincidence between that and Jay's mother's death was too much to ignore. Whoever had taken his father might be connected to his mother's death in some way. He knew, deep in his heart, he had never reconciled that her death was a mere consequence of her job. She was too careful, too smart.

Chloe snapped shut her phone.

Jay glanced over at her. "So what'd Bennie have to say?"

"Not much. He told me he was worn out, was going to take a nap, and then try to get his laptop connected to the hospital's network. I told him we're checking into a hotel." She tapped a finger on her phone. "He was also excited to hear this Stanley Grayson lead panned out, but he was pissed the old guy didn't have anything to do with it recently, except for that brief meeting with the FBI. He wants to follow up with Grayson anyway. Bennie was also wondering where your dad got Grayson's name in the first place. Do you have any idea?"

Jay shrugged. "Me and Dad hardly talked this past year, especially recently. I'm guessing now that it really wasn't a choice. Someone was keeping him quiet, had something over him maybe."

She reached across the seat and touched his forearm. Her fingers felt like small cool breezes as she moved them up and down his arm. "It's been a tough year with your mom, your trouble with your dad, and..." She tried a small smile, but it disappeared from her lips as she clenched her teeth. Her chin trembled.

"What?"

She shook her head. "I can't say. I don't even know if I should. Maybe later. Let me drive. I need something to do."

Jay pulled over at a rest stop in Southington and switched seats with Chloe. He immediately regretted it. His anxiety increased with every mile. Looking for distraction, he popped open the glove compartment and rummaged. He found a laminated foldout map of the eastern United States. He unfolded it and passed a hand over the cool surface, then felt the sharp corners with both thumbs. A real map was a funny thing. It required no batteries, no back-lit display, no network access, and was always on.

They had just passed through Hartford. He searched for the town on the map, found it, and conducted a quick survey with his thumb and forefinger to gauge the distance they had already covered. He wished he had a... a thought struck him.

The glossy texture of the map, his finger tracings, and his need for a pen all coalesced into a single memory—that last outing with his mother. That bizarre, frantic outing to all of those towns. The hectic pace and illogic of their route. How she had mapped the route herself.

He folded the map and stuffed it back in the glove compartment. Had his mother been trying to communicate with him in her own cryptic way? Had she really hoped he could help her or prevent her death? Or maybe she had known her death was a foregone conclusion, and she merely wanted to help him and his father solve it. He remembered his impatience with her that day, his snapping at her, and his sulky attitude.

"Shit."

"What?"

"My mom. Before she died, she *knew* she was in danger. She left me a clue. A transparency in a map book. It's been in my top dresser drawer all this time. It was the last thing we did together, so I kept it. Take me by my house before we go to the hotel." He pictured the constellation of dots his mother had made on the transparency, but no pattern surfaced. Maybe he wasn't remembering it right. There *must* be something to it.

He was glad to have Bennie and Chloe at his side, but nauseated by the enormity of his task. That familiar, crushing need to give up hit him again, but he resisted. *He* was at the center of everything. It was *his* family. *He* had to take the reins and put together the puzzle pieces.

His mother seemed to have been caught up in something huge. His father must have known at least some of it and had deliberately kept it a secret until his art show. Jay had to believe his father had no easier way to share Grayson's name. He must have needed an open venue where he could share the clue without fear of being found out. But had his father planned to disappear? Jay didn't think so, not even after Dad had been acting so funny and distant. The disappearing part seemed like something his father had probably tried, but failed to keep from happening. *RUN* had been his father's warning. His dad, like his mom, had ultimately tried to inform Jay.

A lady had been killed, the jogger, but what did she have to do with anything? Yet, those same bloodthirsty Russian brutes had appeared back at the cell tower. As a further convolution, a fifty-year-old invention, squashed some thirty years ago, was almost revived by the FBI, but seemingly dismissed yet again as an option not worth pursuing. And for some reason, his mother had possessed an up-to-date design specification on her PC.

MD Defense Systems had been stamped on the interceptor device they found on the cell tower. And he guessed from the cached web page Bennie had found that they were, at one time anyway, the same and located in Cambridge and Waltham.

Jay had Chloe pull through a drive-through for two large coffees. They decided they would first check into a local hotel and crash for a few hours. Afterward, Chloe would visit Bennie and see her parents.

With Bennie incapacitated, Chloe unavailable, and his father gone, his list of confidantes had quickly dwindled. He knew of only one other person he trusted enough for help. He looked at his watch. *Better late than never.* "I gotta go back to school today. Can you take me?"

CHAPTER 23

TUESDAY, 1:20 AM

BENNIE

THE FOURTH DIMENSION. ASTROPHYSICISTS COULD rest easy, Bennie thought, for he had discovered it, and ironically, it hadn't been hard to find. It existed in every city, wholly within the confines of its respective regional hospital. As initial proof of his theory, time was affected by the constantly rotating staff of medical personnel every eight hours, which neatly destroyed any reasonable person's naïve notion of time, along with normal sleeping and waking cycles.

He looked at his watch. Jay and Chloe would still be on the road, but hopefully at least halfway to Grayson's. Bursts of chatter, shouts, shrieks, and hearty guffaws drifted through the hallway, no matter the time of day. Nurses shuffled into his room at all hours to look at the wrapping on his leg, check his chart, and inquire about his pain level. A continuous dull drill bit of pain bored its way up his center and tickled the base of his heart.

Normal physical laws of space were also mutable, and in fact violated, especially his, as nurses roughly worked their hands up and down his gown as if he were a faceless mannequin being dressed by hurried store clerks. And gravity, it seemed, changed with each sensation of levitating goodness he received when he self-administered a shot of Demerol, which seemed to raise him a verifiable inch above the bed.

Perhaps due to the stress and the nature of his injury, he had been given an EKG and was still connected to a heart and blood pressure monitoring device, along with an IV set into his wrist for pain relief. After some initial fun, as tempting as it was, he tried his best to keep his finger away from the little red button in order to keep his brain sharp. He was grateful his parents had moved him into a private room that was simple, but functional, with the walls papered in the grayish color of stagnant water stirred cloudy with silt, flecked with what looked like recycled debris to create a texture that reminded him of the coarse, cheap scratch paper from elementary school. To his immediate right stood a large closet where his mother had hung his "Legs" trucker hat and hoodie and an extra T-shirt that read: "Free Tick Inspections."

With no reliable segment of time during the day or night to covertly set up his equipment, he had been forced to operate in a fragmented series of extremely close calls that he would be sure to laugh about later with Jay, but that weren't funny at the moment. His exertions had caused his leg dressing to get out of whack, while, in several abridged attempts—"Hello. Yes, I'm fine—*still* fine"—he spliced into the network jack behind his end table and, with double-sided tape, affixed a small wireless hub to the back of the table. By doing that, he had made it so his laptop could connect to the Internet wirelessly without any clear evidence that he was online, which a bright-blue network cable certainly would have provided.

His doctor had explained the day before to his mother, forgetting Bennie was old enough at eighteen to be directly consulted about his health, that Bennie's broken leg had been placed in a traction harness generally used for children.

A silver arm reached out over his bed like a headless reading lamp, holding his right leg at a near ninety-degree angle. As he had strained to hook up the small wireless hub and hide it, he had pulled out of his dressing and, worse, caused the harness rope on the pulley wheel to derail and wedge itself between the wheel and axle.

A baffled, concerned nurse had re-dressed him, re-admonished him, and fixed the pulley. She had also checked his temperature out of concern for the beads of sweat that had inexplicably accumulated on his brow and upper lip. Despite all of that, he was finally online.

He checked his email and then Jay's. Nothing noteworthy.

He turned his attention to the Brooks' family hard drive. Discovering the schematic on there had been key, but he wasn't convinced that was all he could find. He powered on the hard drive, and the disk spun to life, a whirring, gearing-up sound that never failed to stir and excite him to the core. With his small wireless mouse, he navigated through the personal folders.

The Administrator folder contained nothing of real interest, and by the time stamps on the files, they appeared to have been rarely used. The same held true for a Guest folder in the same location. Additionally, there was a folder named "JJ" for Jay's computer activity, another named "Family," and lastly, a generically named "Work" folder. That folder was where he had found the schematic. He decided to run a software utility against the folder to retrieve deleted items.

The greenest of green hackers knew that although deleted files were not visible to the typical end user, as long as that particular segment of the hard drive memory was not overwritten by new data, the "deleted" information remained. The software program crept through that area of the hard drive like a vagrant picking through litter for refundable empties.

He made a cursory search of the results, flagging his way down over twelve hundred deleted items. He dismissed several temporary files written and deleted by the operating system in its normal operation. He looked through over two hundred deleted emails, quietly tapping out a jazz-like musical rhythm of down-arrow-key presses as he scanned for anything that caught his attention, like attachments or anything that made reference to the *MD* company. After exhuming and then reburying the emails to their original digital graveyard, he dismissed another hundred or so application-specific temporary files. To filter the list further, he searched within the remaining set of files for specific file extensions, particularly for text files, images, and PDFs. As he scanned the final list of ninety-seven recovered items, he stumbled upon what looked like a corrupt Word document. It was only one kilobyte in size and named only by its extension, ".doc." But upon closer inspection, he had imagined the "." The file was a text document, saved *without* an extension at all, as a user would do with a UNIX text file. The file itself was simply named "doc."

Bennie opened it and discovered an alphabetical list of forty names. No titles, addresses, phone numbers, or emails. Just names. His gut told him to immediately cross-reference the list... *But against what?* The FBI's Most Wanted? Massachusetts residents? Cell phone workers?

Deciding to take a break, Bennie closed the file and turned on the TV. He flipped through the hospital-provided television channels, hoping for a *Namaste Yoga* program or perhaps NESN coverage of the National Cheerleading finals. Finding nothing of interest, he lay back and stared out the window. In the upper right corner of his window, he spied a small inverted right triangle of indigo sky so rich it looked to be painted on the glass. He turned back to his laptop screen and was about to open the file again when he got an idea.

He quickly confirmed his suspicion by checking the first few names against an online registry of physicians. He then checked the rest of the list, but limited the search to Massachusetts. All forty names were physicians in Massachusetts. He narrowed the list further to his town and found three. He then filtered by hospital. Two doctors on the list practiced in the same hospital where he currently had a bed. But were the other doctors still practicing? He copied the information for one of the doctor's offices in nearby Sudbury and sent a text to Chloe's phone for her to check it out when she could.

In another two hours, the magenta triangle had turned into a smooth gradient of dove gray, and he had successfully hacked into the local intranet of the hospital. He looked up information on the two local doctors, then he hacked into their personal computers, which were conveniently networked with the hospital's. He also dipped into the hospital's shared network storage space, which was encrypted with a common key Bennie had discovered in the hospital administrator's workstation PC.

A glance at the clock told him it was 3:01 a.m. With the full electronic records of the hospital before him, he decided to poke around, just for the fun of it.

CHAPTER 24

CHARLES SULLIVAN

Charles "Sully" Sullivan had just pulled the steak tips off his grill and was walking through the slider from his back deck when the doorbell rang.

His wife called from the kitchen, "Honey, can you get it? Kelsie's *helping* me, and I can't leave her alone."

"Sure, sure."

Sully kept the platter of sizzling steak tips in his hand and his "Cops do it better because they are trained to use their nightsticks!" apron on to send a message to whoever was behind the door that he or she would be interrupting dinner. Hell, he had to be back for third shift at nine o'clock to cover for Becker, and he hadn't even shaved or ironed his uniform yet.

He swung open the door. Nothing but his empty stoop and the usual garden gnome smiling obscenely underneath the opposite hedge. As he started to close the door, he paused. On the welcome mat sat a package neatly wrapped in shiny black paper—no address, no postage. A gold label was affixed to the top. Black letters spelled out its contents completely: *EMBEZZLEMENT*. Sully scanned the street with a professional eye and saw nothing but familiar cars.

He looked over his shoulder into the dining room. His wife was still in the kitchen. He nudged the package with the barbecue tongs. From the size, it looked as though it might contain a compact disc. He picked it up with the tongs and shook it. *Nothing to call the bomb squad about.* He slipped the disk into his waistband, beneath his apron and shirt.

His wife and daughter entered the dining room from the kitchen.

"Daddy! I helped with the tomato salad!"

"Potato."

"What?"

"Never mind. That's great, honey." He placed the steak tips on the table, seated his wife in her chair, hugged her from behind, and whispered in her ear, "I gotta run upstairs real quick and check on something for work."

She gave him a questioning look.

"Five minutes. Promise."

But he ended up needing more time: three minutes to view the DVD, twenty seconds to read the instructions at the end, and ten more minutes to regain his composure before hiding the DVD in his closet. He re-entered the dining room and took his seat. He kept a frozen smile on his face as he spread his cloth napkin on his lap and mechanically filled his plate.

"Everything all right?" his wife asked.

He nodded, stretched his plastic smile farther, and took his first bite. He chomped the meat between his molars, grinding it as he wanted to grind whoever had sent him the DVD. The video was short, a compilation of his own personal greatest hits with no sound or production value, but all of the evidentiary value a DA would need to put him away for life. From an inexplicable point of view, he watched himself forging timecards, stealing from petty cash, filling out reimbursement forms for phony repairs on the three squad cars assigned to his department, and completing double-time holiday forms for work he had never done.

He left the table, the half-chewed steak in his mouth grown tough and dry, and ran upstairs, ignoring the calls of his wife. In his closet, he tore down his neatly lined uniforms from their hangers, scrutinizing every lapel, button, epaulet, his badge, and even his formal dress hat. Nothing.

He slid the DVD into his pocket. He would have to get rid of it on his way to the station. The video had ended in a final message displayed in similarly unprepossessing letters as the label against a black background:

As you can see, you are being watched. We have everything we need to destroy your life and your family. You have one thing you need to do, and if you do it well, we will destroy the evidence you have just viewed. Capture and detain Jay Brooks of 2 Crescent Hill Road. Work completely alone on this. When you have him in your possession, click the link below, and we will arrange to retrieve him.

Click Here >

CHAPTER 25

TUESDAY, 4:02 AM

BENNIE

INITIALLY, BENNIE HAD BEEN PUMPED about having solved Jay's father's clever clue that pointed to Grayson. But what he found out later in the hospital's electronic records—he didn't think he would let anybody know he knew. He should have resisted looking, but he hadn't been able to resist. The same impulse that dictated one must Google oneself also dictated that when one had illegally hacked into his hospital's medical records, he looked up a few things.

It had been fun at first—cross-referencing Jay's class list with medical records and seeing who had gotten nose jobs, who had Irritable Bowel Syndrome, who was being treated for depression, and who had what STDs.

He turned toward the beeping and flashing equipment by his side. A mountain range of systoles and diastoles etched themselves across the screen as a pulsing amber heart flashed in the upper right corner. He touched a hand to his chest, verifying his real heartbeat with the fake graphical one. But each time, the silence was answered with a beat, again and again, each its own miniature miracle.

CHAPTER 26

TUESDAY, 5:18 AM

STANLEY GRAYSON

GRAYSON WASN'T ENTIRELY SURE WHY he awoke screaming. The echo of his own voice still bounced around his smoke-stained bedroom walls before ultimately finding an exit. He should never have attempted going back to sleep, but his time with those kids had exhausted him.

He had been slipping in and out of sleep as he tried to read, then having trouble finding his place in his book. He laughed, imagining the insulted author. What justice that the book had dropped on his face as he fell asleep reading it. He righted the book on his heaving chest. But hadn't he heard something also?

He was roughly three-quarters of the way through Atkinson's *An Army at Dawn*, and in his sleep-weary, fuzzy mind, Patton had patiently received the same orders four times from Alexander to move toward Gabès. He glanced at his bedside clock: 10:10. He lay rigid in his bed, just as he had when he was a boy and had heard a sound outside his window, holding still with the desperate hope that the advancing monster or intruder would take his brother. *Get a grip, old man.*

Deciding the noise was all in his head, he thought back to his early morning meeting with the two teenagers. When he had been invited back to Washington to provide background information on his long-retired Fight Data Recorder project, he had signed more legal documents than were necessary to close on the purchase of his present home. Although he had only skimmed the paperwork, he was sure the verbiage had centered around confidentiality and whatnot. But he didn't care. Half the people he had spoken to that day were younger than the favorite tie—naked conjoined ladies disguised in a paisley pattern—he had worn to the meeting, all of them looking at him with such condescension. The Fight Data Recorder work was *his* legacy, and he would be damned if it was going to be stuffed into some CIA archive file forever. But if it was being misused, that was another matter entirely.

Those teenagers did seem to be onto something. That design—it was like losing a child and seeing her twenty years later, fully grown and self-sufficient. Perhaps he could have been more careful and not doled out so much information, but his excitement had gotten the best of him.

There. A noise.

He was wide awake, so it definitely wasn't his imagination. He lifted his head off the pillow and listened. The local wildlife had long ago learned what a deadly mistake it was to step a hoof or claw onto his property. So he was genuinely concerned to hear rummaging out back. He vacillated between finally removing his reading glasses and committing to his nap or getting up, grabbing his gun, and running a quick patrol around his property. Then his doorway filled with the shape of a man so broad that if he entered the room, he would have to turn sideways.

Grayson felt his heart shudder. He considered leaping from his bed to the master bath and sequestering himself in there.

The man just stood in place, as if enjoying Grayson's paralysis.

Could he make it to the phone in the bathroom? He could dial 9-1-1 before the intruder could break down the door. But he hadn't leapt toward *anything* in easily a decade. How had the man bypassed his security system? Had he forgotten to set it? How had he not heard some guy creeping down the hallway?

"So?" Grayson demanded, resisting the urge to pull the blankets up under his chin like a cowardly old man and not a highly decorated World War II veteran.

The stranger reached for something. A gun? No, not a gun. It looked like a fancy spatula. Was that glass? Yes. The man held a sickle-shaped section of toxic-green glass in his right hand.

Having had sufficient time to contemplate death, both in the army and in his twilight years, Grayson had always wondered what he would concentrate on in his last moments. He had hoped, of course, that it would be family. He made a hasty, conscious effort to mentally flicker through a photo album of living and dead family members, but couldn't. He was pissed off, pissed off that his family's ignorant smiles in his imagined portraits of them showed no indication that they knew or cared about his current predicament.

The man advanced two steps and was suddenly at Grayson's bedside. He was thickly featured and heavily muscled. He wore blue jeans and a black leather jacket. Bold bastard didn't even wear gloves or a mask. With an expression of barely contained glee, he breathed heavier than Grayson did.

He straddled Grayson and pinned his arms, using the blankets as a straitjacket. Slowly, with apparent relish, he produced a laminated picture from an inner coat pocket and held it up in front of Grayson's eyes. "Look at trees. Look how they seem to move... and the silver undersides. You can see the breeze move through trees, no?"

"I don't know what the holy hell you're talking about, buddy."

147

The intruder apparently didn't like Grayson's response. He raised the glass sickle in one hand, and with the other, he pulled taut the loose waddle of skin below Grayson's chin. He sliced as casually and easily as one would peel an over-ripe fruit.

The horrific pain eclipsed all other sensation and emotion, with the slight exception of a slim, persistent corona of irritation and insult—irritation at his family for not being there, finally, when it mattered, and grave, deep, shameful insult in knowing his technology was out there to vindicate him, but no one would use it for that purpose.

As the man adjusted his grip on Grayson's throat and sliced deeper, he leaned forward and presented his perfectly incriminating, smiling image. That image, that face, settled briefly onto the surface of Grayson's mind before it promptly sank, like a photo into an abandoned well, never to be retrieved again.

CHAPTER 27

TUESDAY, 6:11 AM

JAY

THE THOUGHT OF RETURNING TO his house daunted Jay, but he took solace in having Chloe there, idling in the driveway. Once inside, he sprinted, Christmas morning in reverse, up to his bedroom. He yanked the top dresser drawer so hard that it came loose and emptied onto the rug. He pushed underwear and socks aside. There—the map and transparency.

He grabbed both, ran back outside, and fairly leapt into the car. Chloe gunned the engine and drove down the driveway and back onto the road.

The hotel they checked into was one of three medium-sized hotels built off Route 495 ten miles from Jay's house. He remembered watching the slow construction of the buildings over the last few months. Originally, he and Bennie had hoped the non-specific T-cells of the steel frames would later develop into a new computer or video game store, or even a hobby shop, but they were ultimately disappointed when all three turned out to be competing hotels.

Fearing the men in the black car might be actively trolling

through town for him, they pulled into the first hotel of the three: a perfect square of seven stories with dignified, cream-colored stucco thickly slathered on its sides as if it were a large ceremonial cake. The building was surrounded by a suffering line of terminally diagnosed saplings. Rust-colored shutters adorned each room's window, giving the hotel an out-of-place Mediterranean feel.

The day was starting warm, and the shimmering parking lot shined with beads of fresh tar like an evil extract. He spotted only a handful of other cars. *Good.*

Jay followed Chloe through the hotel entrance, where they were eagerly greeted, first by the doorman, then the lady at the front desk, and finally the concierge, as though their entrance into the hotel had activated a hidden pressure plate that stirred the formerly inanimate staff into smiling motion. Chloe checked them in using her credit card.

The front desk lady shot a glance at Jay, then back to Chloe. "Number of beds?"

Number of beds. Jay couldn't ever remember such an innocent-seeming, but also exciting question. *One bed?* For a fleeting moment, he hoped that was all the hotel had left, but then remembered the near-empty parking lot.

Chloe tapped the edge of her credit card on the marble countertop. "Two, please."

He felt immediate disappointment, but then also relief. He had his hands full already without having to anticipate sleeping with his best friend's sister.

The elevator dinged as if the fourth floor were an idea that had just occurred to it. They stepped out of the elevator and padded down the carpeted hallway to their room. The two double beds occupied most of the space, a disappointingly chaste distance of four feet separating them. Jay resisted the urge to sweep aside the curtains that covered the large window, keeping in mind that a low profile was their highest priority. After they unpacked, he settled onto the bed closest to the window, exhausted from the overnight drive. He flipped on the TV and watched the morning news.

After Chloe took a shower, they ordered breakfast—a bacon and cheese omelet for him and a fruit cup for her. He had already set up his laptop on the tall circular pub table by the window, so they made a picnic on Chloe's bed, placing two stiff bathroom towels together as a makeshift picnic blanket. Chloe had changed into a simple white T-shirt and gray cotton shorts.

They kept the news channel murmuring in the background so they could listen for any local news story that might allude to his father's disappearance, the compromised cell phone tower, the dead woman from Jefferson Park, or Jay's own recent disappearance.

He couldn't remember the last time he had eaten, and the first bite of his omelet fell into the pit of his stomach with no real impact, like a stone dropped down a bottomless well. He took a long gulp of orange juice. "So you never told me why you came back from college mid-term."

Chloe got up and threw her food containers into the bathroom trash can, her still-wet hair swinging as she walked. She sat back on the bed, turning her right foot flat against her inner left thigh. She fixed her hair behind both ears and kept her face lowered. Jay wished he had the guts to reach out to her, touch her shoulder, her knee, her hand, anything—but he simply waited.

Her eyebrows knitted together, then crumpled. A fat tear plopped onto the bedspread and sat there, a perfect silver globule, gaining no admittance into the Scotchgarded polyester material.

He found the courage to reach out to her and touched her elbow. "Hey…" He slid closer, lifting his other hand, but unsure how to offer comfort.

She fell forward into him, leaving her thin brown arms slack in her lap.

"I didn't mean to… I mean… I didn't know it was a sensitive thing, your leaving. It's none of my business. Forget it."

"Oh, Jay." She leaned back, removing herself from his arms. She got up and slouched toward the small coffeemaker. "I don't know what screwed-up mess we're all in. And I know you've got your own problems." She paused and pursed her lips. "I don't want to completely unload on you with... you know, how you're obviously still having a lot of trouble with your mom's death."

Jay's own breakdowns rushed back to him. First, he had cried in her living room the minute she had offered the slightest of condolences. Then he had lost it in his father's attic studio.

Chloe swiped at her eyes. "And now you and Bennie getting into this conspiracy shit, which I guess your dad is messed up in... I don't know, really, if I should say. It could only make things worse."

The mass of his stirred emotions—the loss, the sadness, the shock, even the perverse excitement of it all—he thought that either his nerves were numb or he had become super-humanly strong because he no longer felt intimidated by bad news. "Go ahead, Chloe. You can tell me." His tongue felt thick with dread, as if it were making a clumsy attempt at writing the words in his mouth and not speaking them. "Really, you can."

Her lips flattened into an elongated line, and her mouth and chin twitched as if they were the terminal end of an electrical circuit, sparking with a frantic release of energy. "Bennie's not leaving the hospital," she whispered.

"It's just a broken leg. Or what do you mean? You mean, not soon?"

Chloe shook her head. She spoke into the carpet as one hand fiddled with the coffeemaker. "When I was four, when Bennie was a year old, my parents explained to me that my little brother was always going to need special attention and protection... you know, because of his handicap. There was hope that he might be able to get around, like with crutches and braces, but they didn't know then. But that wasn't the real problem—the real risk. The real problem was... *is* his heart. He's always known he's had a fast heart rate, but it's more serious than that." She raised her hands and made air quotes. "Permanent junctional reciprocating tachycardia. It's been monitored, my mom says, without Bennie's knowledge. His heart often races at twice the normal, healthy rate, and anything he does above his elevated, resting heart rate is life-threatening. My parents didn't feel he needed that burden to shoulder along with his handicap. So the idea had been to monitor his heart at frequent checkups, and when he was older, and hopefully stronger, he could sustain some kind of heart surgery when the time came and maybe even more advances had been made. I've been fighting with my parents, long-distance over the phone from college, ever since Bennie turned eighteen. He needs to know. Right? And they refused to tell him. They wanted to buy more time, since he seemed okay at his last checkup."

Jay realized he hadn't been paying any attention to Bennie's health. His stunted growth, instead of alarming Jay, had conveyed a false sense of permanence. Bennie did not change. He would always be around. Why wouldn't he? "So what's changed?"

She sat back down on the bed. "Breaking his leg. It was too much stress on him." She looked up and met his eyes for the first time. "Have you noticed his color? The stress and shock was too much. A valve is now nearly completely blown, the doctor said. Bennie's never really gotten outside. He's never really done anything physical at all."

She didn't have to say it out loud in order for Jay to feel the unspoken blame she and her parents likely held toward him. Jay should have left Bennie friendless in his computer lab, safely ensconced in his soundproof, fireproof, fun-proof box.

Two images presented themselves at once. The first was the mantel full of pictures in Bennie's living room, the protective shell of family members surrounding Bennie, and how that had been compromised because of his involvement. The second image was of Bennie being carelessly passed around the top of a drug-induced, barely controlled mob every other week at the latest rave.

He didn't want to tell Chloe, but Bennie had never been as safely ensconced in the protection of his house as the family might have hoped. And even when they weren't together, Bennie often used sleepovers at Jay's as a front to venture out to capture new video for his Mnemosyne project. "How much of the family knew about his condition?"

"I don't know. But everybody knows now. Everybody but Bennie."

"So what does this mean?" Jay felt a slight tremor beneath the supports he envisioned as barely preventing a full-blown nervous breakdown.

"He's going to die, Jay, and nobody knows how to tell him."

Without another word, she slipped under the covers and turned her back to him. He couldn't tell if she was crying. After a long pause, he lay down next to her, above the covers.

She began speaking again, barely an decibel louder than the air conditioner, outlining in tired sentence fragments all of her regrets, of her secretly being embarrassed by Bennie when she was in grade school, her later ever-growing resentment of him because of the degree of care, attention, and family resources he had drained, which naturally meant less for her.

Jay responded to each of her questions and doubts, as much as he could understand them, until finally, he realized his words had devolved into a drowsy kind of nonsense, utterances that even he couldn't understand. He stopped moving his consoling hand and let it rest warmly curled over the swell of her hip. Her breathing deepened, and he fell into a deep sleep.

Jay awoke facing the curtained window, which with the morning sun had been silently pantomiming the equivalent of a barely suppressed scream—with light, not sound. He looked at his watch: 8:59 a.m. Only two hours of sleep, but it felt good. Light spilled from the outer edges of the dark curtain, and for the first time, he truly dreaded letting in a new day and all it had to offer. He spied his sneakers on the floor beneath the desk chair. He wiggled his bare toes beneath the sheets. He didn't even remember taking off his shoes.

He turned over and immediately felt the warmth of Chloe's body. She must have awakened at some point and tucked him in. From the appearance of it, she had also neatened the room.

He slipped out of bed, showered, and redressed into his same jeans and T-shirt. He found Chloe's phone on the desk and punched in his own contact information. He then gathered his laptop into his backpack and placed a glass of cold water on the nightstand next to her.

"Hope you didn't mind that I tucked you in." She kept her eyes shut, just moving her lips puffed out in a smooth "O" by the pressure of the pillow.

He squatted and stared at her sleep-pink face.

"Don't worry. I put your pants back on when I was done." A quick smile revealed itself for an instant, and she opened her eyes.

"I feel violated." He smiled back and locked eyes. He had the irresistible urge to crawl into those warm sheets and join her. Not because he was in crisis, and not because it was convenient, but because it was *her.*

She caught his hesitation and lifted her head. "What?"

"I'll... I'll be downstairs grabbing some coffee and something to eat, whenever you're ready to go."

"Right." She flipped back the comforter and sheet in one smooth stroke. Jay was treated to the full expanse of her long brown legs and her perfectly formed bellybutton below her pulled-up T-shirt, like a slight depression made by a master baker's probing thumb.

Downstairs, Jay tried to identify the unexpected lightness

155

in his chest. When he upended the sugar dispenser over his mug, it hit him. *Chloe.*

Yes. He felt so much potential there. She seemed like someone he could make a very deep connection with, a different kind of connection than, say, his friendship with Bennie. But doubt nibbled at the edges of that notion. Perhaps their few shared moments and her show of emotion toward him were just the result of some traumatic bonding. But it felt like more than that. Much more.

Fifteen minutes later, she came downstairs in full dormitory garb—a pink T-shirt, a windbreaker, and navy blue sweatpants with a collegial seal stamped on the behind as if she were literally a product that had been inspected and approved by the university. She wore glasses he didn't know she had, looking like the prototypical nerdy beauty queen who would be transformed three-quarters of the way through a movie by merely removing her glasses and letting out her ponytail.

Jay handed her a Styrofoam cup of coffee he had prepared for her, and she accepted it with a wide smile. She took a sip. "Not exactly Starbucks, huh?"

Since Chloe already knew the way to Jay's school, having just graduated from there a year ago herself, they rode in comfortable silence for the first few minutes.

She braked at a stop sign and looked at him. "You have to promise me you won't say anything to Bennie."

"Promise. Of course. I mean, that's... that's a family thing."

She reached over and placed a warm hand on his thigh before turning her attention back to the road. "I'm sorry, Jay. It's not like you aren't already like family. Definitely to Bennie." She flicked another glance at him. "And to me."

To his surprise, she kept her hand on his leg and opted to drive one-handed the rest of the way. Minutes later, they pulled into the designated drop-off area at the side of the high school. Jay could feel a familiar hard pit of nervousness gather in his stomach. He had never had any real trouble in school, but negotiating the line between complete invisibility and just enough visibility to fill a classroom seat, procure a plastic tray for the hot lunch in the cafeteria, and receive his requisite photocopy of whatever was being taught for the day took some degree of effort and nerve. But as with every school day, once he became acclimated to the sounds and rhythms of the school, and he realized each morning what he had promptly forgotten the night before—which was that it wasn't all that bad and that he would eventually make it through. One more year, and he would be out of there.

Just as he pulled his gaze away from the parking lot to turn to Chloe, he saw something out of the corner of his eye—a blur of black. He rescanned the full parking lot, but saw nothing out of the ordinary.

Chloe braked at the side entrance at the same time the second-period bell sounded. Other milling or late-arriving students grabbed their book bags and scurried up the entrance ramp. She put the car in park and placed her hand on his knee, finishing a palate-cracking yawn. "I'm going to grab another coffee and then work my way to this doctor's office in Sudbury." She pulled a crumpled piece of paper out of her jacket pocket.

Jay nodded. "Yeah. Oh, how's Bennie supposed to get anything done in the hospital with his parents there all the time on watch?"

Chloe shook her head. "I wouldn't worry about that. They don't want to raise Bennie's suspicions until they decide to tell him. They're going to visit, but keep doing normal stuff, so he doesn't get any ideas."

He pulled his backpack onto his lap and opened the car door. For an embarrassing second, he seemed to have caught some part of his red parka on something, maybe the gearshift, because he immediately fell back in the seat after attempting to take his first step out of the car.

Jay squeezed his eyes shut as he inwardly cursed his clumsiness, then felt the warm press of Chloe's lips on his. A bluish-red explosion bloomed in his head, and an uncontrollable smile spread across his face. He pulled back. "What was that for?"

She looked toward the windshield and ran her hands along the steering wheel. "For being there for me, for listening to me. It means a lot. I've never been able to dump on anyone about all this. You can't know how much it's helped."

"Well, sure. I'm here, Chloe. Any time. You'll be okay today?"

She nodded.

"Okay, I'll see you right after school, and we can go in together to check on Bennie. Okay?"

She smiled. "Yeah, that sounds good."

Jay, still unable to contain his idiotically wide smile, jumped out of the car.

At the end of sixth period, an announcement came over the intercom: "Jay Brooks to Vice Principal Chomney's office."

The entire class glanced up at the yellow box to the right of the classroom clock and then at Jay. His lab partner gave him an irritated glare through his scratched Plexiglas goggles. With an apologetic shrug, Jay handed over the beaker he was holding. The lab purpose was to analyze condensates from wood smoke, and a smoldering splinter of wood sent gray tendrils of smoke out through the partially corked top. The entire room smelled like a marijuana den.

The teacher, who was helping lab partners in the far corner of the room, gave Jay a nod.

"Sorry," Jay said to his partner. He gathered his books and backpack and stripped off his lab coat. He had kept his jacket on, anticipating the possibility of leaving early.

Jay trotted down the hallway. After visiting the vice principal, he would pop in to see the only other person he felt he could trust with his delicate situation: his guidance counselor.

At a comforting grandfatherly age, Mr. Henderson was

older than the other counselors were. He had large tent flaps for ears and an ever-growing nose. Above his brown eyes hung twin nests of wiry, unkempt eyebrows. His stern jaw supported a tight, lipless mouth. But as Jay knew, Henderson's appearance was a decoy concealing a nuclear reactor core of mirth. Henderson had also been the first to notice how Jay's grades were silently mutating through Bennie's crafty hacking. And although Jay had been too embarrassed to thank the counselor for not reporting him, he would never be able to fully express his gratitude.

The school was laid out as a large capital E, and as he journeyed out of his wing from the top left corner of the E to the middle wing where the front office resided, he resisted the urge to sprint out the exit. He couldn't just run out of school and raise yet another alarm.

As far as Jay could figure, whoever had taken his father didn't know how much Jay knew. But after the kidnapping, they were surely aware that he would eventually try to appeal to some kind of authority. He thought it was just a matter of time before he was grabbed, too. If he could just reassure the vice principal that all was okay, quietly describe the real situation to Henderson, then get back to the hotel, he would be a lot calmer. Then he and Chloe could follow up on some of Bennie's leads and start to piece things together.

Jay pushed in through a low hinged door and entered the front office. The secretary glanced up at him.

He cleared his throat. "Jay Brooks?"

She indicated the door behind her with a long red nail. "Go ahead. Mr. Chomney is waiting."

"Um, right after this, can you check if Mr. Henderson can see me?" Jay asked, looking around. Two other guidance counselors were consulting with students in their open offices, another student was picking through scholarship applications along the back wall, and a kid with a purple Mohawk waited outside another office.

The secretary nodded curtly, setting into motion the loose

flesh of her cheeks, which sagged just enough to mimic the droop of her eyeglass lanyard, and returned to her monitor.

Jay stepped past her desk and approached Chomney's door. He placed a hand on the knob, picturing the expression of disapproval on the vice principal's face. Chomney was a squat, nattily dressed man who, despite his sour demeanor, looked like Richard Dreyfuss. Jay sighed.

He started to turn the knob, spying the vice principal's vague silhouetted form through the frosted glass, like Death himself waiting, ready to close the deal with a cold, fatal handshake. The guy could be a real dick, but Jay knew he *had* to check any attitude at the door. He swung open the door and stepped into the office.

Chomney stood behind his desk. "Mr. Brooks, please, have a seat." He gestured to the empty chair in front of his desk. Jay looked to his right. The other chair was filled by the hulking, leather-jacketed man who had murdered the cell tower engineer the previous day. The man slipped a hand inside the flap of his coat.

Jay didn't wait. His brain made a lizard-quick leap back into the deepest recesses of itself, shutting down everything except what was necessary for one task: escape. He simultaneously turned and ducked.

Chomney said, "Hey, what are you—"

A loud screech came from behind. He glanced back to see Chomney's large wooden desk smash into the stranger's legs. The air unzipped before Jay's eyes, and a neat hole appeared in the metal file cabinet just to the right of the door. He sprang up from his crouch and sprinted past the secretary.

Nobody in the front office moved or seemed to notice much of anything. He didn't understand at first. Then he realized he hadn't heard a shot, either. The shooter had used a silencer. That screamed "professional." The sound had been no more jolting than an everyday punch of a stapler, but for that same reason, that ramped up Jay's fear.

"Run!" Jay yelled. "He has a gun!"

Two doors slammed, and Mohawk scrambled under a table covered with college pamphlets. Jay moved to hurdle over the small swinging door at the front of the office, but his injured leg buckled at the knee. Instead, he crashed through the small door, grasping for the front counter. Instead of hard wood, his hand found a wire basket of school forms, which went flying into the front hallway. He fell to his knees.

Kneeling on the other side of the counter, he took a second to get his bearings. Where was he? Where were the exits? He tried desperately to remember the endless fire drills he had suffered through over the last four years.

Instead of taking the obvious exit out the door he had used to enter, Jay crept left to the side door. If he could make it, he would exit to the parking lot through the gym. As he moved, he raised his head a fraction above the front counter to check for the gunman. Chomsky looked like a poorly folded card table that someone had tried to shove through the doorway. The secretary sat slumped over her keyboard. To her left, the shooter shrugged off the slumped form of Mr. Henderson, who had apparently tried a heroic move.

Jay took off through the open door and sprinted down the hall. His adrenaline made his strides seem fantastically long, his sneakers hitting the floor only twice between classrooms. At the end of the hallway, he threw his shoulder into the double doors that separated the wings. The shooter's booted feet stomped slower and heavier as each of the man's steps sent a booming echo down the empty hallway.

Jay's pumping arms made sharp zipping sounds against his parka. He raced to the art and music wing, passing through a cloud of glue and paint, then a floating chord of classical violin. Classroom doors opened and then quickly shut, like the pad cups on a saxophone's valves.

The double doors of the gym were propped open, and Jay could hear shouts, screams, and the squeals of rubber sneakers on wood. He ran straight through four volleyball matches. The gym teacher stood from a side bench and began to yell, but a much louder voice drowned him out.

"Stop, Jay Brooks. I will shoot you."

Jay kept running toward the locker room, anticipating his head exploding like the stop-action photo he had seen in physics class of a bullet penetrating an apple.

But no shot came.

He crashed through the boys' locker room and burst through the same exit he had entered that morning. He scanned the area for a tardy student getting out of a car he might be able to use. But with a cold shock, his eyes instead locked on a black Dodge Magnum that sat in the middle of the parking lot like a heeled Doberman awaiting its master.

He kept searching. Instead of a helpful classmate, he found something better. At the edge of the lot where the pavement met the adjoining baseball field, a police officer was just getting out of his squad car and closing the door. Jay ran up to him and grabbed his elbow. The policeman instinctively lurched and reached for his gun, but abruptly stopped as Jay dropped to the pavement.

"Help me. A man is chasing me. He has a gun!" Jay scrambled to his feet and darted toward the passenger side of the car.

The policeman whirled to face the school. "A man with a gun? Where?"

Jay wondered for a nanosecond why a responding police officer would be so clueless.

"Please!" Jay begged, working at the door handle.

The officer was not the tall, chiseled, hero archetype the police department typically sent to the school for Safety Awareness Week or for Students Against Drunk Driving assemblies. He was haunted looking, middle-aged, and potbellied, with shoe-polish black hair and a peaked blood-pressure pallor.

The officer nodded and slid back into the driver's seat. He simultaneously started the cruiser and unlocked the back doors. Jay lunged from the front door to the back, yanked it open, and dove into the backseat. He raised his head just enough to see through the window.

The school's door exploded open. The shooter ran out, then skidded to a stop, hiding his gun beneath his jacket. The squad car's radio squawked to life with commands for all available units to go to the school. The radio suddenly went quiet. The next thing Jay heard was the clicking of the back doors locking.

The policeman put the car in gear, punched the gas, and peeled out of the school parking lot. Jay raised his head so he could look through the back window. Behind them, the black Magnum roared to life, but to Jay's relief, it went in the opposite direction.

Jay sat forward and hooked his fingers into the cage that separated the back from the front. He started to ask where they were going, but stopped. On the front seat lay a photo of him next to a mini-DVD.

"What's going on? Why were you here *before* the shooting was called in? Are you even a real cop?"

The policeman banged his elbow against the cage, jamming Jay's fingers. "Shut up! Just... s*hut up!*" He threw off his hat, rubbed his face as if to wake up, and rotated a miniature laptop on its pedestal. He yanked the car off the road and fishtailed through a dirt path behind the greenhouse of a florist that was only open on the weekends.

Afraid to say anything more, Jay watched as the policeman logged into a webmail account, opened an email, scrolled down, and clicked on a link. The link opened a new browser window. The domain name didn't look normal. It was an IP address only, and the homepage was completely black.

A voice issued from the laptop's speaker. Jay couldn't tell if it was the quality of the speaker or truly the speaker's voice, but it came across high-pitched and tinny, like a little girl's voice.

"Take Jay Brooks to 11 Elmwood Circle, Uxbridge, apartment number two. Take back stairs. Key is under mat. Gag boy and lock him to radiator in hallway. Leave and mention none of this, and we will destroy our evidence against you. You are expected within the hour. Otherwise, we turn the evidence over to the proper authorities."

CHAPTER 28

TUESDAY, 2:36 PM

BENNIE

By early afternoon, Bennie's new cast was set and his leg was lowered. He was enjoying a cup of tapioca pudding when his room phone rang.

"Yo," he answered.

Chloe's voice exploded through the receiver. "Bennie! Have you seen the news? Have you talked to Jay?"

"No... hold on." He dug for the remote under his sheets, turned on the television, and flipped to the first local channel he could find. "It's at commercial. I haven't talked to him. Why? What's wrong? You're still picking him up after school, right?"

"Well, I went to the Sudbury doctor's office this morning like you asked... but I'll tell you about that later. I came back and was going to chill in the parking lot in case Jay slipped out of his last class early, but when I got to the school, the campus was in complete chaos. *Chaos*! I couldn't even get within a block of it. I think some parents were getting through, but it was completely sealed off. Police were everywhere and news vans and at least two news 'copters. The entire school was being evacuated. SWAT guys were swarming with people running in all directions. It was like Columbine. It's crazy. I don't know what happened, but I'm scared for Jay. I tried calling his cell, but he won't answer."

The commercial ended, and the news returned. "Hold on, Chloe. Let me listen." He cranked up the volume.

A pretty blond reporter, red-faced and flushed, spoke with a superficial level of seriousness and concern, but her eyes were bright with a glimmer of excitement. "... and initial reports are that three victims, all school staff, were shot at point-blank range in the front office of the school at approximately two twenty-five this afternoon. No names are available yet or their status. So far, no student casualties have been reported. Fortunately, local authorities have acquired office surveillance footage of the assailant that they hope will help them in their manhunt. They also want to locate one particular Broadside High student who has gone missing after this horrible, senseless massacre..."

A freeze-frame, low-quality, black and white picture was displayed. The image was of Jay, both feet suspended off the floor, as he was apparently running from the front office, a spray of loose paper frozen in the air behind him. Bennie could make out a tall dark form out of focus nearer to the surveillance camera and facing Jay's direction. The guy looked to be holding a gun. The picture was replaced by a younger, full-color photo of Jay that Bennie recognized from the yearbook.

Then, an unsteady aerial shot of the school's campus filled the screen, showing the large *E* of the school at an angle, along with the adjacent woods and the nearby pond. Concentric circles of chaos surrounded the school: bands of people running outward and away, another circle of police cars with the black and white numbers on their rooftops like gameboard pieces, and a final band of parents' vehicles and news vans racing against each other. The camera zoomed out for a fuller view.

Bennie's mind raced. "Look, this has to be related. I don't think we can wait until he contacts us. What if he's been taken, just like his dad? Shit. How did they even know Jay was back in school?"

"Who knows? Maybe they were looking there every day for him, but didn't find him because he was skipping. Maybe his dad told them where he went to school. But of course, that's not hard to find out."

"Where are you?" he asked.

"I'm sitting in my car a couple of miles from the school."

"Chloe, listen. We have to move *much* faster than I thought we would need to, and I was going to have Jay do most of these things."

"Tell me. Anything. I just want to get Jay back before they hurt him."

"Okay," Bennie said. "Get home quick and go down to my lab. There's a police scanner in the closet." He instructed her how to tune his scanner to the police band and hook a speech-recognition microphone to it. He had rigged the speech recognition program to "tweet" via his Twitter account. He also told her to take his netbook to the Cambridge cell tower and pull up by the cemetery with the wireless adapter activated. The Trojan Horse program he had planted in the cell tower would dump all the video files, if there were any, to the netbook. "When you've downloaded all of them, come back and see me and fill me in on the doc's office you visited. Call me the minute you hear from Jay, if you do. In the meantime, I'll try to find out if he's checked into an emergency room."

Half an hour later, his Twitter account sprang to life with tweets. His program still had some glitches, since he had coded it to become familiar with his own speech patterns, and there would be more problems when the voices interrupted each other. To complicate matters, each tweet was limited to one hundred forty characters.

LATEST: *unit 33 what's your twenty*

LATEST: *error -15: sound source too close to microphone*

LATEST: *could you ten nine that over*

LATEST: *ten twelve we're checking the location of unit 33 uh says following a ten thirty seven possibly the shooter*

LATEST: *roger*

LATEST: *all units to secure band*

The tweets stopped.

Bennie had to search online to find out what each police code meant. From what he could tell, a police officer in the area had not been responding because he was in pursuit of the suspect involved in the school shooting.

He studied his twitter page again: *unit 33 what's your twenty.*

Bennie returned to the television and frantically punched through all the major network channels and then the twenty-four-hour news channels. None carried the exact aerial video view of the campus he had seen earlier. Had it been live? Most live broadcasts were on the ground with their embedded reporters, relaying the chaos up close and personal on the scene. He needed to see that aerial view again to confirm his suspicion. He really wished he were home and could just rewind his TiVo.

He went online and browsed CNN.com, boston.com, and some local news stations. He finally found the view on a local news team's website. The video was on the home page, captioned, "Minutes after the shooting at Broadside High (aerial)." He started the video and recognized the exact footage he had seen earlier and the same unsteady view. He kept his mouse pointer hovering over the pause button for the second of video he needed to see again. The view panned out wide enough to take in the small pond beside the school.

Hold it... hold it... there! He clicked the pause button. The video was of extremely low quality, but he easily spotted the black-on-white number *33* on the rooftop of a squad car that was not in pursuit of the suspected shooter, but sitting idle behind what looked like a greenhouse. Bennie brought his laptop screen up to his face. The slightest hint of red was visible in the backseat—the exact shade of Jay's parka.

He pulled out his cell phone and typed a text: *Are you okay?* He stopped just before hitting send. What if the captor had Jay's phone? He waited, staring at his message. His indecision only increased as he stroked the send button beneath the pad of his thumb.

CHAPTER 29

TUESDAY, 10:23 AM

STURGEON

STURGEON'S PHONE VIBRATED ACROSS HIS desk like a possessed Ouija board planchette. He slapped at the phone and brought it to his ear. "Yes?"

"Sir, I was able to intercept the woman at Mount Auburn and cover the autopsy—"

"But?"

"Yes, well, it's just... I'm not sure I can do this anymore. The hospital administrator's been all over my ass. Someone reported me leaving a spinal surgery last week. I was gone only an hour, but someone sold me out. I can't keep doing this. I'm going to lose my license, at minimum."

Too bad Bolshoy was still on his way back from Connecticut, Sturgeon thought. And once the Russian returned, he would be going to the school to grab Brooks's son. Sturgeon had the father, but he also needed the boy. With those two contained, he could finish his work. Sturgeon was half-tempted to meet with the good doctor and work out an agreement in person using Bolshoy's special brand of persuasion.

Sturgeon hummed and ran his fingers along the edge of

his desk, shaking his head.

"Hello? Are you there? Listen, I'll do whatever you want. Sign whatever you want—a non-disclosure agreement. Anything. *Please.*"

Sturgeon laughed. He laughed and laughed, filling his dark office with ripples of heartless laughter, gales of it, until his head became light. He let his laughter dwindle at a leisurely pace while the doctor waited on the other end. "An NDA? Oh, of course! But I won't be able to send anybody until late. I hope that doesn't inconvenience you? Say somewhere between midnight and the rest of your life? Just give me the go ahead, and we can arrange it."

Sturgeon ended the call, and his laughter crested and crashed again.

CHAPTER 30

TUESDAY, 3:19 PM

JAY

THE POLICEMAN SLAPPED HIS DASH-MOUNTED laptop shut and got out of the car. Jay readied himself as the man circled around to the back door. The cop wrenched open the door. Jay fell onto his back, ready to kick, but froze at the sight of the gun.

"Don't friggin' move. Are we clear?"

Jay nodded, unable to speak. The man grabbed him by the elbow and flipped him facedown. He dug his forearm into Jay's neck and cuffed him. Jay tried to squirm, but it was like trying to move beneath a landslide.

"Calm the hell down." The officer slammed the back door and slid back into the driver's seat.

Jay righted himself and kicked against the grate. "Let me out of here!"

The man shook his head and started the car. He made his way onto Route 495 South, maneuvering so other cars would jump into the passing lane, but he kept his strobes off.

Jay considered shouting at the other cars. Then, he realized no one was going to pay attention to a screaming handcuffed maniac in the backseat of a police car. He kicked again, hard enough to cause the policeman to lurch in his seat.

The man grabbed the rearview mirror and angled it so he could make eye contact while they shot down the interstate at eighty miles an hour. His hard black pupils flicked from side to side. "Listen, you little twat. I have a fully charged Taser and a can full of pepper spray, and I am *really* tempted to use both and make a friggin' human fajita out of you if you don't shut the hell up. And I mean *now*!"

Jay's heart was ready to beat its way out of his chest. The overflow of adrenaline in his system was clouding his thoughts, setting each line of thinking ablaze like so much dry kindling. The officer was actually right. He *had* to calm down. He forced himself to sit back and watch as they passed exit after exit. He shifted to try to keep the handcuffs from digging into the small of his back. "Please, just tell me why that voice wants me to go to Uxbridge. What's there? Has someone found my father?" He fought hard to keep his voice level, but he heard the edges give way and splinter.

"Let's just say you and I are both in a really tight spot." He darted another look at Jay in the mirror. "What the hell just happened at your school?" He looked down at his radio as if tempted to turn it back on and find out.

Jay shrugged. "Hell if I know. I got called to the VP's office, and a Vin Diesel guy pulled a gun on me. So I ran."

The policeman raised his eyebrows.

"Okay, here's the whole story. Five hundred words or less." Figuring he had nothing to lose, Jay recounted the events of the last week to the officer. At the end, he explained he had only returned to school to avoid a home visit from the truant officer.

The policeman nodded. "Yeah, the jogger lady and the repairman. Both done in the same area. The entire state's gone friggin' haywire. But MD Systems? Naw. Doesn't sound familiar." The officer took the Milford exit, which would eventually get them to Uxbridge.

They pulled off the two-lane road and turned onto a residential side road. "Listen, I appreciate your trying to explain your situation. Whatever the hell it all means. But I can tell you two things. I can't change my mind about where I'm taking you, and I can't share my reasons." He slowed and parked in front of a redbrick ranch, then leaned back in his seat and worked a wrinkled soft pack of Newports out of his front pocket. He flicked a cigarette out of the pack directly into his mouth and depressed the car lighter on the dashboard.

"We all make mistakes. I've made my share for sure, but what wouldn't a guy do for his family, right?" As he spoke, the unlit cigarette in his mouth bounced like a conductor's baton. "I'm real sorry for your dad, and from what you've told me, it seems like you'd likely do anything to help him. I get that. Well, same goes for me and my family. I wish I was in a position to help you out, help you find your dad, figure out who it is that wants you, and try to see what the hell went on at Jefferson Park with that lady and the technician."

The lighter popped out. He lit up and inhaled deeply. The cigarette burnt down like a slow fuse. "But the bottom line is I can't help you. For the sake of my family, I'm dropping you off, no question, and forgetting everything we've talked about today. I got to somehow explain to the chief why I didn't respond to the Brookside shooting. I got my hands full enough." He stopped as if considering what he'd just said for the first time.

"Shit!" He banged the steering wheel with the edge of his hand. Lit ash tumbled onto his pants. He cursed again, brushing frantically at his crotch, then tossed his cigarette out the window. "Goddamnit."

Jay studied the thickness of the backseat windows. He'd seen enough *Cops* episodes to doubt he could break one. He remembered seeing recorded video of car thieves shattering driver's side windows with a pointedly thrown pebble, but that wouldn't work on the reinforced glass of a police car.

The policeman put the car back in gear and made a

three-point turn. Jay saw they were back on the highway to Uxbridge.

"What? You're still taking me?" Jay was devastated. He had no more ideas. He would never see his father again. He would never again see Bennie, whom he would ironically outpace in their footrace to the grave. He would never find out what kind of future he and Chloe might have had. He fell back in his seat and for the first time felt his phone in his back pocket. His phone. With his hands cuffed, he blindly worked his cell out of his pocket and felt around the casing, finding the power button to orient his fingers. For once, he was grateful his father hadn't been able to afford a touch-screen phone.

He closed his eyes and reconstructed his phone's keyboard layout by memory. He pressed the mute button first. He then let the pad of his thumb skate along the keyboard until he found the joystick switch button and pressed it. He worked the button, navigating down what he hoped were three rows of program selections, then over one to the contacts list. He depressed the joystick to select it. If he was in his address book, the top name would be for Acapulco's, his and Bennie's favorite Mexican restaurant. He navigated up once to circle back to the very end of his contact list, which should be "Welch," if he remembered correctly. He depressed the joystick again to go down to the send text option.

He opened his eyes and looked around. They were already pulling into Elmwood Circle, a teardrop-shaped road that hung suspended from the eyelid of the main two-way thoroughfare through Uxbridge. The road was dominated on both sides by closely constructed two- and three-family homes, all sharing common driveways.

He had to hurry. What should he type? Help? Where was the *h* on a number pad? On the number three? He couldn't remember. Forget a coherent message. He mashed several of the keys, moved his thumb back to the joystick, and shifted it right to what should be the send button. Hopefully, Bennie would get the message and know Jay was alive, for a few more minutes anyway. Maybe they could locate him since the text would ping a cell tower. He stuffed his phone back into his pocket.

The officer turned into a driveway between a gray shake-shingled two-story home and a three-story white clapboard. The houses on the near side of the street were built on a downward slope. Number 11 reached out from its first-floor entrance downward toward the street with a set of cracked, psoriatic cement stairs and a black wrought iron railing. The car stopped next to the partially exposed basement level. Jay thought he could taste death at the back of his throat.

The policeman dug through his duffel bag and brought out a roll of duct tape and a handkerchief. He got out of the car and came around again with his gun drawn. "No fighting now. There's no reason for you to get hurt. Just open your mouth."

Jay eyed the gun, then did as he was told.

The cop stuffed the handkerchief into Jay's mouth, then wrapped duct tape around his head to secure it. His jaw set tight, he avoided Jay's eyes. He pulled Jay out of the car and shoved him up the driveway with the gun pressed to his back.

Jay's feet performed a reluctant kind of gallows trot to keep up with the policeman's quick pace. The cell phone felt huge in his back pocket. Hoping to hide the square bulge, he turned toward the policeman as they ran and got a deeper jab of the gun for it.

Behind the damp cloth ball in his mouth, that same taste of imminent death gathered like thick mucus in the back of his throat. Silent, distant supernovas burst deep within the folds of his brain, as if he might pass out from fear. The broken cement of the ascending driveway skated past. They turned at the crest of the driveway, and Jay tripped up the wooden back stairs to a second-story deck.

The policeman grabbed a key from beneath the welcome mat, unlocked the door, and shoved Jay inside. All lights were off, and the blinds were drawn. Jay stumbled through a small food pantry, a kitchen that was not much larger, down a narrow hallway, past a dining room, and down another hallway leading toward what looked like a living room with a curtained bay window at the end.

The policeman twisted Jay around and pushed him face-first into the wall. His hands slid down his torso and then around his belt loop. Jay could feel the guy's hands on his keys and then his cell phone.

"Shit." The cop grabbed Jay's cell phone and tossed it to the corner of the room. "You won't be needing that." He then shoved Jay's shoulders down.

Jay resisted, not out of defiance, but out of petrified stiffness, but his knees eventually gave way, and he slid down against the cool plaster wall, beside a radiator. A second pair of handcuffs appeared, and the policeman attached one cuff to Jay's current handcuffs and the other to the radiator pressure valve. Jay pushed his shoulder against the radiator to test its give; it felt as if it were rooted to the Earth's very core.

The policeman straightened and placed the handcuff keys on a highboy behind the dining room table. He stood in the darkness of the hallway for a second, giving Jay a moment of hope. Jay rattled his handcuffs against the radiator and howled behind the gag. If he could get him to remove the gag, he could at least make a final plea.

Please. They are going to kill me. Do you understand? Kill me! Right after you leave. You can't do this.

But the man turned and left without a word.

As soon as he heard the squad car start outside, Jay flopped and bounced on his back and side, nearly wrenching his arms out of their sockets, trying to work free of the old radiator. He stopped only out of fear of breaking his wrists. He vaguely remembered hearing a saying that there was no such thing as an atheist in a foxhole, and he couldn't deny that he was indeed sending out his own prayer to whoever or whatever would listen, broadcast with all the electricity and energy his body could summon. Down the hallway, a door cracked open against its doorframe.

Jay's prayer lent itself more energy and became a muffled plea against his gag.

With none of the movie drawn-out, attenuated suspense or even the infamous bad-guy soliloquy to justify his actions, the killer was on him in three easy steps.

CHAPTER 31

BENNIE

CHLOE BURST INTO BENNIE'S HOSPITAL room. She ran over to his bed and pulled him up in a fierce hug.

"Hey," Bennie said, rubbing her back. "Easy, easy. We'll figure this out."

"But what about Jay? What's going on? Is he even alive?"

"He is, I think. I got a text." Bennie showed her the recent text from Jay's phone: Ajjttwwmm. "It's nonsense, but I think he just wanted us to know he is alive." Bennie filled her in on his chance discovery of the hidden police car in the live video feed.

He held back from giving her his honest opinion. He wasn't completely sure of anything. He felt compelled to soothe her, but the entire situation had spun out of control so quickly. He was impatient to grab the purple netbook out of her messenger bag to see if it had acquired any video feeds from the cell tower in Cambridge.

Her added weight on him placed uncomfortable pressure on his freshly cast leg. He gently parted from her, and she sat up on the end of his bed, slumped and shaking her head in disbelief.

"I should be the one crying. He's my friend, right?"

She snuffled.

"You really care about him, don't you?" he asked.

"Well, of course I do. Don't you?" she asked him accusingly, her red, raw eyes and wet lashes blurred in anger and desperation.

"Chloe..." He touched her arm. "You know what I mean."

She dragged her sleeve across her eyes, swallowed hard, and took a deep breath. "Yeah, I do."

"He's still not over his mom dying. It's been really hard on him. Just so you know, there's a negative side to Jay. He gets moody, depressed, and kind of checks out more often than he should. But I'm glad you feel like you do with him. Maybe you're what he needs to get through this."

"He needs both of us, Ben."

"You're right. So let's get to it."

"Why would someone try to kill him inside the school? Also, he escapes, and then he quietly leaves with a policeman who then goes off the grid?"

"We can't be sure of any of that. We have to be careful of making assumptions. I don't think Jay was meant to be gunned down in the school. Think about it. What'd they say? Three or four were killed in the front office? And Jay was right there, but he wasn't shot? I'm thinking they still have him. Maybe. Like that policeman is in on it somehow."

Bennie shifted to try to get more comfortable. "Listen, we know these people have power, and they've exercised it. We've seen that today, and we saw at the cell tower with the repairman that they'll kill whoever gets in their way. We've seen they'll kidnap people in broad daylight, like Jay's dad and maybe Jay himself. And they gotta have money. Think of what it takes to get all that equipment together, to manufacture, install, and monitor all those cell tower overrides across the state. They have advanced technology and know-how from the way they wired the cell tower. They obviously have government connections into this black-ops project. What did you say Grayson called it?"

"ARGUS," Chloe said.

Bennie nodded. "Can they bribe or control a small-town policeman? I think so. Let me check the netbook."

She pulled the netbook out of her bag. "I didn't get to the cell tower as quickly as I wanted. Mom caught me at home and didn't want me going out at all because she was so freaked over the Broadside shooting. You should see downtown. It's a mess, like when the Boston Marathon comes through. I promised her I was just coming straight to see you."

He powered up the computer and started the file transfer to his laptop from a USB connector. "Yeah, she called an hour ago to make sure you were here. I said you were, but that you had headed downstairs to get me a Coke."

"Good."

He looked back at the screen to check the progress bar. "Holy crap. When did Jay put that device back on the tower?" He thought back. "What day was that... the day I broke my leg? Monday?"

Chloe nodded.

"The flash drives I arrayed on the device I hacked into had ten gigabytes of space. From what I can tell, the drive became completely full in the first *hour*. Come here."

He loaded up the several videos to play in sequence in his media player.

A net moving left, right, zooming in, out, white sneakers flashing in and out of the bottom of the screen, a green ball bouncing toward and away, rapidly, most often staying within frame. Several minutes of this passed, then the camera view steadied and bobbed toward a green bench on the inside of a tennis court. A tennis player who looked grim, sweaty, and arrhythmic collapsed next to the camera's point-of-view and sucked water from a sports bottle. The picture went black, then resumed again, mid-game, from the point-of-view of the person serving.

"No sound?" Chloe asked.

"Nope. The other one didn't have it either."

They continued to watch the tennis match with the picture occasionally going black, then returning. Bennie recalled the original video he had seen of the murder Jay had witnessed at Jefferson Park. That video had abruptly cut out exactly the same way.

"Why does it keep blinking in and out? Is there some kind of video limit or something they're reaching?" Chloe asked.

Bennie shrugged. "Dunno." He watched another few seconds. "Well, this sucks. What the hell is going on here? Why would the government be interested in a *tennis match*? And why would *this* guy be outfitted with the ARGUS device?"

Chloe hopped across the room and pulled a wrinkled flyer from her messenger bag. She handed the paper to Bennie. "It's from my trip to the Sudbury doc's office this morning."

Bennie smoothed out the flyer on his lap desk. "Discount RK surgery?"

"Yep. Laser eye surgery was offered at this clinic. So cheap you couldn't refuse. The office space is empty now. There was no business sign or anything. I tried getting in, but the front door was locked. I peeked through the window and saw just an empty front counter and a little sitting area with some chairs. From what I could tell, most of the office space was behind this counter wall, but there was no way to see back there. So I went around back to see if there was another entrance, and some old biddy who was letting her dog out yelled at me, saying she would call the cops. I told her I was looking for a doctor that used to work there. She told me to wait a minute while she went into her house. She came back out and handed me that flyer. She said she had been considering the surgery and was going to get a consultation, but then the entire clinic just up and disappeared. Overnight, it seemed to her."

"How long were they in business?" Bennie asked.

"I wondered the same. She wasn't sure. So I thanked her

and then went into the beauty salon next door. They were a bit more talkative once I bought a manicure." She flashed orange-colored nails. "The woman who did my nails said the clinic opened up at the beginning of last year, in February, and she got the surgery herself. She was really proud of it. She showed me her beautician's license with a picture of her in these horrid thick glasses. She held the license up right next to her cheek to show me the difference. That's when I saw it."

"What?"

Chloe pointed at his computer. "Pull up the schematic."

Bennie opened the file and switched to full-screen mode.

"This." She pointed at the screen, indicating the microscopically thin, red vascular tube labeled "EPI Detector" that led away from the device along the surface of the sclera. "I know it's small, but this girl had these incredibly bright eyes. They did a really good job of trying to match the other... um..."

"Blood vessels."

"Right, blood vessels. Hers were a real light pink, but in the one eye, a portion was thicker than the others. And she complained about it. She said the surgeon said that thicker or burst blood vessels can show up on occasion from heavy coughing, or sneezing, or strain. I swear, Bennie, this woman had that implant and didn't even know it."

"Great find. So I'm guessing we go to Springfield, and we'll find the same story. Fly-by-night office is set up, patients— God knows how many—get unknowingly implanted with the device, and bam, you got yourself a sweet, real-life set of beta users trying out the government's new ARGUS program." Bennie nodded, agreeing with himself. He resumed the video on his laptop. "Let's finish this up."

Chloe sat back and watched the rest of the video with him. Although the tennis match continued, a ghost-like overlaid scene presented itself—another video layer. A jogging trail bounced into view as a dense gathering of trees, shouldering against each other, jogged by in the opposite direction.

Other activity at the park was captured, more joggers, several frog-legged men on carbon-fiber bicycles, and a game of soccer in a distant field.

Chloe pointed at the screen. "Hey, look! There's the tennis court. And over there... those guys playing tennis."

Bennie slapped his forehead.

"Of course! This tower is receiving *multiple* feeds at the same time, just as it would for cell traffic. My overnight hack couldn't handle it, though. Shit. This could get ugly."

Sure enough, as if in response to his prediction, three layers of video presented themselves, and Bennie and Chloe soon had trouble discriminating one scene from the other. Fortunately, forty minutes into the forty-nine minutes of video, the tennis match dropped out and ceased its video feed altogether. The most recent layer, on top of the jogger feed, was what looked like a man, by the size of his work gloves and hairy forearms, who had begun to remove a heavily rooted stump from behind a house.

"How does the tower decide what signal to pick up?" Chloe asked. "It seems kind of random."

"It doesn't. That's not the nature of a cell tower. The cell tower *reacts* to input. Something about each of these people is deciding to send the video upload. The tennis player, and not his buddy, has this device for some reason, and it's active. This jogger has the device, and it's active. And this guy in his backyard. What do they have in common? Is there some kind of timer-based trigger?" Bennie switched his attention back to the PDF schematic of the ARGUS device. He traced the pointer of his mouse along the design and its labels. He habitually stroked the left arm of his glasses with his finger, his lips moving, reading to himself.

Signal Booster. EPI Detector. TEG.

He pointed his mouse at the several-pointed star shape in the middle of the model eyeball. "This middle part, the star over the middle of the eye that looks like an iris, could be a kind of transparent layer, an antennae of sorts, like in the windshield of a car, a signal booster. But what the hell is EPI?"

He googled "EPI" and received a discouraging twenty-four million results. The letters were an abbreviation for a stock fund, the Economic Policy Institute, and something called the Environmental Performance Index. None seemed appropriate. He tried again, adding other key words, such as "biology," "human," and "eyeball," but found nothing useful.

Chloe bounced on the bed. "Maybe it isn't an abbreviation. Maybe it's a prefix. Like what I have for bee stings, an *EpiPen*."

Bennie perked up. "That's it! That's *exactly* it. Epinephrine. *Adrenaline*." He reviewed in his head—the murdered woman, the tennis player, the jogger, the yard worker—all had produced adrenaline at the moment of video upload. "This little red wire must be an adrenaline detector. If so, that's the trigger that initiates video transmission, when it detects adrenaline in the bloodstream. It's ingenious. The adrenaline also dilates the pupils, like a camera aperture seeking more light. And when the video blinks out and stops, the adrenaline level must have dropped. This ties in completely with what Grayson wanted to do originally. Yeah, adrenaline is produced by the fight-or-flight response. Any person with this device who gets into a situation stressful enough to release some detectable degree of adrenaline will transmit."

"So either the heartbeat or the adrenaline level could trigger an upload?"

Bennie typed "TEG" into the search box. He quickly found what he wanted. "Thermoelectric generator. Converts heat to energy. It must take body heat and power itself. So I take it back. The full equation is as long as there's adrenaline, body heat, and a signal, *then* a video transmits. This makes sense. Anyone with this device is protected in a way, like sending an SOS video transmission of any and all real or perceived danger or life-threatening situations."

Chloe nodded. "You sound like Grayson. He said the same

185

thing when he was talking about the first time he thought of the invention. His daughter was raped and murdered. With this, she could have transmitted where she was and who the guy was, real-time. Maybe they still couldn't have saved her, but they'd probably have nailed the murderer sooner."

"But what if people got wise to these devices?" Bennie asked.

"So much the better. I'm guessing these things would act as pretty good deterrents. Even the possibility of a potential victim having one of these would probably make someone think twice before committing a violent crime."

Bennie shifted in his bed again. "And that's not all. Just look at what we've collected, useless records of people exercising and doing yard work. I'm guessing if we collect enough video, we'll eventually see something worthwhile, but how the hell would any of this get filtered through, the right way? How would anyone triage all of it?"

Chloe shrugged. "Think of it. All those cheating spouses, people running red lights, shoplifting, mugging, raping, murdering. I remember researching adrenaline when I first learned I was allergic to bees. Adrenaline can come from stress, excitement, and even bright lights or noise. Seems like a lot of static for any criminal agency to get through to find the meaningful stuff."

They watched the final minutes of the collected video. The man in his back yard finished his project, pulled off his gloves, and collapsed on a lawn chair. The sole remaining feed was the jogger, a fabulously fit and healthy female, who kept her adrenaline pumping.

Chloe pointed at the screen. "Hey, you told me earlier that cell towers of this type have about a one mile radius. I remember that area from following you guys up there. Look how far she's gone."

From the surroundings, the jogger was just beyond the rough one-mile radius Bennie figured the cell tower would cover. Her signal weakened as they watched, jittering uncertainly and creased with bands of static.

"She's *definitely* more than a mile from the cell tower now," Chloe said.

Bennie watched until the video played out to the end. Something in the very last second caught his eye. He backed up and slowly advanced a frame at a time until the very end. Before the jogger's video abruptly stopped, a solid black screen flashed textual output. He paused on it. Dim gray characters were printed in the bottom right corner.

```
12.147.112.147  165.193.93.106  TCP  ufastro-instr  >
http [RST, ACK] Seq=580 Ack=1 Win=0 Len=0 twr beacon
hndshk cell7—cell8
```

"What is it?" Chloe asked.

Bennie lay back on his pillow. "Goddamn it. These rigged-up towers are *networked*." He pointed at the cryptic transmission text. "This is a hand-off acknowledgement of the jogger's signal from cell tower seven, at the park, to an adjoining cell tower."

He sat forward again, holding up his finger. "Hold on. I have this program I built for Jay that might help out. It was normally used to figure out how many wireless signals can be daisy-chained together so that someone could possibly travel without losing connectivity. I might be able to modify it to tie into this first cell tower, spoof the upload handshake signal, and feed it some bytes of this unique type of video upload. Next, it can make a request to hand me off to the nearest GSM signal tower and keep doing it until I reach the edge. As long as the towers keep handing me off to the next and accept this video fragment, we know the towers I connect to are part of this ARGUS program network."

While Bennie worked, Chloe sat in the visitor's chair and watched television. Bennie glanced up occasionally to see the networks still saturated with the school shooting. None of the victims had survived, and the frenzied scene had transformed into spontaneous outcroppings of candlelight vigils on the periphery of the dusky school grounds, which were cordoned off from the public.

After a full accounting of the kids who attended that day and several corroborated reports from Jay's sixth-period science class, police had figured out that Jay was missing. A hotline number flashed on the bottom of the screen. The reporters also mentioned that the police hadn't been able to get in contact with Jay's father.

"Hey!" His parents walked in with a box of Bennie's favorite—New York style white pizza.

Bennie inwardly groaned. Dad was still in his guardhouse uniform, having come straight from his shift to the hospital. His mother gathered more chairs from adjoining rooms and arranged them in a semi-circle around Bennie's bed. They asked Bennie about Jay right away, but he was able to sincerely admit he didn't know where his friend was.

"Well, the police stopped by the house already," Dad said. "I told them that I didn't want you bothered at the hospital. They threatened a warrant, and I think they'll get it. They'll be here tomorrow, I'm sure. So, uh, be ready to answer some questions, son. I want to be here, so I told your doctor to call me the minute the police come by. Damn straight, I'll be here with you."

His mother moved about the room, ensuring everyone was satisfied, as if they were sitting around the dinner table. She delivered pizza slices and napkins, then ran down to the nurses' station for free soda.

Bennie did his best to suffer through the uneasy small talk. He knew what he had found out about himself in the hospital records was drawing his parents toward him, but as far as pizza parties went, theirs was sucking, and he felt guilty for thinking so. His parents would eventually have to tell him about his illness, and perhaps then they could have more meaningful conversations. But until that time, the uncomfortable silences and stiff smiles were intolerable. He turned back to his computer and began altering and compiling code in distracted fragments, with one hand, as he ate. After everyone had their fill of pizza, Bennie stretched his arms in mock-fatigue, telling his parents he needed to turn in for the night.

Chloe agreed to follow them home. "Oh, shit. I almost forgot." She pulled the map book with the transparency out of her messenger bag.

"This is the transparency Jay told you about."

"Throw it in the drawer," Bennie said.

She tucked the book neatly into the end table's drawer.

As she bent over him to give him a hug and kiss, he whispered in her ear, "One hundred thirty-seven."

"One hundred thirty-seven what?"

"That's how many towers are receiving these uploads in Massachusetts."

CHAPTER 32

CHARON

HE SAW IT AS SOON as he got out of his car. He wasn't sure what it was until he approached close enough to set off his motion-activated front porch light. A slim black package. *But mail doesn't come on Sundays.* That meant only one thing: solicitors. Charon, as he liked to think of himself, did not tolerate solicitors, invaders, or anyone who would compromise his privacy. With gritted teeth, he snatched up the package and was about to fling it like a Frisbee when his eye caught the stenciled lettering on the front. He shifted the face of the package to read it clearly beneath the light: *FOOL'S GOLD.*

He immediately felt for the small hard bumps in his pocket. Still there. He looked down the walk behind him. Nothing there but his quietly ticking car in the driveway, an empty street, and the other homes in differing stages of retirement with only select windows still aglow with unattended lights.

He let himself into the house and placed the package on the coffee table. He stared at it for a full minute, fighting back a sense of dread. He moved to the kitchen, poured a vodka and Coke, and returned to the sofa to sit before the package. He took two big gulps, then turned his front pants pockets inside out. He scooped up the shiny fragments and spilled them onto the coffee table as if preparing for a game of Jacks.

Another sip. He was being foolish. He was Charon. The ferryman. He would not be so easily intimidated. Picking up the slim package, he rubbed the black cellophane between his fingers, then pried free one end. A slim cardboard case lay inside. He opened that and found a black, unlabeled DVD.

After another sip, he moved to his entertainment center and powered on his television and DVD player. He slipped the disk inside the player and stood before the television, challenging himself to withstand whatever might appear.

The video segments were choppy, with little production value. But the view was beyond explanation. It was as if his conscience had filmed itself. The video didn't contain all the bodies he had helped cross the river Styx, but it showed all the recent ones, with the exception of the one that night.

He tried to make sense of it. All of the segments skipped the early preparations he'd made at the mortuary—the disrobing, the cleaning, and the flexing of the dead limbs. But each and every portion showed his strong, but careful hands extracting the corpse's fare. Some had just a single gold crown; others had two, four, five, or even six. The older corpses were easy, and pulling out the teeth was no harder than yanking a weed from dry soil. The ones middle-aged and younger were a bit harder, but with the right angle and plier grip, his task ended up being no more difficult than removing a stubborn nail. Each segment terminated at roughly the same point, just after the bloodless extraction as he prepared to wire the maxilla and mandible permanently shut, like a purse that had made its last payment.

He looked at the coffee table behind him, at the teeth spread out in what looked like a mocking, four-toothed grin.

Whoever had sent the video had him absolutely red-handed. He didn't need to see more. He moved to eject the DVD, but the screen went blank, and a message appeared:

As you can see, you are being watched. We have everything we need to destroy your life and your family. We are not concerned with claiming your fool's gold. But we may on occasion need to rely upon your services and your discretion. If you don't comply, we will personally mail copies of this to your local newspaper, your director, and to all the families of those whom you've violated.

CHAPTER 33

TUESDAY, 6:50 PM

JAY

JAY BRACED HIMSELF FOR THE worst—a vicious wrench and neck snap, a knife slipped deep between his ribs, or at the very least, a new gag soaked in chloroform. The figure suddenly stopped, as if unsure, then lunged again, and Jay was enveloped in a warm embrace.

"Jay, I'm so sorry I had to do it this way." The woman pulled back. "Are you okay? Did he hurt you?" She pulled apart the gag.

Jay coughed and nodded. "I'm fine. What the hell is... who are you?"

"Where are the keys?"

He jerked his chin toward the highboy.

The woman switched on a nearby standing lamp, grabbed the keys, unlocked both sets of cuffs, and rubbed his wrists. "My name is Stephanie. I would have gotten here sooner, but I was stuck at work. I work for, I think, a very bad man."

Jay stood. He stared at her dumbly, the realization that he would live another day dawning on him. "Couldn't you have called? Shot me an email? Jesus. How'd you get the police involved?"

"I can explain. See, I only just today started to catch on."
She shook her head. "Let me back up. I was a dupe. I was
nabbed right out of school by this guy. I only know him as
Mr. Sturgeon. He gave me a huge signing bonus and a terrific
salary. I was only too happy to be made the admin of these
top-secret servers that housed some kind of sensitive video
data. I knew the stuff was being gathered from cell towers, but
I thought the videos were being uploaded from cell phones.
I was thinking maybe it was like some kind of Homeland
Security-type project, that maybe the US was spying on itself
to gather intelligence around possible terrorist activities."

Jay retrieved his cell phone from the floor across the room.
"I gotta call my friends, tell them I'm okay."

"Wait. I'm sure they're worried and looking for us. So
I'm not using my landline, and I don't want you using your
cell phone. Put it in airplane mode, or I throw it in the
garbage disposal."

Jay grimaced and turned off his phone. "There. Okay?"

"We can't be careful enough. I'm not putting my ass on
the line like this only for you to get both of us killed."

Stephanie helped him down the hallway to the front
sitting room. He fell back onto a sofa, suddenly exhausted.
She disappeared down the hallway and came back with two
Cokes, then handed him one.

She sat next to him on the couch and moved a laptop
from the floor to the coffee table. "So just to explain to you,
our boss had me, and some other programmers mostly in
India, pretty compartmentalized. We didn't know how we fit
into the overall business. At least, I didn't. One thing I did
know, though, was our business was dealing with incoming,
streaming video. None of which we were allowed to see. Only
my boss had the decryption key. So we all worked in this
weird, abstract way. Even the two other programmers who
worked locally with the video content had to develop their
filters and editors with sample content and provide them to

our boss, untested on the actual content."

Jay took a sip of his soda. "Weren't you the least bit curious about what was in the files?"

"Not really? I'm embarrassed to say that. But I was just happy that I'd landed a job and was making serious bucks. I got a new car, started advance payments on my student loans, you know. But then on Sunday, I was monitoring the incoming videos. We get all these feeds from local cell towers, and these towers have amazing up-time. But on Sunday, I found out that one of the towers we piggyback on was compromised. Then, it went black. At the time, from what I could tell from the activity logs, it was either one of two things—blown up or unplugged. Then suddenly, it was back online again the next day."

Jay nodded. "That was me." He explained his discovery during wireless cruising and how he and Bennie had highjacked the cell tower at the park. "I don't know if my friends have been able to get any collected video back. My friend's sister was going to drive by today and grab it, but I haven't talked to them since this morning, before I was hunted down by those two guys. The cop and the Russian." The thought of Chloe venturing out alone to the tower sent a slick slither of fear through his stomach.

Stephanie sat up straight. "Wait. Did you say Russian?"

"Yeah, the Russian dude shot up the school, and then there was the cop."

Stephanie shook her head. "Shot up the school? I don't... I only sent the cop. Seriously, there was a shooting? Jesus, I gotta get back online. What did the first guy, the shooter, look like?"

Jay described the mean-looking Russian—his huge, towering form, his furious face like a side of raw roast beef, his auburn whiskers, his military-like hairstyle. "Same guy that killed a repairman right in front of my eyes at the cell tower."

"What? Are you sure? Hold on." She got up and half-ran down the hallway. She returned with her purse, rummaged through it, and pulled out a cell phone.

"So you get a phone, and I don't?"

"I absolutely can't go off the grid. If Sturgeon tracks me with my phone, he'll know right away if I go dark." She pushed a few keys, scrolled, and turned the phone's display to Jay. "Is this him?"

Jay looked at the picture. The guy was definitely the Russian, but not as furious looking. He was looking to the side, wearing a dreamy, foggy expression.

She tapped the screen with the edge of her manicured nail. "Once I felt things were going south at the office, I took pictures of everyone. I originally thought I'd need this for a sexual harassment case against him, the horny bastard. His name is Bolshoy, and his brother, or cousin, his name is Malenky. Mr. Sturgeon seems to have them do a lot more extra-curricular type stuff. Sometimes, they'll be out of the office for days, sometimes, a week at a time—leaving their laptops behind, of course, and me picking up the slack. And Sturgeon's completely losing his shit. He sends out the boys and then is looking for them again five minutes later. He's started repeating himself. Lately, he's been having us work in the dark. Like every few minutes, he races up to the blinds and peeks out. But there's never anything there."

"Can I see a picture of him? Sturgeon?"

Stephanie flicked down with the pad of her finger. "Here." She handed him the phone.

Jay stared into Sturgeon's large, dark eyes. The guy looked like a catfish that had taken human form, but only half successfully, still a bottom-dweller. "He doesn't look familiar. So, if you only sent the cop for me, then Sturgeon probably sent Bolshoy. That makes sense, since he also has my father."

Stephanie explained how she was similarly tasked to track encrypted uploads for a particular target and was to forward them to Sturgeon immediately, as they streamed. "I wasn't able to view the feeds myself. Only Sturgeon could.

But I'm a hacker at heart, and when I saw stuff getting weird at the office—Bolshoy and Malenky out most of the time, and Sturgeon, too—I poked around. I got into Sturgeon's laptop with no problem. I saw he was spending a lot of time viewing his bank accounts. There was one that he hadn't signed out of, which was growing at a ri-*donk*-ulous rate, almost doubling every month in recent statements. I kept searching and found that Sturgeon left some of the unencrypted video files on his laptop, too. All the videos were incriminating, and all of them seemed to involve high-ranking public servants, state government officials—that sort. The videos showed them doing some pretty nasty things—sex with prostitutes, getting blowjobs in Boston Common, accepting bribes, beating their wives or their kids. I'm serious, a TMZ wet dream. But what's bizarre is the camera's point of view is right there, in the middle of it all, like one of those helmet cams you see in sports. So, here are all these ISOs, compilations of all these acts, with a message at the end of each, usually a demand for payment threatening the release of the videos if the person didn't pay up. But all the while, what I couldn't figure is why *so* many people would risk exposure like this, taping all their dirty deeds so thoroughly, and how Sturgeon got a hold of them. The big discovery was finding these videos packaged into ISOs."

Jay nodded. "DVD images."

"Exactly. So I mounted a few, since I didn't have the DVDs themselves, and they were amazing. I actually saw two videos from your dad."

"*My* dad?"

"Yeah. The first one was of you up in an attic maybe? You were looking at some paintings."

"Yeah," Jay said. A synapse fired in his brain. "Jesus! Dad must have the ARGUS device."

"What's that?"

Instead of answering, Jay pointed at Stephanie's laptop. "Can I borrow that for a second?"

She picked up the laptop, but held it on her knees. "Why?"

He pulled out his key ring and dangled a thumb drive. "I want to show you what recorded everything you saw."

She raised the screen, tapped in her password, and handed over the laptop.

Jay plugged the drive into one of the laptop's USB ports. He opened the PDF schematic and returned the laptop to Stephanie.

She studied the screen for a moment. "What? What are you showing me?"

"The source of it all." He explained everything he had learned from Grayson. "So, it all makes sense now. It's the only way my dad could've been taped like that, the only way you would have seen that video of us in the attic."

Stephanie chewed her lip. "But that's not what lit a fire under my ass. The next video from your dad was him running down the stairs and seeing Bolshoy and Malenky, the two Russians, breaking into your house. They tossed your father around. Real bad. It was ugly. They had him on the floor, and they kept shoving a picture in his face, pointing at it."

"A picture of what?"

"You."

Jay felt as if the cold soda had jumped straight into his bloodstream, chilling him from head to toe. "Me?"

"Yeah, that's when I started scrambling, thinking of a way to get you safe before they got to you, too, since they already had your dad. I used Sturgeon's own blackmail scheme to get a cop to rush to your school. I couldn't risk taking off in the middle of the day to find you. I'm glad the cop got there in time. Sounds like he wasn't a second too soon."

"Actually, minutes too late. Bolshoy beat the cop to me."

Stephanie studied the laptop again. "God, all those video uploads... all those files. All those incriminating scenes."

Jay shook his head, thinking about his father and how he had seemed to be tearing the house apart, probably looking for some kind of hidden camera. "My poor dad. I'm pretty sure he was about to snap and go insane. He was being monitored, literally through his own eyeballs. I really think he wasn't going to be able to take it much longer. He was scared for his life, I think, for at least a year straight. I didn't understand what was going on, but now I do. Why do you think Sturgeon cared so much about tracking my father?"

Stephanie shrugged. "I don't know. Where'd you get this schematic? From your dad?"

"No, my mother."

"And where is she?"

He shook his head. "Dead. But before that, it seems like she was involved."

Stephanie put a hand on his knee. "I'm sorry, Jay." She sighed. "Well, Sturgeon seems completely in control of this program. If your mom used to be involved and she somehow got in the way... I don't know. And if your dad got suspicious and started snooping around? I'd see why Sturgeon would want to keep tabs on him."

Jay stood up. "Wait a second! I remember something like that. My mom was put in charge of winding down, or 'decommissioning,' she said, some top-secret operation. It must have been the same thing. Maybe she was working with Sturgeon originally, and then they both had to work together on closing it down. And if Sturgeon didn't want to see this operation go away because there was too much for him to gain by it personally, then that makes sense why. If he was crazy enough, he'd have my mom killed, and I guess take my dad and me hostage."

Stephanie raised her eyebrows. "From what I'm learning, I wouldn't put it past him." She sniffed. "I guess I won't be putting Sturgeon on my resume."

"Listen, if I can't call him from here, I need you to hook up with my friend, Bennie, in the hospital, to let him know I'm okay. And then see what you two can do about bringing this entire operation down." He grinned. "Now that we have an inside programmer."

Stephanie considered it. "All right. Tell me what hospital he's in, and I'll see what I can do. Do you promise to lay low until I get back tonight?"

"I'm not gonna just sit here on my ass and do nothing. How about you give me the address for Sturgeon's office? I want to go there and have a look around. Like you just showed me. Sturgeon *has* him. My dad might be there."

"No way. These are kidnappers, Jay. Maybe killers, if that was actually Bolshoy at the cell tower and at the school."

Jay put down his soda, feeling his face burn in anger. "I'm going."

She blew out a puff of air. "Absolutely not! Are you insane?"

Her phone buzzed. She grabbed it, tapped the screen, and frowned. "Shit. Sturgeon's calling for a meeting tomorrow morning at nine thirty. Don't do anything stupid, Jay. Stay here tonight. I'll come back from visiting your friend, and we'll plan our next steps. At least let me go to the meeting tomorrow to learn what Sturgeon knows. That can only be to our advantage."

Jay stood up and whirled around. "I have a better idea. A compromise. I lay low here tonight, like you want. But tomorrow morning, when you go to the meeting, I get that time to search the building for my dad while all of you are gathered for the meeting. It's perfect."

Stephanie closed her eyes and ran her hands through her hair while a long moment passed. Jay considered bolting right then and there if she denied him again, but she opened her eyes and grabbed her purse.

She pulled out a small pad and pen and scribbled something on a piece of paper. "Here's the address. Three-story beige building. There's a backdoor fire escape. Before I see your friend, I'll stop by the office. I'll pull down the fire escape ladder and leave my security badge on the top stair. But promise me you won't go inside. Just look through the windows. These are desperate guys, especially Sturgeon, and I think they're going to realize soon that this entire operation is crumbling around them. The only thing they do have on their side is they have your dad. And if they don't already know, they'll soon find out that I've hacked into Sturgeon's laptop. He must know now that something went absurdly wrong at the high school and that you've gone missing."

Jay grabbed another sheet of paper and scribbled on it. "Here's where Bennie is and his room number."

She took the paper and packed up her laptop. "This Bennie better be a freaking genius, Jay. I'll get back as soon as I can tonight. Probably late. Leave the doors locked and don't go outside in case they come lurking around." She left through the front door.

Jay sat in the quiet apartment for a while and collected his thoughts. He could only pray he still had a chance to save his father. If he could make it through one more night, he was sure, with Stephanie on their side, they could find him. Save him.

The furniture in the dim parlor seemed to tense along with his mood. Without turning on any lights, he made his way upstairs to the second floor. A short hallway led to a spare bedroom, a bathroom, a storage room, and eventually a small office, where he found Stephanie's computer. He shook the mouse, and the screen blinked on. Thankfully, the system wasn't locked with a password.

He felt bad for going behind Stephanie's back, but he wanted to talk to Bennie and Chloe himself. He downloaded a voice-over-IP program and dialed, hoping he correctly remembered Chloe's cell number.

"Hello?"

"Chloe, it's Jay."

"Jay! Are you okay? Where are you? Thank God you called! Can I come get you?"

Tears pricked his eyes. He hadn't had someone express such concern for him in what seemed like years. "I'm fine, Chloe... for now. Are you okay? Are you with Bennie?"

"I'm at home, trying to calm my parents down. I can't tell

you how relieved I am. We were *so* worried. Bennie and I saw you on the news. Are you at the police station?"

"No, I'm with a... a friend?"

"Jay, you don't have other friends."

His paranoia had hit an all-time high, but he knew he had no reason not to trust Chloe. "It's a long story, but a programmer saved me. She works for the people that kidnapped my dad. She saved me, and I'm at her apartment. Safe."

"Thank *God*. I can't wait to tell Bennie. He was so worried."

"This woman, her name's Stephanie. She's on her way to see Bennie. I want to see if they can work together on bringing down this guy's operation. Can you let Bennie know she's on the way? I don't want to risk making too many calls from here."

"No problem."

Something Chloe had said came back to him. "Did you say I was on the news?"

"Well, not on purpose. The news of the school shooting caught you in the backseat of a cruiser that wasn't part of the others on school grounds. Behind the plant place there? We didn't report it yet because we didn't know who to trust. The police are looking for you right now. Good and bad, I guess? Could we just at least try, Jay? Just stop this crusade and let the police take over? They can't all be bad."

Jay considered it for a second, then shook his head. "I don't know who I can trust right now. It was actually a good thing that I was picked up by the cop. He saved my life and didn't even know it. But it's no thanks to the local police that I'm alive. I'll tell you later. Listen, we're closer than ever to getting my dad back and stopping this Sturgeon shithead and—"

"Wait, slow down. Who's Sturgeon?"

"That's his name, the guy in charge of it all. I know where he is now, and I need to see if my dad's there."

Chloe filled Jay in on the details of her last hospital visit to Bennie, explaining how they had viewed video uploads from Jefferson Park. She told him about her visit to the empty RK surgery clinic and the unknowing recipients of the ARGUS device. Then she related the news that a network of over a hundred cell towers in the state were receiving similar such feeds.

"Didn't your dad have eye surgery last year?" Chloe asked.

"Yeah, Stephanie said she saw a video from him. When she described it, I realized my dad must have had one of those implant thingies."

Chloe gasped. "We figured out how to see if someone has it. You can see a slightly out-of-place blood vessel. The video upload is triggered during stress or excitement."

"I can't believe this is real. Listen, Stephanie said she has a staff meeting at Sturgeon's tomorrow morning at nine thirty. If they're holding my dad there, it might be a good time to sneak him out while they're all collected somewhere else in the building."

"Alone?" Chloe asked, panic in her voice.

"Don't worry. I know the meeting time and the building details through Stephanie. I can go through safe parts of the building to look for him. If he's there. If he's alive." He hung up before Chloe could object. He had tried sounding confident with her, but it was all bluster. What if he found his father dead? What then? Or what if he wasn't dead, but unconscious? His father still had three inches and at least forty pounds on him. Only a year ago, the last time they had mock wrestled in the living room, Jay had felt as if he were grappling with a bridge abutment.

Stop it. He couldn't afford to let in any more doubts. He sat in the study with his head in his hands, feeling trapped in the end of a long alley, like the one he had been in that first night in the park. He thrust at and killed each new doubt as it stepped out of the shadows, but he was helpless against the fear that steadily advanced as ploddingly and sure-footed as the darkness that crept through the window in front of him.

CHAPTER 34

TUESDAY, 7:03 PM

BENNIE

BENNIE'S HEART RATE SLOWED AFTER learning from Chloe that Jay was alive and okay. He could tell he had worried the hospital staff with his elevated stress and pulse from the way they would pretend to casually pop in with twice the normal frequency—all for a broken leg.

With Jay safe, he knew he had to commit all of his brainpower to learning more about ARGUS. Just as he had found the design schematic on Mrs. Brooks's hard drive, Bennie could only assume that the Stanley Grayson clue also originated from Jay's mother and that Jay's dad had stumbled upon it. But while it gave them insight into the early ARGUS program, it was a dead end for all practical purposes. Grayson wasn't involved in the current incarnation of the project at all. In fact, by Chloe and Jay's accounts, he seemed to have been deliberately shut out. And Bennie had to believe Jay's mother was more careful than to mistakenly leave the master design of the ARGUS unencrypted on her home computer.

Bennie closed his eyes and reviewed the recent events.

Chloe had come by, they watched the newsfeed of Jay, they watched the collected video transmissions from the tower, she handed him the flyer for the RK surgery special offering in Sudbury...

The *transparency!*

He had been so completely wrapped up in the senseless, relatively unimportant video transmissions from Jefferson Park that he had completely forgotten about the transparency. Either that was the clue that would lead to a final breakthrough, or they were all screwed. He looked to his left. The bedside drawer floated on the periphery of his lamp's cone of light like an unattainable, murky mirage. His heart sank. How he was supposed to reach it with his new cast temporarily fastened to his bed? The drawer stared back at him with an obstinate, square smile.

He leaned to his left to see if his fingers could come even close to prying open the drawer. His elbow touched something plastic hanging from his bedside.

The Gripper. Good old Jay, he thought.

After a couple of tries, he managed to open the drawer. He carefully pinched the book in the claw and brought it slowly toward the bed with the spine down so as not to lose the transparency inside it.

With the book safely in his lap, he flipped through the *Street Atlas of New England* until he found the transparency paper-clipped on three sides to the page showing the Metro-West area of Massachusetts. He hoped it hadn't shifted too much. But then again, he wasn't altogether sure that the places Jay and his mother had gone to had more importance than the actual relative position of the dots to each other.

The black dots on the transparency looked hopelessly random. He studied it further, letting the dots float before his vision and approach him with some kind of pattern, like the magic 3-D murals that hid a disguised object within their superficial pattern. A possible pattern eventually revealed itself. The dots over the towns were irregularly spaced, but organized in two distinct rows. He smoothed out a balled-up napkin from his lunch and laid it over the transparency. He began tracing the dots with a pencil, connecting them left to right, hoping for a message. He studied his initial result, raising it up to the bedside lamp. Nothing.

From what he could determine, some segments of dots had to represent slanted lines of varying slopes. Other dots seemed to indicate either circles or crosses, depending upon how he traced them, composed of four points. Or addition symbols? On another quadrant of the napkin, Bennie worked to link the dots as distinct symbols, tracing out the addition symbol and then the horizontal and slanting lines. He raised these to the light. *Minus, plus, bump down, bump up, next line, division symbol, @ symbol, division symbol.* On a new napkin he started fresh again, turning the addition symbol into a circle.

Suddenly, the image of the Brooks's brushed-steel refrigerator came to mind with its tornado of sticky notes. Jay's mother often wrote coded messages to Stephen Brooks, probably assuming Jay wasn't observant enough to discover the shorthand. Jay and Bennie had both secretly acquired an elementary grasp of Gregg Shorthand, and it had become a great way for Jay to head off any trouble by reading the notes. *Jay came home an hour late last night. See if you can talk to Jay about his room. Jay won't be going out this weekend unless he cleans the mess he made in the garage.*

Bennie had never suggested it to Jay, but he had begun to think Jay's mother was cleverer yet. She was too smart to think Jay wouldn't notice these notes and try to use them to his advantage. It was all too convenient. It didn't bother Bennie that his friend was being manipulated by his mother. What were mothers for?

He hadn't used the shorthand in a while, so he found an online Gregg Shorthand chart on his computer. He worked carefully, looking from the napkin to computer screen, making slight corrections in his strokes, and slowly decrypting the clue. The translation wasn't easy because Jay's mother had needed to anchor the points of the symbols as dots over the imperfect system of *real* yard sale locations.

He finished and held up the napkin. A name. First name was either Mark or Marc. The last name looked like Dutch… no, Doitch. Shorthand was vague because the symbols represented sounds, not exact spellings. Doitch didn't seem right. Deutsch or Deustche seemed more likely.

"Mark Deutsche," Bennie mumbled. "M-D."

MD Software Solutions. MD Defense Systems.

He sat back as he reflected in wonder how Jay's mother, in death, had finally conveyed the name of the person in charge of the ARGUS operation, likely the same person responsible for her death.

CHAPTER 35

TUESDAY, 2:55 PM

STURGEON

STURGEON LEARNED OF THE MULTIPLE shootings at the high school well before Bolshoy could come back to the office to report it himself. The bad news spread like malware through the several scrolling television station tickers and online news sites.

The shootings infected all possible media until each host was completely subsumed by the parasite, which then proceeded to replicate, stretch, and mutate itself, interlocking itself and its clones into intricate death-knell tapestries, discernible language patterns, and words meant only for Sturgeon. *Panic, is the man sick, have you heard-er about the murd-er in the Columbine combine, thrash the thrasher, dried the flowers to the grinder to the finder for the hunt, the man-hunt.*

Since he had started exploiting the ARGUS program for his personal gain, he had been putting in eighty-hour workweeks, keeping up checks on Stephen, overloading Bolshoy and Malenky with blackmail visits, keeping the India team productive, and keeping the Leadership happy. He kept the exploitable ARGUS videos for himself and forwarded to the Leadership the uploads they wanted, anything indicating unsolvable crimes—home invasions, auto theft, rapes, and even some murders—that could be used to prove the necessity of the ARGUS technology to the wider world.

Sleep had become an unintended event, like losing one's balance. Caffeine pills filled his pockets and had begun to pulverize into a powder, but Sturgeon didn't care. He simply licked his hand and slipped it into his pocket, then licked the pearl-gray powder from the tips of his fingers, heedless of the dose.

The world had begun to appear to him as a 3-D movie to which he had arrived too late and without the appropriate glasses. He sat at his desk, hitting F5 every few seconds to refresh his account balance. Each time the laptop screen refreshed, he was calmed to see that the balance remained untouched. *$1,138,017.05.*

He placed a finely manicured nail against his laptop screen, and the screen gave in to the pressure, producing a visual halo around the pressure point. He tried coaxing several pixels representing commas and zeroes into larger numbers, greater balances, to no avail. *Scrape the accounts, scrape the pixels, fix the pixels, raster faster the money.*

After kidnapping Stephen Brooks, Malenky had scrubbed through Brooks's cell phone logs and transferred the contents to Sturgeon's laptop. A recovered deleted text message had been received that same day from Brooks's son, Jay.

It read: "where r u? r u ok? what is md software slns?" Sturgeon had some questions for that little turd, Jay.

Although the Leadership had ordered Sturgeon to monitor Stephen Brooks after Elizabeth Brooks's removal, it seemed the emphasis should have been on the son all along. Had Elizabeth suspected something and conveyed information to her son and husband before her death? When she had blown the whistle on ARGUS before its secret resurrection, she had essentially written her own death certificate. She

209

had claimed she couldn't morally accept that the ARGUS participants were unknowing beta users of the software, and each was living with the risk of becoming victim to the program's design flaw, which could cause deadly seizures. But whoever had killed Elizabeth had broadcast their intent ahead of time, and Elizabeth was clever enough to warn her family. *Big mistake.*

Once Sturgeon had discovered the text message, he had immediately ordered Bolshoy to grab the little pissant out of his high school and throw him down in the basement with Stephen. Later, he realized he should have been more specific. Something must have been lost in translation, just as he had worried about what would happen when he originally hired Bolshoy and his cousin Malenky.

Whatever the *hell* had convinced Bolshoy that his only option was to shoot his way out of the school was beyond Sturgeon. He obviously had no real leverage over Bolshoy if the man was prepared to act that way.

No matter. As soon as he got one more big payoff, maybe something from Senator Pearson's personal assistant, he was going to evaporate—leave the government and the Leadership with their dicks in hand and let them try to explain the school shooting, the cell towers, Bolshoy, Malenky, Stephen, MD Software Solutions, and MD Defense Systems. As the government had proved over and over again with their czar appointments and contracts from private security firms such as Blackwater, they never quite had enough time to thoroughly vet each and every person in their employ. They would easily take months just to discover Sturgeon's true identity.

Sturgeon got up and headed for the basement. He paused at the bottom of the stairs to open the padlock and wind the heavy chain. He placed his hand on the door's crash bar, pushed through, and entered the dark basement, where he was briefly blinded before his eyes adjusted. In the middle distance, he spied Stephen's dark form. The hooded head jerked in Sturgeon's direction. He crossed the cement floor, and for effect, added an extra intimidating click with the heels of his dress shoes, just as the Nazis had outfitted their missiles with a foreboding whistle.

And just like a heat-seeking missile, his fist flew out and instinctively located Stephen Brooks's head. He punched through the hood around the left ear area, and then landed a blow to the face. With the third punch, he zeroed in on the nose, which imploded like a rotten baby squash.

Exhausted, Sturgeon tore off the hood to appreciate his handiwork. Stephen's head slumped forward, and a thick thread of saliva, mucus, and blood hung from his chin. Sturgeon needed more to burn off the excessive caffeine. With his knuckles swollen, bleeding, and torn, Sturgeon moved to the corner of the room. He unscrewed the long wooden handle of a nearby mop and beat Brooks like a dirty rug. The captive grunted at the first two blows, but subsequent noises became softer, as if Sturgeon were beating the air out of a sack. He continued striking Brooks, his own grunts taking over until he literally could no longer grip the broom handle. Statue-hard from the exertion, his forearms and fingers tingled from the strain.

Sturgeon let out a long, cathartic sigh. *There, that felt better.*

The adrenaline from the beating and the caffeine caused his thoughts to blur and skate along his brain like small electrical storms across a distant planet, and only the more significant ones captured his attention. *Need to order, make orders, need to come to order, come to me, come to meeting, time has come.*

The time had come.

He slowly ascended the stairs, his thighs weak from the exertion. In his office, he collapsed in his chair and unlocked his bottom drawer. Bolshoy would be coming to report the disaster at the high school, likely with an absurd, thoroughly Russian smug expression. Sturgeon reached into his drawer and pulled out his gun. The silver sheen of the Sig Sauer pistol soon turned a coppery pink as he stroked it. Stephen's blood mixed with his own and cooled to coagulate on the grip. *Shiny pink, blood slipping, slip in the pink, turning pink, deliver the pink slips.*

CHAPTER 36

TUESDAY, 8:0I PM

BENNIE

BENNIE FELL INTO A SHALLOW sleep, his dreams vague and see-through. He was running out of time, but was about to solve the riddle of his dreams and win back consciousness, as he had with the transparency, when he noticed a subtle change of lighting in the room. A long shadow lengthened over his bed. He panicked, remembering he hadn't closed his laptop before falling asleep, leaving the bright screen to advertise the remote network computers and the high-value doctor list he had recovered.

He sat up blindly, wondering why the visitor hadn't turned on the lights. He began to make apologetic noises as he felt for his laptop and slapped it shut.

The shape before him developed slowly, and more detail came to being—short blond hair, a soft smile, and electric blue eyes. *No doctor. No nurse.* He examined her closer and came to the only reasonable conclusion. He was dead, and she was an angel.

"Am I?" he asked.

"Are you what?" she whispered.

"Dead."

She put a warm slim finger to his lips. "Shh." She leaned forward. "Listen to me very closely, Bennie. You and I need to talk."

"Okay."

"My name is Stephanie, and—"

"Oh, you're the woman Jay told Chloe about."

"Jay told... Damn! I told him not to use the phone."

"Don't worry," he assured her. "He called Chloe using a voice-over-IP program."

She sighed. "Okay. Well, that saves us some time at least. What I need you to do now is help me hack into my work network and bring down ARGUS." She handed him a writeable CD-ROM and a small device that looked something like a thumb drive. "Here's the software needed to VPN into my work network, and that's my OTP token. You need to prefix the token's code with my six-digit PIN. 8-8-9-3-3-4."

Bennie shrugged. "Jeez, sounds like my work is done for me."

Stephanie sat on the edge of the bed. "Not *that* easy, big guy. By the way, if I get harassed for being in here, tell them I'm your girlfriend." She lay down beside him, already playing the role. The swell of her left breast weighed upon his elbow, and he nearly fainted in excitement.

He instantly became conscious of every single body part. Blinking, speaking, and swallowing became complex operations. He worked his jaw and tongue as if he were warming them from a deep freeze. "Not a problem."

With great effort, he refocused on his computer and installed the software. His fingers felt twice their usual size. He struggled to remember his keyboard shortcuts, selected incorrect menu items, mistyped directory paths, and fumbled with his mouse. Finally, he launched the application and entered her PIN, followed by the code that appeared on her access token after pressing a button on it.

"Your friend Jay says you're *all that* on computers, so let's see what you can do."

Blushing, Bennie opened a secure-shell terminal window and successfully logged into the machine with user credentials from Stephanie. He navigated around, chewing on the inside of his cheek. "So, I'm guessing this isn't just a matter of killing a service or shutting down the server?"

Stephanie first nodded, then shook her head. "First of all, it's *servers*, more than one, and yeah, it gets a little problematic. Sturgeon brought over some very tricky and sensitive tripwire programs from the DOD, most of which I haven't the foggiest idea how to circumvent. I did kill one of the incoming requests one night by accident—what a mistake. See, we rotate weeks when we're on-call twenty-four, seven with a beeper. And I got an alert that one of the web servers was exceeding available memory and beginning to borrow from half of its swap space, so I logged in to check it out. I isolated the incoming thread spiking the CPU. It was about to bring the server down, so I killed the process. Within twenty minutes, Sturgeon, Bolshoy, and Malenky showed up on my front stoop like some death squad. I had to bring them all into my house and explain what I was doing. Scariest night of my life. Bolshoy and Malenky have never trusted me from the get-go, and ever since then, I can tell they've been keeping a serious eye on me." She shuddered. "Not only do they want to rape me, but I think they'd like to kill me, and not necessarily in that order."

A chill shot down Bennie's back, and he shook his head in disbelief. "Unbelievable. Well, you made it out alive."

Stephanie nodded.

"So where do we start? Do you have the root password for at least one of these machines?"

"Yep. I set up these servers before all the protective software was installed."

Bennie typed the command to change his normal user account into a "root" user that had full access to the machine and its contents. "Okay, what's your password?"

Like any conscientious programmer, she hesitated for a fraction of a second before sharing the sensitive password, even considering the circumstances. Then, she began spelling it out as he typed.

When he finished, he looked over at her. "Your password is 'i_hEART_HackKneed1'?"

"Yeah. So?"

Bennie chuffed. "Well, that's me. That's my handle, *HackKneed*."

Her cheeks turned crimson. She shoved his shoulder. "Shut *up*."

"No, really. That's me." He laughed.

"*The* HackKneed? The same guy that took over that billboard on 128 and posted the governor's credit card bill from the Foxy Lady?"

He nodded.

"The same guy that redirected that Worcester city counselor's emails to his mistress straight to the Globe's online chat forums?"

He nodded again. "Yep."

She grabbed his arm and held it. "I've been following you ever since I took that course at UMass on hacking and civil disobedience. You were essentially the focal point of the course. My professor did, like, an amateur psych profile on you and thought for certain that you were an ex-government software engineer who had soured on the government and started using your skills to re-assert some civil disobedience values from your experience in the sixties."

"Ha! The sixties? Way before my time."

"Oh, my God, my head is reeling. I can't believe you're *him*. He's you." She ran her fingers all along his arm, as if she had discovered an ancient artifact and was examining it for correctness of form, testing to see if it was still in one piece. She gestured at his cast. "I guess you could say HackKneed is knock-kneed?"

He laughed. "More than you know." He pointed at his

wheelchair in the corner. "That's not temporary. I've been in a chair since I was ten and will be for the rest of my life." He cleared his throat. "Anyway, I'll see what I can do with these servers to stop Sturgeon in his tracks without alerting him. I'm going to need some time to check out the architecture and monitor it through a couple of cycles to test it for weak points... you know, vulnerabilities." He pointed at his laptop. "I've brought my entire bag of hacking goodies with me, so I'm sure I can do something. It's just a matter of how much style I can bring to it."

Stephanie grabbed him by the ears and smashed her lips against his. "I still can't believe it's you. I can't believe it." She stood up from the bed. "I need to go move my car to long-term parking. When I come back," she said, pointing to the chair in the corner, "I'll be right there if you need me, but I promise I won't distract you."

As she looked away, Bennie furtively touched his mouth. He couldn't help it. He still felt the warmth of her lips on his. Having never kissed any other girl but his mother, he expected the sensation to instantly dissolve and depart, but instead, it lingered... and felt good.

Still reeling from the kiss, Bennie reluctantly returned to his snooping. He quietly scaled over firewalls, sticking to the shadows as file watchers came trolling by like guards on patrol. His dream had come true. He was not only doing what he did best, but also doing so to save his friend, his friend's dad, and to impress a drop-dead gorgeous programmer.

Half an hour later, Stephanie returned, settled into the chair, and opened her laptop. "I'll send you some server logs I was able to grab from the last time I was installing some patches."

"Sure," Bennie said. "Hey, was anyone else in your office involved in the server maintenance?"

She shook her head. "No, mainly me. Sturgeon would occasionally check my progress. He had the server access to do it, for sure. But I could tell from most of his questions that he was mainly relying on me to maintain them."

The servers had massive, petabyte level capacities and were using an encrypted protocol Bennie had never seen before to translate incoming data at a mind-blowing rate. Even though the logging level was set to report only select server activities, the log files were still huge and had to be archived every ten minutes. Bennie studied a dozen of the logs to get an idea what cycles the servers went through, when their peak times occurred, when they were idle, and if and when they ever encountered errors that he could exploit like a fissure in a wall and insert himself into with his bag of tricks.

Bennie's latest hacking tool allowed him to clone any running process and fiddle with it experimentally, as the new process was maintained within a secure sandbox that could not contact any other service or process on its own. So he could try to kill the process, interrupt it, attempt to inject executable code into it, and see what *would have happened* if he had tried to do the same on the actual process.

The server was a hacker's nightmare and a paranoiac's dreamscape. Every running process had the equivalent of a police escort along the information superhighway. From his experiments with the phony processes he created, nothing could be done to mutate, exploit, or destroy them without setting off alerts at multiple levels. He briefly abandoned that tactic and returned to the server logs to find another chink in the armor. He was getting dispirited, aware that Stephanie was reading the emotions on his face and becoming obviously anxious.

So much for the infamous HackKneed, he thought.

He doubled his concentration. Since he knew what events triggered logging activity and that the logs were updated at predictable intervals, he tried infiltrating a file input/output stream and riding the current into the heart of the server. No luck. He backed out with perhaps a nanosecond to spare before the file log write activity was complete and he was left stranded in an orphaned process, which would have locked up the server completely.

"Shit!" He banged his fist against his head.

Come on, Bennie, you can do this. He returned yet again to searching through the logs. Suddenly, his heart contracted and froze completely with an unanswered last systole. He grabbed the bed rails with both hands and jerked himself upright, attempting to jump-start his heart.

Stephanie leapt from her chair, dumping her laptop on the floor with a clatter. She came over and held him with a hand on his back. Finally, a reluctant *lub-lub-lub* was telegraphed out from his heart through the quiet wires of his circulatory system.

"Bennie, are you okay? Should I get the doctor?" She pulled away and reached for the alert button by his bed.

He grabbed her hand. "No." He massaged his chest and worked on regulating his breathing. Checking the hospital machines, he was grateful they remained unperturbed.

From what he'd read on the latest server log file, his work wasn't even halfway done.

CHAPTER 37

WEDNESDAY, 7:35 AM

JAY

JAY STOOD ON **STEPHANIE'S BACK** steps, waiting for the cab he had summoned from a payphone down the street. He was concerned that Stephanie hadn't returned the previous night. An almost overwhelming temptation to text her returned every few minutes, but he remembered her warning. *I'm not putting my ass on the line like this only for you to get both of us killed.* Maybe her work with Bennie had taken up most of the night. Or maybe Sturgeon was several steps ahead of all of them. Maybe Stephanie, Bennie, and Chloe were all dead, and Jay was the last loose end. Maybe they knew he had called for a cab and were about to pick him up.

A flash of yellow passed the end of the driveway. He heard the squeal of brakes, then the cab backed up into his line of sight. He froze. Should he get in? What would he do if he didn't? Call for yet another cab he didn't trust? Acting quickly and decisively was his only option. His father was waiting.

He glanced behind him, then at the windows above and the street ahead, before trotting down the driveway. He slipped into the back of the warm cab and gave the cabbie the address. Clipped to the dashboard was the driver's identification: *Sergei Burov.*

No.

The man's shaved head remained still, comfortably seated upon the several fat folds of his neck, like a boulder dropped into wet soil. The cabbie turned. "I have question."

Just shoot me now.

"Vich vay you prefer?"

"Get it over with already."

The Russian's scarred brow creased horizontally, but then also vertically, like two dried-up tributaries working their way down a pink-sand desert. "What? Eh... I mean Valtham. Some say 'val-thum.' Some say 'val-tem.' Some say 'val-tham.' I like last."

For a moment, Jay was nonplussed, not understanding. Then, he translated the question. *Waltham.* The street name. Relief coursed through Jay, and he fell back in his seat. "Listen, man. I'll give you thirty bucks to get me to any of those places... fast. Your choice."

CHAPTER 38

STEPHEN BROOKS

STEPHEN **B**ROOKS'S GREATEST CONCERN OVER the last few days was to restore two of his five senses: sight and touch. The sack over his head had been tied at his throat with what felt like a drawstring that had zero give. He never realized how long a day could be until the simple act of swallowing had become a task that required a conscious decision. And his sense of touch, at least in his hands, was completely gone after having them bound behind him for so long.

He had initially tried twiddling his fingers against each other every few minutes to keep the blood circulating, but he was eventually unable to endure the death-like touch of his own fingers. He settled for flexing his fists at regular intervals.

Thrice daily, he was allowed a bathroom break. One of them would unbind his hands, grab him by the elbow, and guide him to the corner, where he would be handed a bucket and a balled-up handful of tissue, then left to employ all of his powers of balance, aim, and imagination to complete the task blindly with some degree of dignity.

The Russian thugs who had grabbed him at his house had been brazen enough to let him see their faces, their car, and even their license plate number. He had memorized the license plate, but as time passed, his panic had acted as paint thinner on his memory.

When they had moved him from the car to the apartment, Stephen had filled his lungs in order to call out for help from a passing pedestrian. In a blink, his full lungs were expertly deflated as two steel-tipped fingers fired into his ribs. The pain was blinding and unspeakable, and it folded his legs neatly beneath him as if a release button had been pushed. They dragged him along the rest of the sidewalk and up the narrow stairs to the top-floor apartment, his legs trailing behind him like a doll's. Until the head honcho arrived, he had been tied in a sparse living room dominated by a black leather sectional, a coffee table littered with soda cans, a half-eaten pizza, and a large-screen television.

"Why, *helloooo,* Mr. Brooks," the man had said. "You can call me Sturgeon. May I call you Stephen?"

Sturgeon was dressed like a mafioso mortician in a black knee-length overcoat, a white shirt, a black tie, and black leather gloves. His face was downright ugly, and Stephen had trouble maintaining eye contact with him. He looked as if his original head had been removed and a second one was trying unsuccessfully to sprout in its place. He was mostly bald but for a small struggling thatch on top and a greasy wreath of hair around the back and sides.

"What the hell do you think you're—" Stephen began, but a crushing elbow to his mouth ended that line of questioning.

The Russians nudged each other and the squatter one let out a sympathetic, "Oof."

Sturgeon scolded the two for not having put a hood over his head earlier and told them it was time to go. Stephen opened his mouth to ask where they were taking him, but was rewarded with another elbow. Before he could again focus on Sturgeon, the Russians slid the hood over Stephen's head and drew the string tight.

From what Stephen could tell, he had been placed back in the Russians' vehicle, and they followed Sturgeon to another location. He was yanked out of the backseat approximately thirty minutes later. He guessed they were near either Route 128 or the Mass Pike. He'd maybe been taken to an office building, because they had stopped once, where he heard a small ding, as if from a scanning device, maybe for work badges.

Bound to yet another chair with his legs and arms tied, Stephen had tried to make some educated guesses as to his whereabouts. From the intermittent whoosh of air that shuttled over his head like a distant elevated train, the occasional gurgle of rushing water on his right, and the strong smell of unpainted, corroding cement, he thought he was in the basement of a business complex of sorts.

The first day of his capture, struggling within the darkness of his hood, he had tried hopping his chair toward a dim light source. He had hoped it was a doorway or window, but in a panicked moment, he nearly tipped himself over when the chair leg caught on some kind of metal strut bolted into the floor.

Occasionally, one of the two Russians would enter and scuffle heavily booted feet over to him. More often than not, after a grunt of satisfaction, the person would just leave. Other times, he would feed him crusts of pizza or half a corndog and give him a sip of water through a tear in the hood. When the mouth hole was made in the hood, Stephen's head was still in it. The knife had also sliced both corners of Stephen's mouth.

The only true, discernible milestone throughout the last few days was the impatient, carbonated burst of the sprinkler system, which he was fairly sure went off somewhere between midnight and three a.m. Each night, exhausted from struggling against his bindings, he resigned himself to waiting for what was to come in the silence of the musty basement, listening to his breathing and heartbeat like the most enlightened of meditating Buddhists.

Finally, some interminable hours later, he would hear the tell-tale drumbeat of the awakened water compressor and then the eventual hiss of the sprinkler system.

His signals to sleep. Acquiesce. And he did.

CHAPTER 39

WEDNESDAY, 8:08 AM

JAY

JAY CALLED STEPHANIE FROM THE cab.

She answered with, "Shit! Where is he?"

"Stephanie?"

"Yeah, where'd he go?"

"Bennie? Aren't you still with him at the hospital?"

She sighed. "I *am* at the hospital. We were up... up late. I fell asleep when Bennie said he was finished, but now he's... I don't know where the hell he is!"

"Calm down, Stephanie. They probably took him for a test or an x-ray or something. No matter what, you have to go to that meeting on time with Sturgeon. He can't be made suspicious of anything more. I'm *depending* on you."

"Yeah, yeah. I know. I'll be there. Listen, like I promised."

"Awesome. If things break up early, send me a text."

"Okay. Good luck, Jay."

"Wait. If you hear from Bennie, can you call and let me know?"

"You got it."

The Saturday morning traffic was light on Route 128,

and he had the cabbie drop him off in a restaurant parking lot three blocks down from Sturgeon's office building. The morning sun was bright, glinting off everything chrome and silver with extra brilliance, as if Mother Nature had come out the previous night and scrubbed away the dull patina.

He scrambled up an artificial cliff of cut rock slabs and smooth stone that separated the restaurant from the next adjoining business, a six-story building housing a vaguely familiar software company. He skirted that building by going around the back. He wanted to steer clear of the road in case one of Sturgeon's team decided to come in earlier than the appointed time.

Sturgeon's building was in the worst repair. The mulch was worn thin, revealing exposed dirt in several places, and only the hardiest of shrubs were still barely alive, maintaining the last dim shade of green. He crouched behind a blue transformer, spied no cars in the lot or entering it, and sprinted toward the back. The fire escape ladder was extended to the ground. He raced up the stairs, looping around until he made it to the top. He grabbed the badge Stephanie had left for him and used it to enter.

Inside the building, he stood still, collecting his breath. He could feel beads of nervous sweat pop free on his forehead. He pulled out his phone and sent a text message to Stephanie.

leav ur keys on back left tire. text me back when mtg done, i'll pick u up.

He hoped he wasn't putting Stephanie at too much risk. But his father was his priority. Stephanie would be okay. She had credibility with Sturgeon, and he had no reason to not trust her.

He looked at his watch: 8:21. He would have time for an initial sweep of some of the building if he kept an eye toward the windows facing the parking lot.

He made his way past a gray sea of empty office cubicles and toward a glowing, red exit sign. On his way to the stairs, he passed the elevators and nearly missed the floor directory above the elevator buttons. He stopped and read. MD Software Solutions was on the second of the three floors.

Jay guessed it would be too high risk for Sturgeon to keep his father hidden on any other floor but his own. However, he figured he should still check the first and third floors. He backpedaled out of the stairwell and walked down the hall. He opened and closed the office doors, peered under workstation desks, glanced in every utility closet, and searched the two sets of bathrooms.

He hissed, "Dad?" He waited a second. "Dad?"

He strained to hear a muffled response from anywhere, from the ceiling tiles, from within a cabinet. Nothing. The third floor was absolutely empty. He again glanced at his watch: 8:32. He still had time to make a quick sweep of the first floor if he rushed.

As he passed the second floor, he had an idea. *The basement.* He toed aside a pile of heavy chain coiled before the door, and it hissed in protest.

Just then, from the parking lot, the piercing squeal of tires sliced through his body like a knife. An angry slam of a car door followed.

Shit! He skipped the first floor inspection and headed straight to the basement. Random utilities flickered green, red, and yellow lights in the dark. Against the far wall, a dim red bulb in a protective steel cage emanated enough of a glow to allow him to make out the dim outlines of shapes. He made his way toward the light, avoiding several large steel storage cages filled with mountains of boxes and rows of file cabinets. The basement air contained a cold dampness that smelled of aged cardboard, copper piping, and the pervasive septic odor of old plumbing.

A door on the floor above squealed open and slammed shut again, sending vibrations through the ceiling. The elevator engaged. *That could be Sturgeon himself,* Jay thought, *the devil incarnate.* The realization both unnerved and infuriated him.

He spun around, scanning the basement. A french drain

surrounded the basement floor perimeter and also met in a cross in the middle of the floor. He followed one trough in the sparse light and abundant shadows. He dragged one foot like a rudder inside of the shallow indentation in the floor. The far side of the basement seemed impossibly far away.

He knew he had made it to the center drain when his sneaker squeaked on the moist drain cap. Despite the lack of recent rain, the drain seemed active, still shiny and damp. He revised his plan. Instead of making it to the far side of the basement toward a light that would give him away, he turned left. He followed the dampness, seeing nothing but more locked storage cages.

Tall cabinets in the cage to his right blocked what little ambient light was available. He reached out, his fingers curled poised to brush aside anything before his face did.

Another car door slammed above, followed immediately by a third. He picked up his pace.

Ah ha. He froze as his fingers touched something cold. A janitor's wet mop, he guessed, feeling the cold wet tendrils of a resting mop head. He took another sliding step, extending his other hand down to grab where he imagined the mop handle would be.

He touched bare skin.

Jay forced a painful scream back down his throat. The form jerked violently, as if electrocuted, and Jay fell. He and the person both hit the floor at the same time. Jay scrambled up and defensively kicked at it. The person spun in place, but didn't move. He or she was in a chair. No, *tied* to a chair. *Captive.*

"Dad?"

The only response was ragged, labored breathing. Jay felt around and removed a large, wet cloth from the person's mouth. "Dad? It's me. It's Jay." He crouched over his father, shocked not to find one spot of warmth on his body. He wrapped his arms around him, trying to transfer his own body heat.

He tore at the duct tape that fastened his father's ankles to the chair legs and his arms behind him. He tried pulling his father up from behind, under his arms, but he staggered under the weight.

"Dad, come on. We have to go. We can get out of here, but we have to hurry. They're coming." Jay tried to prop him up against the far wall.

His father moved his feet like a child pantomiming obedience. Jay ducked his head under his father's limp left arm and began to drag him, shouldering most of his slack weight.

Halfway to the exit, Jay leaned his father against a storage cage to catch his breath. He looked at his watch: 9:00. Sturgeon and his team would be in the meeting if everyone had come on time. He sent out a silent prayer that Stephanie had received his text message.

"Dad, I need you to concentrate and try harder. We have one set of stairs, then we're out the door, across the parking lot, and we're home free. Can you do it?"

His father moved his mouth without opening his lips. *Dehydrated,* Jay thought. He could see that his father's left jaw was sorely out of place, the skin at the jawbone made bloodless where the dislocated bone pressed outward like a popped spring.

"Ggggg... ggggo wi.... ou... mmmmeee." His father's right eye was fixed in place, the dim red light from the distant bulb lending it an ember-like madness. His stare was urgent, but still feeble, without its familiar authority. His lips were shredded into a red pulp, making them look like two leftover grapefruit rinds. Despite the tangled system of burst capillaries in his father's good eye, Jay could see where the implant had been ripped out.

"I... tried... warning you... *run,*" his father hissed, then feebly pushed Jay away and slumped toward the floor.

Jay tried speaking, but it was like trying to operate a nonexistent muscle. He wanted to fall to his knees and weep out of an uneasy mix of gratitude and abject fear. He wished his father could take over then, but seeing him in such a bad state, with such a needy, desperate look in his eyes, he knew that would not be an option. "I know, Dad. I know you did. But I can't leave you."

Four sharp pops echoed from above and reverberated through the plumbing as if someone had tapped a pipe with a small stone. *Gunshots?*

Jay yanked his father back up and pushed him against the cage. "We're out of this, Dad. They got Mom, but they're *not* getting us."

Jay threw his father over his shoulder in a fireman's carry, his fear and anger making the weight manageable. As he made his way toward the exit, the physical strain and stress tunneled his vision. The upright steel cages seemed to bow outward, and the flat cement floor appeared concave under his weight, curling up at the sides. Everything was skewed in the reflective ball of his absolute concentration. Even the door appeared to open unassisted...

He froze. *The door was opening.* A second later, a shadow formed against the blinding daylight streaming through the doorway. He heard a laugh, and the basement was flooded with fluorescent light.

"Ask, and ye shall receive! How wonderful!"

Jay recognized him right away from Stephanie's cell phone picture—Sturgeon. His knees started to buckle. He knelt and put his father in a seated position against the nearest steel cage, then he straightened and faced Sturgeon.

In the candid, bright light, Jay saw all he needed to see to understand how their meeting would end. Blood spattered Sturgeon's face, and his collar was a bloody cravat. A valiant struggle had taken place upstairs, but Sturgeon was the victor.

Sturgeon raised his hands. "I am just simply *slammed* today! Meetings back-to-back."

Jay spotted a flash of metal on the man's hip—a gun.

231

"What do you want?" Jay asked.

"What do I want? What do *I* want? I just want what everyone wants in this economy, simply a *return on my investment*." He spoke in a hysterical warble curdled with false pleasantry. "Remember, I warned you? I said, 'Stop asking questions, and no one will die.' Or maybe that was your father. No matter."

Sturgeon stepped closer, moving with a limp. Blood dripped steadily onto the floor from his right leg. His voice rose to a still-higher pitch. "And I was almost *there,* until my little wards got a bit too ambitious and started snooping around, getting bold. If you could have just kept your asses in place for two more months maybe, I would have been home free, out of the country, mission accomplished. I'd disappear, and you, your dear daddio, the ARGUS, and the Leadership could all go screw yourselves." He wiped his mouth and looked at his blood-spattered cuff.

"You were using the ARGUS to spy on people and blackmail them."

"Well, aren't you clever?"

"And you killed my mother because she found out." Jay figured that if he and his father were going to die, he could at least get the truth out of Sturgeon.

Sturgeon released his gun magazine, checked it, and slapped it back in place. He snickered. "You think *I* killed your mom? Someone *much* higher up than me took care of that. Sure, I considered having her killed. She was the impetus behind the program *officially* closing down. But that didn't last. As soon as your mommy was removed from the picture, I was contacted to resume the entire operation in secret, fully funded, to allow the ARGUS program to complete its full test cycle. And of course, I had to keep an eye on your father and make sure he didn't stick his nose in where it didn't belong, in the *mysterious*, unfortunate death of his wife."

"To do what? What was the program supposed to do?" Jay slumped down and covertly checked for a pulse on his father's wrist. He felt a thin, but persistent beat.

"What did they intend it to do? Take your pick. Prove to the *top-side* government what kind of full-scale data gathering could be accomplished if they had access to the most intimate details of everyone's personal lives. Solve rates for crimes that would exceed all expectations. Break up burgeoning terrorist cells before they could shout 'Allah Akhbar.' It's where everything is going anyway—the city surveillance, the automatic tolls, the wiretapping, the email and Internet snooping. The government has a good idea where you are and what you're doing at all times, but what they really want to know is *where* you are when you're doing the *really bad* things. Anyway, whatever. I couldn't care less."

Sturgeon shrugged and pointed upstairs with the barrel of his gun. "So I was supposed to send all 'criminally significant' feeds to the darkly mysterious Leadership, but I kept a select few for myself, you understand, to recoup the money I lost from the original launch of the program."

Sturgeon moved toward the cage opposite Jay and his father, producing a large key ring. He opened the cage. "Let me show you something. Get in here, both of you."

Jay struggled to drag his semi-conscious father into the cage, then dropped to the floor beside his dad.

Sturgeon stepped over them and moved toward the back of the cage. He pulled a tarp off a stack of cardboard boxes. "There's a network of almost a hundred fifty cell towers in the state, all configured to receive ARGUS uploads and transmit them to our servers here. These boxes represent all of the falsified medical records we had to manage for over five thousand ARGUS RK surgeries."

He pulled the lid off one of the boxes and began throwing file folders over his shoulder. "Of course, you probably know all of this by now, don't you?"

The contents of the folders scattered all over the floor. Jay spotted what looked like dictation notes and a bunch of different kinds of forms like those he'd seen in doctor's offices.

"That's five thousand little dutiful cameras documenting

the worst of human behaviors, the most despicable acts you could ever imagine, and supplying it in a live feed, straight to the government. I don't care what the hell they do with it as long as I get *my money*. I need about three more days for my largest payoff. But I can't have you, dear old dad, and my retarded staff screwing things up."

Sturgeon raised his hands and smiled. "All right, all right. I admit it. I rushed the hiring process. Mea culpa. Perhaps I didn't build the team as solidly as I could have. Maybe I could have done more background checking, broadened my interview team beyond myself. Maybe I should have asked a couple of hypothetical questions during the interview process, like, when I tell you to go retrieve a target, a mere *boy*, mind you, out of a school, does that mean that I want you to quietly grab the little snot by the short hairs during lunch, a bathroom break, maybe at a bus stop, or even walking home? Or does it mean I want you to shoot up the entire place like you're the Terminator and ensure that every goddamned news agency and law enforcement agency on earth comes looking for us?

"But on the bright side, I'm admitting all my mistakes and taking ownership of them. I am *accountable*. But I also will be bailing *myself* out, thank you very much." Sturgeon screamed the last sentence, the cords of his neck standing out like reptiles in attack stances. His angry red eyes seemed to glow in the darkness at the back of the cage.

"What about Stephanie?" Jay asked.

"Never mind her. One more loose end for me to wrap up after I dispatch you two."

"And who's this Leadership? Who are they?"

"Hell if I know, kid. I've told you enough now. So long." Sturgeon raised his gun and pointed it at Jay's father.

Jay grabbed his father's limp hand. He was too weak to pull him anywhere, never mind trying to outrun a bullet. He looked into Sturgeon's contracted eyes and could smell the stress hormones in the room, a blend of bleach and citrus.

Sturgeon tightened his grip as he began to place pressure on the trigger.

Jay heard, or might have imagined, the crunch of cartilage in Sturgeon's finger joints. He squeezed his eyes shut in fear, but then opened them because of the same fear. He saw a piercing burst of light, then heard a loud bang. *This is what it's like to be shot.* But then, he heard an out-of-place sound—the squeal of metal on cement. Light streamed in from the same doorway Sturgeon had used, and Sturgeon's eyes flicked toward the disturbance.

Jay suddenly understood the metal-on-cement sound. In one fluid motion, he leaned away from his father, out the cage's doorway, and picked up the gun as it slid to a stop. He snapped his arm forward as if cracking a whip. He pulled the trigger. Again. And again. And again.

CHAPTER 40

ANNIE TOWNSEND

ANNIE PINCHED HIS INNER THIGH, careful not to use her nails. She did it just enough to hurt him and stop the screaming for a shocked second. The baby's eyes grew wide.

She loomed over him. "Shut up!"

He tried to claw at her face. Little baby's mommy had told her to keep the baby safe in his portable crib when not feeding and playing. She would think the little bastard would be grateful for the freedom.

Usually, the little shit would get interested enough in some object in the house that he wasn't allowed to touch when Mommy was home. That way, the nanny could buy herself at least enough time to get in a cooking show or maybe the first half of *Judge Judy*, sometimes all the way to the verdict.

Yesterday, she had hardly heard a peep out of the baby the entire morning, although she was aware of his presence: the needy white bump of his swollen diaper floating between the ottoman, the coffee table, the sofa she occupied, and the two easy chairs. He was as quiet as one of the cats, right up until he started barfing up the dust bunnies he'd been collecting and eating from under all the furniture. *Dumbass.* Yet another mess she had to clean.

That day, he hadn't shut up since she'd gotten there. "Wah-

Wah-Wah!" All morning. Face like a frigging boiled lobster.

"I don't know what you want!" She pressed the baby's thighs against his stomach. Not gas. "What do you want?"

It was the end of the road for the two of them, she thought. There was hate in his tiny red-rimmed eyes, disgust even. She wouldn't doubt he could sniff out her infertility, the way an animal could sense danger.

Warning: Barren Womb Ahead.

Bastard. She pinched him on the other thigh, and something miraculous happened. His voice went hoarse. The shrill pierce went away. She grunted, straightened, and tweaked her back. She returned to the sofa. Her spot had cooled.

She fussily repositioned her knitting, cursed, and got up again. "You made me lose the remote. See what you did?" She snapped the device from between two of the sofa cushions and turned down the volume that she had previously set on max to drown out and frustrate the baby.

Goddamn kid knew more than anyone gave him credit for. He knew exactly what he was doing. The breathless grunts from the baby were easy to ignore. She soon found herself guffawing again at the screen as she picked up on the thread of the current court case over some hair salon coloring mix-up the day of a bride's wedding. *Hah. Snooty bitch deserved the bad dye job.*

She ripped out the last row of knitting she had nearly completed. It took all her restraint not to get up again for one more cathartic pinch.

Then, she heard a mewl.

Only every other word from the show registered as she counted her loops.

A louder mewl.

You've got to be kidding me. The bastard had found his voice again. She looked over at him as he half-reached for his pacifier. She normally enjoyed getting it for him, after dragging it across the floor to collect as much cat hair as possible.

His whine spread rash-like into an angry red scream, but with a new gurgle. She threw down her needles and sat up, half-expecting to see the baby drowning in his own blood from all the screaming. Her own throat felt raw and burred. "Get it yourself!"

She pointed the remote at the TV to pause the DVR, but turned and threw it at the baby instead. Missed. She felt a burst of relief, but immediately afterward, something caught on the relief like a barbed snarl catching on its end. She would rather have nicked him, shocked him into silence.

"Oh, you want your beebee? Huh? Go get it. You're right next to it. I'm over here."

The baby didn't move any closer to the pacifier, which he had thrown himself, for Christ's sake. He could have reached it if he would only stretch his arm across the carpet. Instead, his little crimson body curled up in a knot and snapped out, straightening like a diver coming out of a tuck. Again and again, a bucking, suffocating fish.

She shot to her feet. Instead of the slight light-headedness that normally filled her head when she stood too fast, fury shot through her. Red, hot, stinging nettles shot out of every pore, piercing her skin. "You want me to get it? From over *here*? You try it then!"

She lunged, picked up his bucking body, and threw him in the general direction of the sofa. She meant to throw him in more of an arc, but her limbs had lost all sense of proportion and depth. The baby bounced off of the back cushion, then the seat, and fell to the floor.

Still screaming, she thought. *Still fucking screaming!*

In a flash, a solution presented itself. Since the boy liked playing under furniture so much, she would leave him there.

She squatted and leaned her side into the heavy coffee table. "Rawwwww!" she yelled, feeling her face bloat and grow hot, her body somewhat relieved to channel the pressure of her anger toward a simple task. The heavy marble coffee table resisted her, but soon relented. She felt it move, and she could see in her blurred, teary vision a lighter colored, newer beige section of the carpet reveal itself. The large piece of furniture slid easier once she had a little momentum. One, two, three inches toward the sofa. Already, the baby's cry was quieting, stifled.

The table stopped. She grunted and pushed once more, but it wouldn't budge. *Oh, isn't that just perfect.* The very nap of the carpet was against her. The entire house. Her womb. The world.

The dim idea that it might be the body of the baby resisting her presented itself. She growled, deep and primal, and pushed again with what she thought would be enough power to lift a small car, her back grinding into the ornate side of the coffee table. The table would either slide or tip over. But it *would* be moved.

In sudden release, instead of the coffee table sliding to the baby or tipping on its long side on top of it, the floor itself gave way. The bright floor had decided to succumb instead. So bright, it hurt her eyes.

Unlike any death she had ever imagined, a trapdoor opened and closed behind her, and unimaginable darkness swallowed her whole.

CHAPTER 41

JAY

AS THE ROOM TOOK SHAPE again, Jay grabbed his right ear. The loud reports still burrowed into his ear canal like scared animals digging into a too-small hole.

"Jay!" Chloe rushed to his side, Stephanie in tow.

Chloe placed a warm hand over Jay's and firmly pulled the gun from his frozen fingers.

Jay got to his feet with a little help from Chloe and went to stand over Sturgeon's body. The man had at least two hits to the chest, and a neat hole in his pock-marked forehead cried a solitary red tear.

"I don't... I don't know what just happened," Jay said, unable to stop shaking his head.

"Stephanie called us in a panic. She said she heard gunshots upstairs at work and didn't know where you were exactly. So I grabbed my dad's gun and rushed here. I'm a good shot, but I couldn't get one off from the doorway. It was all on you, Jay."

Jay looked at Stephanie. "How did you get out of the meeting?"

"I lied and told Sturgeon there was an urgent server issue and I'd be a minute or two late. Then, I heard the gunshots and called Chloe."

Stephanie knelt beside Jay's father, shaking him a little and gently slapping his hands. "Your dad's out of it. We need to get him to the hospital, *soon.*"

Jay nodded. "I know, but I think he's going to make it. He was talking a bit earlier." Then, a funny thought hit him. "Let's put him in with Bennie."

Chloe looked at Stephanie.

Jay felt his heart plummet. "What? What happened? Is Bennie okay? Stephanie mentioned he was away from his hospital bed." A dreaded possibility occurred to him. "No, no. His heart. It was his heart, wasn't it? Shit! Did his heart give out?"

Chloe grabbed both of Jay's hands. "No. We don't know what happened. No one's seen him since this morning. The hospital's in a tizzy, accusing *us* of taking him home. Stephanie was the last to see him. She said he was hacking into the ARGUS network to bring it down when she fell asleep. Did he say anything to you?"

Jay shook his head. "No. Was his laptop in his hospital room, all his equipment?"

Stephanie said, "No. All his stuff was gone. After we reported he was missing to the hospital staff, the local police taped off his room. But I'm sure of it. None of his equipment was there."

CHAPTER 42

WEDNESDAY, 11:01 AM

JAY

FOR **J**AY, THE SATISFYING AFTERGLOW of killing Sturgeon cooled quickly and became a gelatinous, curdled porridge in his stomach, the more he learned about Bennie's disappearance.

They decided it would be best to drop off his father at the ER. For the days his father had been captive, he might be severely dehydrated, and the severe beating might have caused some kind of concussion. They came up with a plan for Stephanie to guide Stephen into the hospital and tell the front desk she had found him looking delirious just outside the hospital. As hard as it was, they knew the best decision was to get his dad professional care.

Back at Chloe's house, they broke into Bennie's locked lab. Inside, they found a note displayed on all the wall-mounted plasma screens. Apparently, Bennie had remotely terminated the hundreds of girly sites he had been hosting and replaced them all with the same message: "If I can't enjoy 'em, neither can you."

Chloe kicked over a computer tower, and it fell flat to

the floor with a loud clap. "He's done so little in this little computer lab, in his little world—a lonely little computer nerd virgin. And he has no idea about his heart condition. He could die even sooner if he overexerts himself."

Stephanie chuckled as she seated herself in front of Bennie's keyboard.

"What?"

Stephanie turned toward Chloe and scratched at a pink splotch that had begun to spread across the base of her throat. "I... I don't know how to say this. But if he was a virgin two days ago, he isn't now."

Jay guffawed. "Are you serious?"

Stephanie nodded, her neck blush spreading. "And I'm guessing you don't know about his online alter ego?"

Chloe and Jay shook their heads. Stephanie told them about the world-renowned HackKneed and his hacker exploits.

"*My* brother?" Chloe asked.

Jay had heard of some of the lesser exploits, but hadn't realized the extent to which Bennie had already upset the hacker world.

"And he *does* know about his heart condition already. He told me that while he hacked into the hospital's network, he thought he might as well look into his own records and see if they think he's a closet gay or a psychopath or something. If he didn't know before, I guess he's known for a couple of days now. Whatever he plans on doing, he's going to do it, and I don't think anyone can stop him."

Chloe laughed through her tears, shaking her head.

Jay's greatest fear had been that the Leadership group Sturgeon had referred to had taken Bennie. No other evidence pointed toward where Bennie might have disappeared to, but it became obvious that wherever he was, he had gone under his own free will.

From one of Bennie's terminals, Stephanie connected to her Waltham office and searched for whatever, if anything, Bennie might have uncovered before he had left the hospital.

She could be more brazen in her search since Sturgeon and his two comrades were dead.

After thirty minutes had passed, Stephanie yelled, "Ha!"

Jay jumped to his feet. "What is it?"

"I was about to give up. I can see that Bennie had been trolling through these huge server logs, but couldn't find anything significant in them. So I decided to take a break and check my email. The answer was sitting in my inbox. It arrived six minutes ago. He must have delayed delivery on purpose."

Stephanie dragged the opened mail message off her monitor and onto a larger wall-mounted screen so all could see.

Stephanie, Chloe, and Jay,

I'm sorry I had to leave like this. I hope all works out with Jay and his dad. Early this morning, I discovered some scary shit, something I don't want to share just yet, but trust me, if I uncover it, you'll all know for sure. The entire world will know. Shit. This thing is much bigger than this little network here in Massachusetts. I hope you understand why I didn't tell you right away, but I needed a big head start, and I wanted to keep all of you out of this. The attachment is for Jay's eyes only. Jay, please do not share.

- Bennie

Jay leaned forward. "Screw that. Open it."

Stephanie double-clicked the email attachment, and a neon-yellow flyer appeared on the screen.

LOST DOG
$800,000 reward
Answers to Shibuya
Email contact- 900knockneedboy@yahoo.com
Dog Breed: Akita
Age: 11 1/2? (not positive)

"What the hell does that mean?" Stephanie asked.

Jay nodded. "It's a local code used to announce raves. We cracked it earlier this summer. He's using it to tell me where he is." Jay scanned the flyer. "I don't understand the huge reward yet. Let's see... The pet name is supposed to be a street name, the email contains the street number. The age of the lost dog is the time, always at night, so eleven thirty. He says 'not positive.' So whatever he plans to do, he wants to do between eleven and midnight maybe?"

"But what day?" Chloe asked.

Jay had to jog his memory. They usually only watched for the colors of the weekend days. "Yellow... Thursday. It's for a Thursday." He frowned. "The dog breed is a new thing. I don't get that, either."

Chloe grabbed Jay's arm. "Shibuya is Chinese or something, isn't it?"

Stephanie popped open a browser and did a Google search. "Shibuya's in Tokyo. And Akita is a breed native to Japan."

Jay pointed at a line on the flyer. "The reward is supposed to be the cover charge for the rave, if you move the decimal twice to the left. But that's still eight thousand dollars."

Stephanie brought up a travel website and typed in some information, then scanned a table of available quotes. "Just a guess, but not an unrealistic price for business-class airfare to Tokyo."

Chloe grabbed Jay's hand. "Do you have a passport?"

Jay turned. "I... yeah. What? But what about my dad? Who's gonna take care of him?"

"Your dad's in the hospital. Stephanie will still be around, and she can tell my parents where he is. They can check on him. There's nothing more you can do for him right now. But you can help me find Bennie and bring him back. I'll tell my parents everything and have them promise to go check on your dad. That'll actually give us good cover to get out of here."

Jay paused to think, but nothing came. The scope of what

she was proposing was too large to fit in his brain. He shook his head. "I don't know. I mean, we just killed a man. *I* killed a man. Aren't I supposed to tell someone about it? Explain it or something?"

"Jay, let them sort it out. Who knows? Sturgeon was so deep under that they may not even open a public investigation. We can't sit around while my brother is risking his life for us halfway across the globe."

"But what if I'm wrong about Japan? Bennie broke that code, not me."

"Answers to 'Shibuya,' and the breed is 'Akita'? No way. You know you're right, and you're coming with me." Chloe stepped toward Stephanie and pointed at the website. "Book us *now*."

CHAPTER 43

THURSDAY, 12:07 PM (TOKYO LOCAL)

BENNIE

DESPITE THE SLEEP SUCCESSES OF his more travel-experienced neighbors, apparent by their rich snores, Bennie hadn't been able to do more than nap for a few minutes at a time. He battled with his nerves, his doubts, and the craziness of what he hoped to accomplish. So instead of sleeping, he worked on his computer. He had been quietly plied throughout the night with assorted meals, snacks, treats, some of which he wolfed down, others which he didn't quite understand or know what to do with. The attendants removed and replaced these offerings with no look of frustration or condescension on their faces, blamelessly blank, calm, smiling, as if his dismissal of these treats were an admirable choice.

Bennie had feared that flying halfway across the globe would belittle the urgency of his mission or make his loved ones and Jay seem smaller, even insignificant. During wakeful periods, he watched out his window, scanning the featureless blackness below. At any given time, without consulting the onboard flight progress screen on his monitor, he wouldn't know if they were over ocean or land. But the cold relief of nothingness served as the perfect backdrop on which to project his thoughts. He saw the helpless look on Jay's face when his friend discovered his house had been broken into. He saw the fear and uncertainty in Chloe's face as she had poked her head around the tunnel and found them. He saw his parents' faces, smiling, but delicately, as if a single faltering expression would trigger the complete collapse of whatever was so fragile in the structure of his heart. Finally, he saw Stephanie's stern expression as they held each other in the darkness afterward, the glint of each eye like a signaling semaphore asking the same question between slow blinks: *Can he do it?*

Sixteen hours after leaving Logan airport and thirteen after connecting in Chicago, the plane was touching down at Tokyo's Narita airport. Bennie raised his business-class leather seat from a flat to an upright position, kicked off the complimentary slippers, and swiveled his private television screen away from him. Remainders of unidentifiable, raw seafood snacks and a glass of sparkling water had been whisked away, along with the heated towels he had learned to use on his face and fingers after eating.

A shock of nausea snaked across his stomach. He tried to dismiss it as a reaction to some of the treats he had eaten in desperate hunger, but he knew it was panic, or at least anxiety. He was too far out of his element to feel confident that he could do it all, but he had to believe that he could.

The flight crew worked their way down the aisle, passing out more steaming towels. He took one and scrubbed the previous night's oils from his face, then wiped his throat and the back of his neck.

As the plane taxied to the terminal, a male attendant retrieved Bennie's slimmer, travel-ready wheelchair from the forward cabin and helped him into it. His nametag read Takahiro. The guy wore a surgical mask, which Bennie thought humorous, but he resisted asking about it, not wanting to insult anyone when landing in a strange land.

"First time to Tokyo?" Takahiro asked in excellent, but muffled English from behind Bennie's shoulder as they worked their way up the narrow tunnel from the plane into the terminal.

"Uh, yes, first time."

"Meet someone?"

"I hope not," Bennie muttered, dreading the idea that any of his family or Jay would have figured out where he had gone so quickly.

"Excuse me, sir?"

"No, I'm not meeting anybody."

"Where you stay? You stay at hotel, then?"

Bennie gave the guy the name of his hotel. The attendant made a call from a small kiosk in the terminal, and a neat little indoor shuttle arrived. The attendant loaded him up and guided him through customs, then helped him retrieve his one suitcase and returned him back to the main concourse.

As the attendant drove the baggage cart over the carpet, a dark sea of silk and wool parted before them. As the crowds made way, a refreshing shock of almost tropical life appeared: a teen boy in dark double-denim and copper-toned hair; a platinum blonde wearing a short blue-and-white gingham dress; another boy, effeminate with caked-on makeup, hair spiked sideways, and a shiny red shoulder bag flashing by his side. Not all of the younger kids dressed in such garish ways, but the ones who did caused Bennie an unexpected pang of jealousy. Still another boy passed, with a stiffly gelled pompadour, a leather jacket over a brilliant white T-shirt, and black jeans. His garish belt buckle was as shiny as a Bentley hood ornament.

Bennie studied the streaming crowds. Without question, absolutely all the kids he saw, and at least half of the adults, were connected—either through cell phones, tablets, or at a minimum, with MP3 players. Most had devices in-hand or strapped to purses, backpacks, shoulder bags, or belts, and several walked by with the universal sign of actively using a cell phone—neck crooked as if nursing a toothache. Then, there were the masks.

Bennie tapped the shoulder of the baggage transport driver. "Excuse me? Why are those people wearing masks?"

The man looked back. "Germs are not for sharing, yes?"

A silver-haired gentleman waved his hand to get Bennie's attention. "Ess-change? Ess-change?" He pointed at a small desk off to the right of the ticketing counters.

"Exchange? Yes, right!"

The attendant helped Bennie into his chair and over to the exchange area. Bennie took out a wad of cash and exchanged three hundred US dollars for yen. The foreign paper bills he received looked like faded, invalid gift certificates, and the coins had holes in the centers.

More workers helped Bennie onto the back of the bus and settled him in a handicapped row with the seats removed. Four men stood nearby, each closely studying thick comic books. From his window, Bennie took in what he could see of Tokyo as it passed by. He didn't see much difference from the scenery in the US, except for the occasional house or building that peeped through the ginkgo trees with curved, layered ceramic tiles that scooped up at the corners like a skirt caught in a breeze.

Every Japanese announcement broadcast over the PA was promptly followed by one in almost British-sounding English. Once off the highway, the bus swerved along streets like a car from the movie *Speed*. The roads seemed barely wide enough to accommodate the bus. The driver worked the large steering wheel as if he were at the helm of a large boat and enjoying all the room of an ocean in which to navigate.

Bennie was dropped off at his hotel shortly before three in the afternoon. The first-class hotel was a tall, shining spire of gold-tinted steel and silver-plated glass, strangely alone on a wooded hill in the center of an otherwise completely urban district. The landscape was immaculately maintained, as if the shrubs had been carved with a laser and the small stones in the gardens scrubbed each night by hand. Even the seams between concrete sections of sidewalk were completely free of debris.

In the lobby, a volley of courtesy was fired at him by an ambushing hotel staff. Bennie checked in, and with the help of a young boy, he finally made it to his room. He wheeled over to the edge of the bed and struggled onto it for some badly needed sleep.

Bennie awoke famished. He checked the clock: 8:12 p.m. Smacking his sleep-stuck lips, he slid into his chair, wheeled to his eighteenth-floor window, and looked over Tokyo. The city truly did resemble a circuit board. The streaming lights from the traffic below looked like the stop-action movement of electrons navigating the traces of a computer chip. Instead of conveying power and authority by the sheer magnitude of its size, the place betrayed a sense of precariousness. Everything was so interwoven and closely constructed that the layout truly did look like some awesome damage could be wrought either by a large tsunami, or for that matter, a mutant dinosaur sea-creature waging war with nuclear breath.

Or by something much, much smaller...

Intuition told him what he was going to hopefully uncover in Tokyo would rock the country, and possibly the world, to its core. But he couldn't save the world on an empty stomach. He studied the pamphlets on the desk and decided he would get in his night of fun in the Roppongi District. And after dinner, maybe he would have some of that hot sake he had read about in the flight magazine. He changed into comfortable black sweats, a long-sleeved silk shirt, and his black leather jacket.

The concierge called for a taxi that could accommodate Bennie's wheelchair. Ten minutes later, a cab driver arrived, wearing a dark suit, a white shirt, and white gloves. He expertly folded Bennie's chair and helped him into the backseat. Bennie settled back and watched the mechanized door close.

"Where to?" the driver asked after putting the chair in the trunk and getting behind the wheel.

"Rapun-*jee*... Rapun-*gee*?" Bennie responded.

The man removed his hovering gloved finger from the dashboard-mounted GPS and nodded. "Ah, yes, of course." After ten minutes of breathtakingly fast driving, the driver slowed. "Where in Roppongi?"

Bennie leaned forward. "Something to eat?"

Three blocks down, the man stopped and pointed at a building. "Very good miso."

After an awkward transaction and what he hoped to be a sufficient tip, Bennie was installed back into his wheelchair. He made his way into the restaurant as the cab pulled away.

A long counter stretching the full depth of the place was empty, except for a young couple at the very end. Steam rolled out of the kitchen, and a sweat-shiny chef moved briskly behind the counter. He glanced quickly at Bennie and then resumed his work.

Bennie sat at the counter and ordered miso soup. He glanced at the couple. *Why not?* Without missing his first international Mnemosyne opportunity, he covertly turned on his camcorder via remote control and positioned his laptop bag so it faced them.

When his food was served, he brought the first spoonful to his mouth in hope and the next out of obligation. The soup tasted like briny, tepid salt water scooped from a low-tide concavity of sand. After finishing half of it, he powered off his camera via remote and headed back outside.

As if capable of smelling the combination of his loneliness and the yen in his pocket, representatives of local gentlemen's clubs began to solicit him. Bennie had never had much luck outpacing any kind of sidewalk solicitor in his wheelchair, which typically annoyed him, but there, he didn't mind.

Quite the opposite. He began to enjoy being sought after so aggressively.

He *was* essentially a mobile lap dance waiting to happen. He didn't take long to a notice a clever pattern in the salesmen. The men would approach him about fifty yards be*fore t*heir respective establishments. Those fifty yards represented the window of opportunity, their cold call, in which they could try to convince him to come into the club.

"Hey, little dude. You like Latina girls? We got Latina girls. *You* like those Latina girls, those big booties... right, my man?"

It quickly become obvious that Latina girls were some kind of exotic import in Japan. Out of curiosity, he eventually agreed. The man led Bennie down an alleyway, into the tiniest elevator he had ever ridden, and through an extremely dark, smoky room lined with reclining women who lazily cat-called him in broken English, referencing "nice boys" wanting to have "nice times." He struggled a little with rolling his wheelchair across the thickly carpeted room. The carpet was everywhere. The floor, walls, and ceiling were covered with a mottled dark-maroon and black carpet, making it look like the inside of a cancerous lung. Bennie finally made it to the far end of the room.

"Nothing you like, my man? Come with me. I know what you're looking for. I know exactly what you're looking for."

To Bennie's relief, the man led him into a twin elevator, and they made their way back down and through another set of alleyways.

"I'll be straight. I wanted to give you the option of the cheap stuff. I'm sure you want to stretch out your yen. Am I right? This place is more 'spensive, but the girls are gorgeous." The man put a firm hand on Bennie's shoulder, a mockingly sincere, sober look in his droopy eyes. "And *clean.*" He straightened, satisfied, as if he had beyond a doubt seen straight to Bennie's soul and finally intuited the greatest of his needs. And it was—*cleanliness*? "Top of the line, my friend."

For the novelty of it, Bennie let himself be led through three more establishments, each of them much the same. In fact, the last one may have even been the first one, approached from the opposite direction with one or two girls cycled out for new ones. The man who brought him lingered in the shadows by the door as if waiting for a commission or perhaps to see if Bennie would conduct a business transaction that would earn him a finder's fee.

Bennie waved the man over and gave him fifteen hundred yen—approximately fifteen dollars, he guessed. "Thanks for trying so hard for me. I guess I have my mind on something else. Can you point me to somewhere I can get some roadside sake, and I'll leave you alone?"

The man gave him a tired smile. "The name's Anyim. Here's my card if you change your mind." He handed Bennie a business card. "Why don't you give those little arms a rest?" He pushed Bennie back out into the Tokyo night.

Anyim left Bennie beside a roadside cart that had set up shop on a small cobblestone street off the main thoroughfare. An ancient Japanese man busily tended to the steaming treats on his cart—triangle-shaped tofu, pork on wooden skewers simmering in a brown sauce, curled octopus and squid legs embracing each other in mutual agony, hugely bloated cylinders that looked like hot dogs about to burst, and other sundry unidentifiable, gelatinous items. The old man, with the scientific exactness and care of handling nuclear materials, ladled a tall glass of hot sake into a glass for Bennie.

"This first one free. I like you." He pointed at Bennie's head. "When I was young boy, I had cowlick, too." He spun around and rubbed his bald spot. "I now have dragon lick." He giggled.

Bennie lifted his glass and poured half the drink into his mouth. The sake warmed his tongue first. He then tasted a half-hearted sweetness that lasted for a second before turning into something less appetizing, nearly spoiled. He downed the second half, and his jumble of nerves began to unwind.

After two more glasses, his thoughts blurred. A slow, luxurious explosion was occurring in his head, and he closed his eyes.

With no clear indication of how much time had passed, he awoke in his chair, chilled by the night air. His head was thrown back, and he looked toward the plum-colored night sky. The constellations appeared foreign and misplaced. The high-rise buildings seemed to lean toward him in his peripheral view.

He straightened his neck and looked for the old man to tell him that he'd had enough, but the magical cart was gone. He studied his watch as the digital numbers performed smooth hula-dancing maneuvers. He forced the multiplying digits together and focused. 1:37.

Shit! He had some serious work to finish before the afternoon, some of which he had accomplished on the plane, but the rest, the critical portion, needed to be done against live systems to see if what he wanted to do was even possible. He wondered if Chloe, Jay, and Stephanie had received his last note and if Jay had cracked it. What would they do next? Would they try to contact the authorities and get some international cooperation over here to try to stop him? Hell, he hadn't done much of anything yet and would regret that bit of grandiosity in his email if he fell flat on his face. *The entire world will know.*

CHAPTER 44

WEDNESDAY, 2:15 PM

JAY

STEPHANIE DROVE JAY BACK TO his house to pack. Afterward, they picked up Chloe, and Stephanie dropped Jay and Chloe off at Logan Airport. They sprinted to the terminals and barely made the three fifteen flight. Boston to Chicago, Chicago to Tokyo. In the air again after a short layover at O'Hare, Jay, for the first time, really understood how small the world could be, and the thought depressed him. In one flight, he and Chloe were biting off about half of the globe in one fell swoop. Never before had he flown over so much ocean—thousands of miles of cold, dark water patiently waiting for a hydraulic valve to give or for a misthreaded bolt to snap and puncture a fuel tank. Whatever Bennie was planning, Jay hoped he was increasing Bennie's chances of success by joining him.

They arrived in Tokyo just before ten in the evening on Thursday, with less than two hours to meet Bennie's cryptic deadline from his email flyer. They took a cab from the airport and encouraged the driver to go as fast as possible toward the address in Shibuya. Jay had a strong suspicion that they were already too late.

An entirely new country's exotic, brightly lit landscape whipped by the taxi window unnoticed. Instead, Jay projected the same video clip over and over again in a loop: Sturgeon's head snapping back and the body collapsing to the floor. The image haunted him. *I did that.* Sturgeon had simply collapsed like a marionette with its strings cut—cut by Jay. He didn't regret killing Sturgeon, especially since it was in self-defense. He wished that it had been in retribution for his mother, but Sturgeon had seemed to be telling the truth about not being involved in his mother's death.

Someone else much higher up took care of that for me.

If Jay had to kill someone again, to avenge his mother, he would be ready. He would find a gun shop in downtown Tokyo and hunt down the person. But maybe it wouldn't come to that. Jay guessed Bennie already knew where to find the Leadership headquarters and at least had some kind of plan for bringing them down.

Jay had to hand it to his friend. Bennie sure was scratching off items from his bucket list fast. He looked over at Chloe, who sat forward in her seat, looking out the windshield as if hoping she would by chance see Bennie rolling along the Tokyo streets in his chair.

Jay studied the lost-dog printout. They had an address and a time: that night, 11:30 p.m., Shibuya Crossing.

CHAPTER 45

BENNIE

IN A SAKE-SOAKED STUPOR, **BENNIE** put in an hour of hacking in his hotel room, trying to get into the ARGUS headquarters' computer system. It was a losing battle.

He broke a little before ten o'clock and resumed work at an Internet café in downtown Tokyo.

Only occasionally sipping a latte, he let his fingers and mind spin. He had enough trace information from the log file entry he had found to narrow down its source. The process he discovered used a tool that essentially copied, or "scraped," an entire operating system's contents, bit by bit, in order to duplicate it elsewhere.

The log entry had been from at least a year ago, but thanks to poor maintenance of the servers, it had not been archived or deleted. Some remote entity had been attempting to duplicate the Massachusetts network from a location in Tokyo. The scraping process would have been obvious to any serious and diligent system administrators, but given Sturgeon's obsessive greed, the Russians' need to spill blood, and poor Stephanie being stuck in the middle, Bennie wasn't surprised the action went undiscovered. The server that had been completely scraped had presumably been duplicated somewhere, unknown to Sturgeon's team. The other servers in Waltham had shown no traces of such intrusion, but that made sense, since there would be no value in copying each because each was a duplicate of the other, working together in a multi-server cluster.

That was their one mistake. They had assumed Sturgeon would complete his task of eliminating the entire Waltham team and cut off the India team's access. No one would have thought to disallow network access of a supposedly dead person. With Stephanie's still-active privileges, Bennie could hack into the remotely duplicated system through a tiny crack in their superstructure and drive himself like a wedge into the wider system.

Once inside the ultimate source of the network server scrape, he began to poke around. He made it past the corporate firewall and acquired several pieces of information that helped him. In his pillaging, he unearthed emails, business plans, prospectuses, and even some engineering server code. The worldwide headquarters were completely self-contained in Tokyo. Two dozen investors from around the globe were apparently financing its operation. The secret company had over three thousand people in its employ, four hundred of which were scientists, computer programmers, and IT professionals from all over the globe. Tokyo had been chosen as the base of operations because of how interconnected the city was and how dependent it was on technology.

Bennie recovered ARGUS work schedules, personnel lists, contracts, work agreements, and design specs. He thanked God that at least for the time being, English, and not Mandarin, was still the premier international business language. In the personnel directory, he found thirty-three of the original forty doctors who had been part of the Massachusetts RK surgery network. Additionally, he found a how-to HR guide on badge security, what points of the facility required badge access, and even a picture of the badge, which included a photograph, a name, an access level, and presumably their corporate logo: an ideographic representation of an eyeball overlaid by a thin net.

As if in a game of Operation, Bennie carefully probed what seemed to be possible vulnerabilities into the final set of internal firewalls, but was ultimately unable to penetrate them. Whenever he could sense the small electric vibration of detection come up his digital arm or the dim red bulb began to glow on the nose, Bennie backed away instantly, into the safety of the digital shadows.

Once, he was sure he had blown his cover when he had discovered and decrypted an especially secure document that outlined the upcoming maintenance schedule for their control center. The document showed which areas of the labs would be down and when for the rest of the year. Bennie had just made a copy of the document for himself when a network sniffing alarm went off on his computer, alerting him a bit later than was comfortable that the document had been tethered to a network resource that had detected his illegal access. Bennie quit the original document with probably only about three milliseconds to spare before he was completely exposed.

He had completed half of his hack, and the script was ready and waiting on his laptop to be deployed. But he was unable to get deep enough into the servers to do everything he needed to do. It was becoming apparent that his only way to bring down ARGUS was from the inside. He slammed his fist down on his computer carrel, making the guy in the adjoining terminal jump.

"Sorry. Uh, *gomennasi*." He had memorized the Japanese phrases for *please*, *thank you*, and *sorry*, figuring the last one was likely to be the one he would need most while on his trip.

He studied the document and realized he might have enough information to be effective once inside ARGUS headquarters. In minutes, he had hacked his way into three low-level access workstations. A diagram of the first floor's network setup provided a handy way for him to cross-reference the machines with their offices.

He pulled out Anyim's business card from his back pocket and dialed the number on his computer via a voice-over-IP program.

"Yes?"

"Anyim, it's me. Little dude?"

The man chuckled on the other end of the line. "Little dude! You change your mind?"

"No, but I have another request. I promise all the yen I have in my pocket if you do this one thing for me," Bennie whispered.

"How much you saying?"

"About a thousand American."

"Sure thing, my man. Sounds like my kind of request. Let me finish up here with a customer."

Bennie could hear the guy's grin across the phone line. "Here's what I need. When I was in Roppongi, I noticed there were a bunch of you guys soliciting. You must all know each other. You're a network of sorts, right?"

"Agreed," Anyim said.

"Well, can you part with some of that money? Pull that group together, as many as you can gather to get as much coverage of the district as possible. Start looking for any guys that have Bluetooth phones in their ears. This is an international operation. White guys would be preferred, if not, lighter dudes."

"Bluetooths in their ears? Shit, man, that's every other dude here."

"But I can make it easier. While you're trolling up and down the sidewalk, dial this number."

Bennie recited the general emergency number to call in off-duty employees of ARGUS. "Let it ring once, maybe twice. Anything more than that, and we'll attract more attention than we want. Once you find anyone answering the call, grab him and offer a free lap dance, no strings attached. I'll cover the expense. When you have him, do whatever you need to do to get his access badge, which will probably be clipped to his belt or in his laptop bag."

"Don't tell me one more damned thing about what you're trying to do because I don't want to know." Anyim chuckled. "And not a penny less than five hundred, my man."

Bennie knew he was making a dangerous play. The emergency number probably wasn't used much, and it was going to take Anyim a few tries to find someone in Roppongi who was also connected to ARGUS. But he was sure of one thing, and that was the libido of the typical computer programmer.

While he waited on Anyim, Bennie continued to gingerly probe at the innards of the ARGUS network. Twenty minutes later, he hadn't gotten any further when his instant messenger blinked in the lower corner of the screen, alerting him of an incoming call.

"Easier than I thought, my man. Good plan. Where are you? I got the badge."

Anyim was outside in minutes, honking the horn of a beat-up orange Jeep. Bennie rolled out to the car, and Anyim helped him in his seat and tossed the wheelchair in the back.

Anyim dangled the badge in front of Bennie's eyes. "You have about two hours before the poor dude can't take no more. I got one of the girls watching him in a private room."

Bennie handed over his remaining yen and grabbed the badge. He clipped the badge to his shirt pocket.

"But the guy I grabbed was fair complected, as they say, but wasn't, uh... You know, he could walk. He wasn't handicapped."

Bennie laughed. "Trust me. No one questions a guy in a wheelchair. If they do, I'll make a big embarrassing scene of it. When I get done, they'll be giving me a police escort inside to get me to shut up. So listen, where I need to go is an industrial park. Chiyoda-ku?"

"Got it. That's about ninety minutes from here."

Bennie looked at his watch: 10:25 p.m. "As fast as you can."

Before they even made the final turn to approach the access gate, Bennie could see the bright glow of the ARGUS complex over the tree line, like a grounded asteroid. When they got closer, he spotted at least four armed guards milling about the gatehouse.

Anyim's easy smile faltered a bit. "What's the plan when we get there?" He pointed at Bennie's leg cast. "You look like you've gotten into enough trouble already, my man. Besides, you don't speak any Japanese, right?"

"Don't worry," Bennie said. "They'll speak English. And several other languages, I'm sure. This is an international enterprise, like the Hadron Collider."

"The what?"

Bennie handed his glasses to Anyim. The man in the badge picture didn't wear glasses. "Just take me to the gate and let me off, then turn around and forget about me. Your work is done, Anyim."

Anyim squinted out the dirty windshield as he drove down the dark access road. "Listen, little dude. I'll be waiting about a mile out, back toward the highway. If you need anything, you get in trouble, give me a call."

"Okay, but I don't know how long I'll be in there." Bennie found his heart was amazingly calm, as if luxuriating in its final allotment of beats, stretching out his life just that much longer. "They have shuttles that take the employees deeper into the complex. I'll take it from here."

A white-gloved hand tapped on Anyim's window, and he rolled it down. Bennie handed over his badge.

The man squinted, then leaned down to look through the window. "If you come in from off duty, no need. We had false alert. Someone compromise our emergency number. We're turning dozens away."

"Oh, no," Bennie said. "I am here for actual work."

The man returned the badge and waved behind him toward the guard post. The chain-link fence opened, and Anyim swung the Jeep alongside an idling shuttle.

"There's your fellow employees, little dude." Anyim raised a solidly knuckled, chapped fist to Bennie.

Bennie bumped fists. Anyim went around back, pulled out the wheelchair, and helped Bennie into it.

Bennie slapped his head. "My laptop. Can you grab my laptop?"

Anyim grabbed the laptop and put it on Bennie's lap. Doubt and worry creased his brow.

"Thanks, man. I can take it from here. The shuttle has a lift." Bennie looked up at his newfound friend. "I really appreciate all you've done."

Anyim bowed his head slightly. *"Gokouun o inorimasu.* That means 'good luck.'"

Bennie remembered one of the only three phrases he had memorized. *"Arigatou."* He nodded and wheeled over to the shuttle. The driver activated the chairlift, and Bennie was soon rolling toward the heart of ARGUS.

CHAPTER 46

THURSDAY, 10:45 PM

BENNIE

FROM STUDYING THE MAINTENANCE MAP he had acquired while hacking, Bennie knew that the largest of the rooms in the complex, labeled A1 Control, would be down for general maintenance from six p.m. until midnight. If he missed that maintenance opportunity, he wouldn't have another until two weeks later. If he could get in there and plug in, he was confident he could shut down the entire system.

He studied the marquee at the security entrance, which directed him to follow the orange stripe along the wall. His obvious, mechanized presence in the hallways drew a good deal of uncomfortable attention, but as he had guessed, no one had the guts to question the handicapped kid.

After some meandering, Bennie's wheels eventually traded highly waxed linoleum for carpet. Bennie headed straight to the first office he had hacked into from the café. It was dark, but locked. Perhaps because of the late hour, or because of the maintenance schedule, most offices were unoccupied.

The second office was also dark, but fortunately unlocked. He slipped inside, closed the door, and let his eyes adjust to the darkness. He rolled around the L-shaped desk, feeling on top of it with one hand—a monitor, keyboard, something that—*shit*—was tipping over! A quiet clink and a gurgle told him he had just knocked over a vase. He forced himself to remain calm and continued to feel along the desk's surface. A phone. He trailed his hand to the back and felt for the outgoing phone cable, hoping it was a nice thick one.

The cable was indeed thick—not a typical phone wire, but a network cable. That meant that ARGUS's phone network was indeed a voice-over-Internet-protocol network. That type had a little known vulnerability Bennie had discovered earlier in the year, but hadn't had a chance to exploit. These phones connected directly to the same network that the computers and servers did, but utilized a different, weaker firewall. He took the phone off the hook and stopped.

He had to think for a second and remember where the number "9" was on a phone's touch pad—third row down, third key over. He pressed "9" to get an outside line, then attached a small speaker he had purchased at one of the ubiquitous electronics stores in Tokyo, rigged with a small battery and computer chip. He ran a program that would quickly go through a series of sounds to place the phone into a debugging mode used by repairmen during service, which also conveniently disabled the firewall.

He looked toward a smoked glass window, making sure no one was passing by and no new lights had turned on. Reassured, he powered on the computer workstation and logged in as Administrator with one of the three passwords he had memorized. He connected via secure shell to his home computer lab, downloaded the re-routing program he needed, and installed it on the workstation. Next, he opened his laptop and overloaded the re-routing hack with the custom code he had written in the Internet café. As long as the office owner didn't show up or VPN into the computer in the next hour, things would be good.

Bennie left the office and rolled down the carpeted hallway

to the back of the complex, toward his final destination—the A1 control room.

"Uh, excuse me," a voice said behind him.

Calm. Bennie stopped. *Shit! Couldn't evil take a Thursday night off once in a while?* Bennie turned slightly in his chair, hoping to give the air of being too busy to be interrupted and to keep from exposing his badge.

A young Japanese man in a white lab coat stood behind him. "Could you please direct me to cafeteria?" the man asked and bowed.

Bennie closed his eyes, awash in relief. He had to squeeze the bridge of his nose to pinch off tears and hoped the gesture came across as impatience. He resurrected the office map in his mind. "You know the south elevators right out this way?" Bennie pointed in the opposite direction of where he was headed.

The man scratched his head, issuing a sharp sucking sound through his teeth. "I think so?"

"Go past the elevators, past the restrooms, take a left when you see the spiral staircase heading up, and you'll see it on your right. Can't miss it."

The young man bowed again, and Bennie was able to read his badge—"VISITOR." *Wonder what it takes to get one of those,* he thought. Maybe there was some kind of legitimate reason for the company's existence, at least on the public face of things.

Bennie waited for the man to leave, then rolled deeper into the hive of offices and labs. After five minutes of working his chair down antiseptically clean hallways, he located A1 Control and a series of labs that flanked the large auditorium on either side. He rolled past A1 and stopped in front of the third door on the left, the one he had located earlier in the day on the floor layout. He wasn't sure what kind of access his stolen badge had, but the floor layout had not indicated a badge swipe, and it was accurate. He pushed his way in and found the room empty of personnel. Waist-high cabinets were pushed against three of the four walls. He rolled along the cases, studying the labels above each drawer handle. Although he was unable to read the full label descriptions, the notation seemed standardized. Even some of the English abbreviations had remained constant. He went down the row and stopped. By how the values of the numbers were grouped together, he was fairly certain he had found the right set. He pulled out a box with a label that read, "OD SPH 225. OS SPH 3." He shook the box. "Got it."

Back out in the hallway, he sat by a water bubbler, pretending to drink, so he could get up his courage. He hoped the maintenance schedule was correct and there had been no last minute changes, or God help him, a notorious IT delay.

He consulted his watch—11:23 p.m. Time was flying. He made his way toward the door just as an array of maintenance engineers burst through with several crash carts filled with monitors, keyboards, and other diagnostic peripherals.

Shit! Shit! Shit! Why had he assumed the maintenance would be done remotely? They had been in the lab the entire time, and if Bennie hadn't paused in the hallway, he would have had a lot of explaining to do.

He gathered his nerves. At the very least, they had apparently finished their repairs early. Once the engineers were out of sight, he rolled into A1 Control. For the first time, he was impressed by the otherwise-bland facility, but also uncomfortably overwhelmed, feeling his plan begin to unravel. The room was not what he expected—at all. In anticipation of what he might find, he had subconsciously begun to formulate an image in his head as he made his way through the complex. He had envisioned the typical setup—tiered rows of computer terminals all facing four or five screens that projected large-scale city maps in live-motion, with real-time analytics and graphics dancing in multi-colored display, numbers and charts and flowing formulae, a throughput of digital information on a God-like scale.

But what he found was different. The recessed lighting

was dim, just enough for Bennie to discern the general layout. The space was auditorium-sized and perfectly square. The individual stations were not desks or shared tables, but enclosed pods that looked like dinosaur eggs.

The pods sat upon concentric square tiers, each tier descending down toward a central pod. The entire room resembled an inverted Japanese pagoda. Each successive tier held fewer and fewer pods, until ending at floor level, where a pod twice the size of the rest sat alone on the glassy black marble floor, appearing as a smooth lotus bud floating in dark, still water. Where the smaller pods measured at most a tight four feet in diameter, the central one measured at least eight feet.

His chair's rubber wheels squeaked across the black polished floor as he approached the center pod. When he got closer, he cursed. The job wouldn't be as easy as plugging into a USB connection and installing his virus. The pod appeared to be constructed of thick, semi-opaque glass, supported at its base by an eight-to-ten-inch transparent glass column that routed several network cables, power lines, and other peripheral cables through a complicated anti-twist spindle system, which then fed directly into the floor. Some exposed gearing on the base of the pod made it appear capable of rotating 360 degrees side to side and vertically to a lesser degree.

His stomach sank even further as the necessity of employing his backup plan became apparent. The pod was as smooth as mirrored glass. He ran his hand over it, relying upon his touch more than sight, and found a fracture. He followed the crack as far as he could reach.

A hatch.

No matter how far he reached, and how hard he tried, he couldn't find any obvious button or latch to open the pod. The semi-opacity of the outer shell allowed only a dim view of a bucket seat with complicated armrests. He could see no other equipment, as he would have expected, like a monitor and some kind of computer workstation. At one spot, he detected a slight vibration, so he placed his palm flat against the glass shell.

Instantly, an electric blue halo glowed around his hand, reacting to his touch like a lightning globe. Startled, he jerked his hand away, but realizing he felt no pain and heard no alarm, he put it back. A muted chime sounded from the top of the pod, and digital Japanese text scrolled across the curvature of the shell, coming to rest above his hand.

A soft female Japanese voice spoke what he guessed were those words. He heard a click, and for a moment, he thought the pod was about to open, but then he realized with sudden dread that the sound had come from behind him. An icy bolt of fear traveled up his spine and split its current down both arms.

"I know you're good at math, Bennie, but I imagine after spending so much time on the right side of your brain, you don't have much facility for foreign languages?"

Beyond all logic, he knew that voice. He continued staring at the pod, terror and confusion freezing him into place.

"To help you translate, my workstation just told you 'access denied.'"

No longer able to stand not knowing, he wheeled his chair around in an about-face movement. Recognition and realization were a couple of two-by-fours striking him in the face, one immediately after the other, as he faced Jay's long-dead mother. His mouth went dry as his mind frantically tried to absorb the incomprehensible idea that not only was he sharing the room with a supposedly dead Elizabeth Brooks, in Tokyo, at the very nucleus of the conspiracy, but his best friend's mother was also pointing a gun at him. Her hair had been cut short and dyed a brilliant copper orange. She wore dark slacks, a blazer, and a light-blue blouse buttoned up to her neck. Her access badge with her photo was clipped to her vest pocket.

"Mrs. Brooks?"

She kept the gun directed at him as she walked back toward the entrance and raised the lights. He got a better look at the resurrected Mrs. Brooks, and despite her new haircut and sharp suit, she didn't look well. She was significantly skinnier than he remembered, and her clothes hung as if on a hanger. Her skin was an unhealthy, splotchy yellow, and exhaustion and stress were visible under her eyes like an athlete's eye-black.

"You look different," Bennie said.

She strode toward him. "So do you, Bennie. I couldn't immediately put my finger on it exactly, but I see now what it is. You've acquired some male bravado. Some balls. It's done wonders for you." She stopped in front of his chair. "I'm surprised you got this far and still didn't know it was me. I've been watching your silly attempts at hacking our system for the past few hours. From an Internet café? Really? Do you really think you snuck your way in here? I all but rolled out a red carpet for you."

Damn. Questions swarmed into his head. He picked one at random. "Who died that day? Who was it in your car?"

"Let's just say that's one less homeless person in Boston for the municipality to worry about. I switched out my dental records with hers... fairly trivial matter for hackers like us, right?"

He was immediately relieved he had diverted Jay and Chloe. His original intent was to keep them out of danger, but he had also inadvertently spared Jay an incredibly painful, perhaps fatal family reunion.

Time to break the emergency glass. Plan B was the only option.

He gripped the penknife in his pants pocket and slipped it up under his shirt. He had to keep her talking and distracted. "You're part of this?" He dug the blade two inches into his side and bit his lip to stifle a swelling yelp that raced up his throat like a gas line explosion rushing topside, hungry for oxygen.

"Part of it? I *run* it. I created it. I *am* the ARGUS project, 2.0. I see you broke your leg. I hope dear old Mark Deutsche didn't do that to you?" she asked.

He successfully smothered his scream, but couldn't prevent the tears that welled in his eyes and slid down both cheeks. He shook his head. "Long story."

She suddenly reached out and pulled his wheelchair a few feet away from the pod. She manually set the brakes on both wheels, then came back around to the front of his temporary wheelchair and slammed the butt of her gun into the cheap plastic armrests. Each blow punctuated a word spit from her mouth. "God. Damn. Bennie. Sticking. Your. Damn. Dick. Where. It. Doesn't. Belong."

Plastic shards exploded across the marble floor in every direction, some debris flying up to sting his face.

Eventually, she stopped and leveled the gun at his face. "Don't move." She jabbed the muzzle into his forehead. His head snapped back.

She straightened, tucked the gun into her waistband, walked calmly toward the pod, and placed her palm on the surface. The pod immediately split into uneven halves. She took off her jacket and expertly slipped into the inner seat.

She does this every day, he thought. *This is her office. This has been her daily existence for who knows how long.* Although the pod was open, he couldn't see the full interior from where he sat, but he could make out a mini-split keyboard, half on each chair arm, two joysticks, and two embedded roller-ball mice.

She typed briefly on the small number keypad implanted in the right chair arm, and the shell closed shut with a hydraulic whisper. The glass suddenly became transparent. Smart glass, he thought—a specialized glass that responded to a slight change in voltage to determine its opaqueness. He watched as she slipped on a headset with an attached microphone.

Bennie twisted the knife farther into his side, feeling the warm blood trickle down into his lap.

Elizabeth's voice boomed over speakers set high in the auditorium ceiling. "First things first. If you try to damage any equipment in here, escape, or hurt me, I'll shoot you right between the eyes." The pod jerked as she grabbed the controls. "I imagine you have lots of questions, but let me start with a demonstration of—"

"Actually, I'm wondering why you abandoned Jay by faking your own death. I'm wondering why you haven't asked me yet how they're doing." He fought to keep his voice steady despite the pain in his stomach.

"You're young. Young, Bennie. And foolishly brave, I'll add. Had you the chance to grow older..." She paused. "Anyway, you would... you will come to realize that life is all about priorities. Life is finite. Ultimately, you have to decide where you want to expend your energy. What is your *most* important duty? What is your calling? And for some, your calling may require, if you are honest with yourself, that you have to make a whole host of sacrifices—sacrifices of your own happiness, of a future with your husband and son, of all that is familiar, all that is loved, all that is cherished, because you want to protect *all* these things, because they're constantly being threatened by those around us that don't have that happiness, that don't share the same ideals. The classic have and have-not scenario. But we now have a solution for taking care of the have-nots who intend to *have* by any means necessary."

She swiveled slightly in her chair. "Let me show you something." She manipulated the joystick, typed on both of the split keyboards, and spun one of the roller-ball mice. The entire pod turned ninety degrees so she was looking straight into Bennie's eyes.

He stared back at her, not knowing what she meant to show him, but soon her face dissolved, and in its place, a facsimile of a computer screen materialized on the surface of the pod.

Hoping she could also no longer see him, he buried the

273

penknife another fraction of an inch into his side. He didn't know how much further he would be able to push it or how much more pain he could tolerate before passing out.

A video appeared on the screen. It was old, maybe from a non-digital Hi8 camera. The edges of the video dissolved into white as if by deliberate artistic decision and not due to the decrepit quality of the original.

A little boy of about five sat on a dark-plaid sofa, smiling and waving at the camera. He had brown eyes and a static-charged mop of dirty-blond hair. Wearing light-blue footie pajamas, he hammed it up for the camera—sticking out his tongue, then pretending to sleep, popping awake, crossing his eyes, and making a pig nose for the camera.

Seconds later, another boy tottered into frame. He was much younger, wearing a dark-green Onesie, his thick, plump diaper pushing out the sides of the Onesie's legs like an overfilled cream puff. He carefully skated along the edge of the sofa, using his hands and shuffling his feet sideways. The larger boy frowned and then leaned forward to pull the younger one up onto the couch.

If Bennie enlarged the younger boy's head, darkened his hair, added a wry smile and a light dusting of burgeoning facial hair, the child would be a spitting image of Jay.

"That," she said, "was Jay's older brother, Jeffrey." She flicked the roller-ball in the arm of her chair, and the video moved to the side as the two boys waved gaily at the camera. "Jeffrey was taken from us. From *me*. I... I literally looked away for a *second*." She leaned around the video and looked directly at Bennie, as if expecting him to dispute this.

He couldn't think of anything to do but nod.

She sat back, once again hidden behind the display. "We were at the food court in the mall. I was having a great day with the boys. They were always such angels together. I was helping Jay into one of those little coin-operated rides, a fire engine. It had lights, sounds, and... Well, we could never pass it without riding it once, or Jay would scream his head off." She coughed out a laugh.

"I was just making sure, as tame as it was, that Jay was holding on good, you know? I left Jeffrey in his booster seat. I had just given him a pretzel. He was right there, quietly licking the salt off the pretzel like he usually did, thinking I couldn't see him. I mean, that's what I don't get. He was *strapped* into his booster seat! Who takes a child strapped to a booster seat?

"I know I couldn't have looked away for more than twenty seconds, at most, and the food court was *full* of families, other kids, other *moms*. We all usually look out for each other. We're each other's eyes sometimes. I just could never understand how Jeffrey could have disappeared so quietly. Not a scream? A yelp? Just disappear so *completely*."

She took an angry swipe at the roller-ball, and the video slid away behind her and disappeared. "Gone."

A long moment passed. In shock, Bennie had no idea how to respond, so he just remained quiet.

"Of course, we never told Jay. He was only eighteen months at the time." She shook her head. "We just couldn't seem to shake the loss in Ohio, so we moved to Massachusetts with the full intention of never letting Jay know what happened."

"If you could have seen—well, you did, there, in that video—how much Jay adored Jeffrey. I know he's aware and misses his brother on some level. We all did. Months after, he still asked if Jeff could come back over for a playdate. You don't know how that hurt. Stephen and I would even call Jay 'Jeff' at times and had to make up a lie to explain why."

Bennie cleared his throat. "Jay told me that Stanley Grayson lost a daughter. That's why Grayson created the Fight Data Recorder that became ARGUS."

Elizabeth nodded. "That's true. We were all well aware of his initial work by the time I was involved."

Bennie continued, "But they shit-canned Grayson's operation because of some fatal error in the software, some video feedback to the transmitter that could cause fatal seizures. So if it's true that you agreed ARGUS should be shut down for people's safety, why would you secretly revive it and leave someone like Sturgeon running it?"

She wiped at the corners of her eyes with her pinkie fingers. "A complete decoy. Once the DOD gave me the order to really kill the ARGUS project, I decided I had to take the entire project out of the country. I needed Sturgeon to keep the project alive long enough for us to—"

"Scrape and duplicate the servers," Bennie interrupted.

"Yes. Apparently, you know a bit more than I gave you credit for." She smirked. "I also needed a way to keep an eye on Jay and Stephen to ensure they didn't get hurt, or interfere too much, or find out too much, for their own good. I wanted Jay to continue thinking I had been murdered rather than have to face the reality of the situation, which is that I *did*, as you say, abandon him and his father, for a greater purpose. I left clues that all pointed toward Grayson and Sturgeon, aka Deutsche. The harmless clue to Grayson was supposed to take much longer and be a dead end. But it aroused too much of Grayson's interest. Did you get the other clue? Pointing to Deutsche? I planted that so his name bubbled up to the proper authorities to eventually shut down the US operations. I didn't expect at all that it would lead to a personal visit. And I thought for sure I had at least one more year before Sturgeon self-imploded. Plus, I needed someone stateside who appeared to be slowly shutting down the program. Sturgeon thought he was part of a secret resurrection of the program sponsored with covert slush funds. And when the revived US operation was discovered, then Sturgeon would take the fall for me."

"And you also made sure Mr. Brooks was implanted with the ARGUS device?"

Elizabeth nodded coolly. "He was always a sucker for a bargain. Yes, it was the only sure way I could have Sturgeon track him, at least when Stephen was excited. As you know, the device triggers video uploads from the implant whenever the person's heart rate hits a designated threshold and adrenaline is pumped through the system at a certain level."

"You mean heart rate *or* adrenaline would trigger an upload," Bennie corrected.

"No, that was the old model, but it generated too much cruft to sort through. Requiring both an elevated adrenal output and increased heart rate is the key."

Shit, Bennie thought. That could affect his plan. "We did figure that out, and that it was powered by body heat."

"That's correct." She then paused, as if considering. "Watch this." She pressed another set of keys, and the entire pod lit up with dozens of video screens wrapped around it from top to bottom, in ten distinct rows, each projected screen about eight inches wide. She worked her joystick to simultaneously spin the pod left and right while the videos remained in a fixed position. Then, she rotated several rows and columns of the screens like working a Rubik's cube. "Each of these screens represents a live ARGUS feed here in Tokyo, events going on in real-time right this moment."

"But how can you continue this program when you already know about its major flaw—the same reason the government yanked it—the random fatal seizures?"

"Grayson was onto a world-altering idea. You couldn't understand unless you lost someone you loved through a violent crime. You just can't empathize or understand the true benefit of such a technology. I became obsessed with Jeffrey's kidnapping and murder, yet I was never able to generate a single lead that would help me find the bastard that took my first baby. Later, I also became obsessed with reality crime shows—cold case stories, forensic stories, unsolved mysteries. All of them had one intensely frustrating thread—every victim had key knowledge in their last moments before death that would have solved their murders almost instantly. More often than not, the victim sees the killer's face. The victim may even learn why they're being killed. They may even know what events led up to their death, key clues that

277

could take decades to discover, if ever. So, Grayson cleverly figured that if we can have black boxes for aircraft, why can't we have the same for people?"

A thought occurred to him. "I'm guessing Grayson's not okay."

Elizabeth shrugged. "I had no choice but to have Sturgeon send someone to pay Grayson a visit. He vowed it would be merciful. The old man deserved that much."

She continued to scroll through the videos. Bennie studied each in wonder. It was a graphical, live tapestry of human need and desire. One person was stealing from an electronics store downtown; another was cutting off several fellow commuters on the highway. An airport traveler stared down at his suitcase while a dog sniffed it. People were exercising. A boy desperately fought what looked like a much larger boy. Each person's life was executing like a mini-software program spinning in a finite loop, the upper index being the day of their death, as they worked their way through several conditional and switch statements, experiencing pleasure when possible or pleasure through pain, until finally exhausting all iterations.

Elizabeth continued scrolling through the videos. "I don't know if you knew this, but my father was in government. He was a key player in our early terror-alert programs. But in my opinion, raising a threat level is not nearly enough. We need to be there, right there, in order to stomp out evil where it stands."

Bennie couldn't routinely watch those videos, even to satisfy his voyeuristic urges, because they contained too much pain—way too much pain, which far outbalanced the pleasure. He wondered what type of person could stare at the innards of human need all the time, day in and out, and not become desensitized. Bennie had to disengage himself and concentrate on his mission. What did he know? He knew Mrs. Brooks had seen him coming from a mile away. He had to preserve any and all advantages. *Play dumb.*

"How... how are you getting so many uploads? Are there that many people that got the surgery here, for real?" Bennie asked.

"First of all, Tokyo is one of the most interconnected cities on the globe. You must know this. You can't escape the reach of a cell tower here. You'd practically have to go a mile underground or miles into space to get out of cell range. And in the latest version of ARGUS, there's no surgery. We've upgraded our client-side software, so to speak."

She smiled. "We're in contact lenses now. *Disposable* contacts. All we require is embedded in the lens itself. Thirteen million people wear contact lenses in Japan. Oh, Bennie, the technology has advanced so *much* in the last year." She brought up a schematic on the main screen.

Bennie looked at it, but was too distracted to study it in detail. The diagram looked roughly the same as the implantable device, but far more sophisticated. "And these people don't know about it? They don't know what their lenses are transmitting?"

"Of course not. How else could they be policed?" She spun the pod left and rotated a column of videos downward. "Look here." She rotated the pod farther so he could see over her shoulder from his vantage point behind her. She dismissed other movies with a key press in order to focus on just one.

The person stepped into a dark room, a bedroom, turned, and closed the door. A nightlight in the corner glowed near a bed, a child's form eventually discernible beneath a puffy comforter. The subject sat on the edge of the bed and placed a hand—a man's hand—on the comforter, where the child's hip would be. He leaned forward, and the girl's face came into full view on the feed. Her eyes were large with fear. Her pink mouth was drawn down at the corners. The man ran a thick knuckle down the soft swell of her downy cheek. The hand moved down, resting briefly on the girl's chest, before brushing the comforter aside to reach her feet. His hand returned up her shin and her knee, raising her pink nightgown along with it. When the hand neared her panties, she tried to push it away, but...

"I think we've seen enough." Elizabeth flicked open a glass-topped panel and turned a key. Her finger hovered over a button on the joystick, then she pressed it.

A message appeared. *"Are you sure?"* Elizabeth confirmed with her keypad.

On the video, the man's viewpoint jerked, then moved to show the ceiling and an idle ceiling fan. The screen went black.

Another message appeared. "Feed disconnected." The single blank screen dissolved, and the full gamut of other feeds restored to the pod's 360-degree view, like a circuit board coming back online after removing a bad node.

"Did you... did you just...?"

She stared at him. "Kill him? On the spot. Sometimes our staff can't react in time to these events, but when we have the opportunity, we take it. That 'fatal error' in the software you mentioned? Well, we decided to take advantage of that and make it a feature. We're testing it on a smaller scale in Massachusetts, and we're now able to control it here. The second the subject puts on our lens and comes online, we construct their signature kill signal and store it in our databases. We can control the random strobe that used to kill people accidentally. We store it now and kill them on purpose. With this enhancement, we actually have enough penetration to cleanse an *entire* city of its evil. Later, we'll broaden our reach to other cities, other countries, the world. Over a long enough period, what we're actually doing is forcibly removing from the human gene pool any DNA that exhibits a propensity for evil. No legislation. No prison systems. Make everyone wear the device. There will be no need to *deal* with these people and lose precious time, precious money over such lost causes. Do you understand? We'll remove this entire strain of miscreant from all human existence. When this program is enforced on a global scale, no government in its right mind would deny it, if not for safety and peace of mind, then for the savings alone. Trillions of dollars can be saved by not rehabilitating, prosecuting, and jailing the slime of the earth."

She chuckled dryly. "Sounds OCD, right? Actually wanting to cleanse the world of evil. But it makes complete sense to me. I have a theory that OCD is a physical vestige of ancient religious rites. Think about it. What other sense could you make of someone who needs to count the four corners of their bedroom ceiling, in a certain order, each night before sleep? Why else would someone spin three times to the left and three times to the right before leaving their house? These are traces of religious ceremonies—physical acts to represent a spiritual commitment. A commitment toward order, cleanliness, justice. Those of us who have a clear understanding of how the world should operate, how it should be *ordered*, I believe, are the most religious. The *most* religious."

So this is what it's like to converse with a crazy person. Her ideas were fascinating in one respect, but deeply disturbing in another. And that she was holding a gun to his head didn't help matters. Bennie pressed the knife into his side with the heel of his hand.

Elizabeth continued, "Eventually, if successful, there won't *be* a person alive who wishes to do intentional harm. We won't need armies, police, legislation. There will be accidents, of course—vehicular homicide, mistaken overdoses. Those are things I think can be handled by our present systems. But murderers, rapists, kidnappers, sexual deviants? The silly hope now is that these people can be rehabilitated. The rehabilitated person is a mythic figure—a griffin, a unicorn. No such thing exists. If you think so, you're lying to yourself. But we soon realized we have to go further than violent crimes. We need to eliminate those people who are developing in that direction."

In disbelief, Bennie watched as she selected several videos at once—a man breaking into a car, a woman stuffing a blouse into her purse, a boy pushing a girl against a brick wall and shoving his hand under her bra.

"Are you sure?" appeared on the screen.

Elizabeth went through the same authorization again, and the three videos blinked out in quick succession.

CHAPTER 47

THURSDAY, 11:35 PM

JAY

JAY AND CHLOE ARRIVED AT 900 Shibuya Crossing five minutes later than they had intended—11:35 p.m.

"Here it is," Chloe said, out of breath. She ran her fingers over the gold numbers on the door's glass, then tried the knob. "Locked."

Jay leaned toward the wide front window covered with newspaper taped up on the inside. He could see past a curled end of newspaper to the dim interior—an empty, dusty reception area with a front counter and three askew folding chairs. If Bennie was in there, somewhere out of sight, Jay had to save him.

"Let's try around back." He pulled at Chloe's elbow.

He ran around the building, looking for an alleyway between the large block of storefronts. He bumped into several people standing still on the sidewalk before he thought to see what had caught their attention. He looked up and immediately froze in place.

Chloe ran into him at a full sprint, and they both went sprawling to the sidewalk.

"Jay! What the hell?" She scrambled to her feet and started to run again.

"Chloe!"

She turned back, and Jay pointed up at the three large television screens, JumboTrons, that dominated Shibuya Crossing.

His mother was staring into the camera and smashing a chair arm with the butt of a gun. Jay gawked at the screen, luxuriating over every live pixel of his mother's face. She looked haggard, sickly, and extremely tired. A hopeful bright light danced in her eyes, but it was an askew gleam, one he had never seen from her. He wiped away the tears that had begun to cloud his vision.

After a moment, he recognized Bennie's chair and his legs, from Bennie's own point of view. He recognized Bennie's T-shirt—"Ask me about my patented teeth-whitening system."

"That's my... my mother," Jay said. He grabbed Chloe and pulled her closer to the screens, farther into the street. His instinct insisted he be closer to her and to Bennie, but then he realized he had no real idea where they were.

"And Bennie!"

The JumboTrons were silent. Streams of people stood still in the middle of the square, stopped in the several overlapping crosswalks. People in taxis and cars honked furiously, not understanding the reason for the congestion. Dumbfounded scores of people spilled out of businesses to watch the screen.

Chloe moved closer and took his arm.

"I don't believe it," Jay said weakly.

"That little jerk tricked us, didn't he?" Chloe started crying.

"I think he did." That was all Jay could say. His mother. All that mourning, all that loss. And she was *alive*.

"We may be the only ones who have the slightest idea what's going on up there," Chloe said, sniffling.

Jay's mind raced. Bennie had discovered the true location of the ARGUS project and had come to end it. But had his friend known Jay's mother was involved? Jay decided that the answer to that had to be no. On the screen, he watched as his mother pointed a gun at Bennie and even nudged his head once with it as the camera swung toward the ceiling and then back again to his mother's retreating form. She stepped into an oval-shaped pod that looked like some fancy chair from IKEA.

Jay noticed Bennie looking down twice to his lap area and saw a flash of something at his side, then blood.

Chloe gasped. "What is he doing?"

"He's keeping his heartbeat and adrenaline up. He got the device, and he's using it to expose the ARGUS project. And my mother." The words sounded strange, but Jay knew with certainty that he was correct.

The volume of honking waned as drivers got out of their vehicles to watch the screens. Frustrated drivers, those who couldn't see what was going on in the square, still honked in the distance. The video changed to show a small boy sitting on a couch. After the kid mugged for the camera awhile, a toddler joined him.

"Who is that?" Chloe asked.

Jay shrugged. "The little one is me. The other one... I don't know, maybe a neighbor."

Next, his mother reappeared. She seemed to be angry, yelling something with spittle forming at the corners of her mouth. The view moved away from Jay's mother and toward a large screen portraying a technical schematic.

"It's another design," Chloe said. "It looks different, though. Is that...? It's a contact lens!"

Jay nodded in agreement and awed disbelief.

More videos—dozens of them—appeared on the screen.

"Those must be live ARGUS feeds," Jay said. He felt as though the entire city watched alongside him as the man on the screen started to molest a young girl. Then, the feed halted, jittered, and went black.

"Did she really just do what I think she did?" Chloe asked.

Jay didn't answer. Did the ARGUS have that control?

Would they really use it like that? Would his mother do that? Did she have such murderous intent to execute people on the spot, however justified it might seem?

The entire crowd collectively gasped as they caught on to the pattern, watching as petty criminals were executed on the spot.

"She can't do that. How can she do that?" Chloe yelled.

His mother, seeming frantic, began selecting several other video uploaders, as if proving a point to Bennie.

On the large screen, Bennie's lap appeared. His hand pulled his right sleeve up to the elbow. In smudged, blurry ink, was a printed message: "Hacked the hospital network. I know about my heart, guys. I love you all. It's *OK*."

Chloe groaned and turned to bury her face in his chest.

Jay put his arms around her. "My mother doesn't know she's being transmitted like this. Bennie's outsmarted her."

"What good is outsmarting her when *she's* got the gun? She's going to kill him," Chloe cried.

Policeman showed up in teams of two and three. The rough insurgence of police, some of them in full riot gear, unsettled the crowd, and people began to scatter and collide in a stampede.

CHAPTER 48

THURSDAY, 11:40 PM

BENNIE

"Y**OU CAN'T DO THIS!**" **BENNIE** blurted. "This is like... like having control of God's own task manager!"

She continued to terminate people at a mad clip, but then abruptly stopped. She breathed heavily out her nose and scrolled through videos, hundreds at a time. "Now, that's how you clean up this godforsaken globe. Remove one goddamned scumbag at a time."

Bennie buried the penknife in his body as far as he could, hoping that final push would release enough adrenaline and increase his heartbeat. "How do you—" A sharp bolt of pain ran through his chest, his body alerting him that it would no longer put up with his bullshit.

Elizabeth raised an eyebrow.

Once he caught his breath, he asked, "How do you explain away all these deaths you're causing?"

"Trust me. It's air-tight. We have battalions of like-minded people from every branch of local government. We have police to forge accident reports, coroners to document completely dull and expected death certificates, and enough presence in the local legislature to quickly squash any heightened concern or awareness of our program." She got out of the pod and stepped toward Bennie, waving her hand at the vacant pods. "We work two ten-hour shifts every day, cleansing the population of these undesirables. I'm guessing you knew that, though."

"You can't possibly think this is the right thing to do."

"Of course it is, Bennie. We've been coddling and siding with the criminal for too long, believing like fools that despite thousands of years of documented criminal history and evidence, people will just 'come around.' These people are broken—broken at birth. It's in their DNA, and that's DNA the world can do without. This is a proven method, Bennie."

She started pacing, in full lecture mode. "We can get Tokyo's low crime rate to go down to almost nothing. A completely peaceful, crime-free city. A utopia. We're already setting up new facilities in Yokohama and Osaka. Then we'll jump to other countries, other continents, like one huge, much-overdue vaccine, but protecting ourselves from ourselves. Intelligence diplomats from several countries have already joined in the effort. Call it a League of Frustrated Nations."

She turned back toward her pod. "That's why, Bennie, unfortunately, I *do* have to kill you, right here, right now, so this can continue. It's bigger than any one person, as I've demonstrated for you already."

She started to reach into the pod. "Wait. What? How am I...?"

Bennie looked to see what had caught her attention. One of the video feeds. *Shit.* On one of her active screens, popping up like digital popcorn, video feeds leapt into place from live ARGUS subjects in Shibuya Crossing. She was seeing several live feeds of herself, video representations projected from the three JumboTron screens in the square, all coming from people in the area with ARGUS lenses, looking at the JumboTrons receiving Bennie's feed.

"You little prick. You have the device, don't you? How?"

Bennie laughed, hoping to sound brave. "I found your original 'doc' list. Three of them decided to follow you here. It was easy to find their office. And I can see so much clearer now, thanks to you. It's really a miracle. I'm just glad you kept the same network protocol. As a customer, I thank you for your commitment to backward compatibility. That made it so much easier to redirect my own signal, once it came online. I may not have successfully hacked my way into this place, but I've just successfully hacked my way *out*."

Elizabeth let out a roar as a quarter of her own screens filled with uploads from ARGUS subjects rushing to the square to view her self-incriminating videos. She rushed to her pod and began killing each of the feeds as quickly as they popped up on the screens. She worked so feverishly, her hands slapping the console and controls, that she appeared to be playing a game of Whac-A-Mole with horrific, fatal results.

CHAPTER 49

THURSDAY, 11:42 PM

JAY

SCREAMS SLICED THROUGH THE SQUARE, glancing off each other, in varied pockets of hysteria. Jay could see his mother knew she had been exposed. He was horrified, watching her frantically kill off subjects.

News crews had arrived and begun filming. Among the incomprehensible Japanese flowing from the on-scene anchors, Jay caught the frequent use of Bennie's name. The technicians behind one of the JumboTron screens finally recovered from Bennie's hack and started broadcasting local live news. A picture of Bennie smiling in a family photo was displayed. Jay hoped they would leave the second and third screens alone and let them continue with Bennie's feed.

People began pointing between the screens as comprehension spread like a wave through the crowd. A surge from a throng of people pushed Jay and Chloe to the left. A teenage girl writhed and jittered against the pavement, bubbles frothing at her mouth, her eyes gone white. A young man, perhaps her boyfriend or brother, tried to hold her still.

More screams rang out as medical personnel ran through

the crowd, helpless and without a single idea of how to control the chaos.

"Shit!" Chloe yanked at Jay's sleeve, directing his attention from the crowd back to the two remaining Bennie feeds. "She's trying to find Bennie's signal now."

Jay watched the screen. His mother had given up trying to kill random people in the square and had begun to rapidly flag through video feeds, with purpose. Chloe was right. Mom was looking for one thing, and it was surely Bennie's original video feed. She used both hands, desperately working the controls.

Jay could no longer imagine what was going on in his mother's head. He just couldn't reconcile the image on the screen with the woman who had raised him. He squeezed his eyes shut. Wasn't that the solution anyway? The solution to it all? Just don't look? He reinforced his blindness by placing his hands over his eyes. *Yes, just don't look.* He didn't want to watch his best friend seize his way into a death sentence delivered by his own mother.

"Don't." Chloe pulled his hands away from his face, her grip on his wrists surprisingly strong. "We owe him this much," she said, crying.

She was right. Bennie was showing courage and self-sacrifice. Jay owed his friend that much, to watch until the end. He looked back at the screen.

His mother worked the mice-balls and controllers like a child playing her first console game. Her search no longer seemed methodical, but purely chaotic, as she randomly flipped through rows and columns of videos.

"Why doesn't he leave? Maybe... Oh, God, why doesn't he just rip the lenses out? Bennie!" she yelled at the screen.

Jay didn't know the answer. He supposed that as soon as his mother saw Bennie remove the lenses, she'd simply turn and shoot him in the head. But while she could, she was going to go for a techno-kill, her clear method of choice.

"I love you, Ben," Jay whispered. He watched with clenched

teeth. What he was looking at would be the last live images of Bennie he would ever see—the first publicly televised death from the dying person's very own eyes.

But instead, something changed.

From what he could tell by the camera's unsteady, but discernible rise, Bennie had begun to *stand*. A roar ripped through the crowd like a holocaust, the city on fire with emotion as Bennie made his way toward Jay's mother. Hot tears singed Jay's eyelids.

Bennie was standing. He stood, somehow, at his fullest height. Next, Bennie fell forward, as if he were on stilts that had been kicked out from under him. The crowd sucked in its collective breath, but the frame corrected itself, and the people responded with another triumphant roar.

Chloe grabbed Jay's arm with both hands, jumping up and down, crying, laughing, and screaming. "That's his scissor gait. I haven't seen him try to walk in three years! That lazy little crazy bastard can do it!" She shook Jay until his teeth chattered.

But it wasn't easy for Bennie, Jay could see. Not only was Bennie not used to walking, but his right leg was still in a cast. The camera view lurched from floor to ceiling, and only a glimpse of his mother could be seen each time, scrolling up, then down, then up, then down. But Jay could see she was still preoccupied with finding Bennie's feed.

The crowd began chanting, "Ben-nie! Ben-nie! Ben-nie!"

Jay couldn't bring himself to chant along with the crowd, perhaps due to some intractable splinter of allegiance to his mother, but also out of doubt that Bennie would reach her before she found his video feed. He worried that what they were witnessing was an admirable, but vain effort. And what could Bennie do once he surprised her? She would quickly overtake him, and her gun was a hand flick away.

CHAPTER 50

THURSDAY, 11:48 PM

BENNIE

BENNIE HAD SWORN HE WOULD never in his life try to walk again, aside from the two short steps he had tried three years back. Never in his *life*. But in *death*, he would make an exception.

When he stood, the collected pool of warm blood from his lap dribbled and soaked his pants down to his shoes. The blood loss affected him more than he had expected. Mrs. Brooks was an impossible distance away, and she had an uncomfortably wide span of time to look back at any time and see his pitiful advance. Still, he continued, feeling like the straw man in Oz as he dragged his folded legs with a lurching, hip-based motion, painfully acquiring his balance by grinding his overlapped knees together and balancing with his arms stretched out to his sides.

He knew what she was attempting to do, to kill him with the reverse ARGUS signal. Ironically, he no longer had the choice of taking out the contact lenses because he wouldn't be able to make his way toward the pod without them.

A banging started on the door, sounding as though an

effort had begun to shoulder it open or use one of those heavy door buster tools. He expected Elizabeth to turn at the sound, but she was committed. She remained hovering over the pod's console, obsessed with terminating Bennie's life with the same technology he was trying to expose.

Each step Bennie took was an injection of a year's worth of memories, dislodging themselves from the inner recesses of his brain and fluttering out like so many previously cocoon-bound butterflies.

His mother, who had unsuccessfully struggled to hide her sense of guilt over his condition. His father, awkward, burly, non-communicative, but in his own helpless way, as devoted a father as Bennie could imagine. His sister, with all of her protectiveness, her awkward period of hating him, rebelling against him and what his condition robbed her of, her eventual coming around. His best friend, Jay, a friend like none he had ever hoped for, who stuck with him *because* of him, not in spite of him, loved him for who he was, and forgave him for the person he disguised himself to be. And finally, Stephanie, for her warmth, her awe, and her passion. If he were completely honest, he loved her all the more for her loving him so much. If not for her being brave enough to breach Sturgeon's firewall and alert them, they would all be as dead as that cell tower repairman.

As if gliding on some other force, he suddenly found himself directly behind Mrs. Brooks. He jammed his left hand into his pocket and felt for what he needed. He pulled out the object and popped off the protective cap with his teeth.

To his horror, he looked over her shoulder and saw that she had finally found his video feed. She was looking at herself, but from a much closer vantage point than she surely expected.

The warning message appeared. "Are you sure?"

She placed her finger on the confirmation button and pressed it.

As he made his move, his last thought was of knowing he

could always *outthink* a computer, but for that moment, he had to physically *outrace* one. *Bennie versus machine.*

He jammed the prepared syringe into her neck—a fatal dose of his Botox. She turned and screamed, grasping for the source of the pain like an enraged dinosaur in a Creature Double Feature movie.

Bennie's knees buckled, and he dropped to the floor as an entire cosmos of light entered his eyes. He knew it was beautiful; he knew it was sad.

He knew it was the end.

EPILOGUE

ONE MONTH LATER

JAY

MOST OF THE UNKNOWING SUBJECTS of the ARGUS program had been contacted and informed of the situation. Not only were their corrective RK surgeries paid for, but generous settlements had also been furnished for all the victims, with the tacit agreement that they would never speak of it, or at least until the full investigation was complete and the findings were shared with the world.

The FBI and local authorities deemed it a waste to destroy the collected video in Waltham. In a weird way, Jay reflected, his mother had been right. Follow-up investigations solved sixty-seven violent crimes in a matter of a week, including the female jogger murdered in Jefferson Park. Several other videos had leaked out, destroying the high-profile careers of several people in Massachusetts local government and that of one professional football player.

Analysis of the ARGUS technology showed a certain expected latency, or delay, of a few hundred milliseconds in the transmissions. Jay liked that for Bennie's sake. Seconds after Bennie's death, after he was killed by Jay's mother, he was still uploading, having opened his last output stream with what Jay liked to imagine as the contents of his soul.

Jay's father learned that he had been stonewalled in the FBI's investigation because they, too, had suspected Elizabeth Brooks's death was related to the shutdown of the ARGUS project. But they couldn't confirm it, and the problem had been compounded by the revelation that one of their junior agents had been bribed by Sturgeon to head off any concerns raised by Stephen.

Sturgeon, if not having the last laugh, enjoyed at least one of them. The FBI had not sufficiently vetted him. He had even used a fake name, Mark Deutsche, a laughably obvious reversal of Germany's predecessor to the Euro, the deutsche mark.

Jay's father had the first of the reversal surgeries and was healing fine. He confirmed for the FBI the spot of his original surgery, the same Sudbury clinic Chloe had visited and found vacant.

Bennie's body was brought back to the US for a proper funeral. An autopsy revealed what Jay, Chloe, and Stephanie had suspected—that he had deliberately stabbed himself throughout his encounter with Jay's mother in order to continuously transmit the incriminating video in Shibuya Crossing.

Audio recordings from A1 Control had been recovered and analyzed, and a soundtrack had been overlaid onto the silent video Chloe and Jay had witnessed live. After watching the video several times, Chloe picked up on the barely discernible segment where Bennie had seemed to lose his composure for a fraction of a second when he learned the new transmission protocol required an elevated heartbeat *and* adrenaline.

"I think he was hoping his tachycardia would transmit the entire time, but he had to inflict pain to increase his adrenaline. I just can't imagine..." Chloe said.

Reviewing the video, they also noticed that Jay's mother came dangerously close to discovering Bennie's plan. She had commented that he looked different. She just didn't realize that he was missing his signature glasses. Records showed Bennie had been fitted with the ARGUS lens after forging a Japanese ophthalmologist's prescription... in Japanese, which was no small task.

With the initial insistent presence of the paparazzi, attempting to go about their normal everyday lives was like wading through tar. In the media universe, the Brooks and Welch households flared like bright planets for a time, each with its own ring of reporters constantly circling their properties, eager to learn anything about Bennie that couldn't be gleaned from the Internet. What were his other exploits? How had Jay met him? Did Chloe and her parents recognize his early genius? Leaving the house inevitably led to a low-speed chase to the mall, or the pharmacy, or the grocery store. A common oath sworn between the families pledged not to feed the media's appetites. After the initial few weeks, the attention predictably turned to something else entirely, just as an infant could be distracted from something they could no longer see.

Jay and Chloe continued to see each other, almost daily, most often to piece together those last days and the incredible efforts and insights Bennie had made. Also, they made a project of distributing Bennie's Mnemosyne video files for free, a small gift back to the world, some retribution for the death, horror, and sadness Jay's mother had wreaked across the globe. In the spirit of the original project, Jay and Chloe redistributed the video files anonymously via mini-DVDs wrapped in pristine white paper.

They watched the videos in advance, meeting nightly for several weeks to convert them to DVD and ensure nothing untoward would be delivered to the subject. Ironically, they found no inappropriate videos of sex acts, shared drug use, or anything else incriminating. Jay was taken aback with the high quality of the videos, surprised to see Bennie'd had the emotional acuity to anticipate the precious moments and to ready his camera to capture them.

Through this common activity, Jay was able to see there was much more between Chloe and him than just an irrational bonding through some crisis. Although chiefly a somber occasion, they often found themselves laughing together as they listened to Bennie's unconscious mutterings and his curses when he was discovered and ejected from wherever he was videotaping.

It filled Jay with great sadness to picture what wasn't captured—the person sitting on the other side of the lens, Bennie feeling his own loneliness exaggerated even more so by those extreme moments of tenderness, sharing, and love.

A month after Bennie's death, on a balmy summer evening, Jay was washing out his father's brushes, a nightly activity since his father had requested his painting materials from the attic. Dad was finally reacquainting himself with the art form he had grown to despise in the last year while under Sturgeon's watchful eye.

Jay stared out the kitchen window, watching the sunset play tricks on the eye by giving the maple trees a look of premature fall. He still had so much to personally process— losing his best friend and losing his mother a second time. Whenever he was driving, the sudden appearance of a black SUV behind him still caused his heart to flub, and the dark, grim features of Sturgeon's face continued to appear in the darker shadows of his dreams, where Jay had to kill him once again. But at least it was getting easier.

As for losing his mother, he had come to recognize the bulk of his mourning had been accomplished after her first "death." In his heart, her betrayal of him and his father had settled that. But the splinter of hope he had clung to throughout the year, that his mom was somehow alive, was still something to be dealt with. It almost seemed to Jay that with his grandfather's involvement with the terror alert system, his mother's allegiance to her father trumped all, above and beyond her own family. He wasn't sure that was everything to be said or thought on the subject and suspected he had years left to consider his mother's thought processes that had led her to possess no more compassion than a common warlord. He had so much to absorb, but he knew he could do it with his dad's help. Re-losing a mother. Regaining a father he had thought he lost, emotionally at least. He also had to work through gaining and losing a big brother in the same split second. His father had brought out an album of hidden photographs of Jay and his older brother, Jeffrey. Jay kept the album by his bedside. He flipped through it most nights, unable to resist taking a few out from behind their protective transparent covers to handle them directly. He enjoyed feeling under his thumb the somehow reassuring, bumpy surface of each picture's white frame as he studied it. He couldn't find a single picture where Jeffrey wasn't smiling. Some nights, as he worked through the pictures, his father would join him, initially talkative, but then soon silent as his words caught in his throat. His father had explained to Jay how the cyan dye was the first to fade in instant photographs, ultimately infusing each with a canyon-like red and imbuing them with an other-worldly feel that was helpful to Jay. But ultimately, the pictures weren't enough. To digest everything and to work through their grief, his father had scheduled them for joint counseling.

Much was being written about the Tokyo event, and several television, movie, and book deals had been presented, all of which were summarily rejected by Jay's father.

Jay found it ironic that he had always dreaded the day when he would have to leave Bennie in order to move on with his life, and instead, had been faced with the opposite. Bennie had taken leave of Jay. But Bennie had gone in the highest of style, rather than waiting timidly for his heart to finally give out in a quiet hospital room.

Bennie's online persona, HackKneed, was celebrated and memorialized over the Internet. The live video feed from Shibuya Crossing had gone viral, bringing down YouTube for a solid day and a half when it premiered. Bennie's efforts were said to have inspired a revolution of philanthropic hacking. In Bennie's memory, an assorted collection of hackers, under the assumed collective name "HackKneers," committed themselves to the greater good. Jay had initial doubts about their long-term success, until one day when he received a postcard from a small town in Colorado with a short message: "Lost any dogs lately? Having fun spearheading HackKneers." It was signed simply: "S."

Jay was consoled greatly by having Chloe in his life, the fact that his father was slowly recuperating, and to some degree, that he had once had a brother.

He lifted the small kitchen window sash, letting the fumes of the brush-cleaning chemicals escape. He was just turning off the kitchen light when he heard a car honk in the driveway. He rushed to meet Chloe at the door.

She stood on his porch, as beautiful as ever. A sweet smile spread across her face, golden in the porch light that had been triggered at dusk. Whenever she was so close to him, his arms literally itched and ached, as if restless leg syndrome had infected his upper torso and could only be relieved by holding her. He gathered her in his arms.

"I have a delivery for you," she whispered.

He led her into the house, keeping an arm around her. "What?"

She dug into her back pocket and pulled out a mini-DVD. "What's on it?"

She just shrugged, took him by the hand, and led him into the living room. "Sit."

She pushed him into the leather sectional, then went over and turned on the television and DVD player. She grabbed the remote and joined him on the couch. She pressed play.

A low-quality video shot from a high vantage point showed a small room. A bedroom, Jay thought. Most of a bed could be seen, along with a dresser, a closet, a single window, and some girly-looking adornments on the walls.

"So... what? Whose video is this?" Jay looked over at Chloe. Her eyes brimmed with tears, ready to overcome the levee of her eyelids, but her smile remained.

Jay turned back to the television screen and spotted movement in the lower corner. A head. The head of someone crawling across the floor. He sat forward and studied the scene, then laughed and fell back into the sofa. Bennie, in the ether somewhere, out in the cloud, had still gotten the best of him.

"That's me," he said.

Chloe reached out and pulled him closer, resting her cheek on his chest. "I know. I've watched it all."

Jay felt a mixture of embarrassment, amusement, and self-pity as he watched himself prowl through Chloe's bedroom... more times than he would have thought. Items slowly changed in the room, varying in levels of cleanliness, position of furniture. Even Jay's hairstyles changed, but one thing remained constant. He watched himself nuzzle his face into her pillow, perform snow-angel-like motions on her bed, and bury his face in her drawers and closets.

"Boy, am I a creep," he said, and flopped into Chloe's lap. She giggled. They continued to watch as she slowly stroked his hair.

He could feel his face turn red, flushed with hot blood. A typical fight-or-flight response. But he would do neither.

Although he *was* embarrassed, he also imagined with wry satisfaction his friend Bennie watching the live feeds from his lab each time Jay had excused himself upstairs. All those nights Jay had thought he was safely alone in Chloe's room, he hadn't been. But that was okay.

A friend had been behind the lens.

ABOUT THE AUTHOR

COLLIN TOBIN LIVES IN MASSACHUSETTS with his wife and two daughters. He holds a bachelor's in English and master's in Education. He has worked in the software industry for the past twelve years.

He was the lucky recipient of the Mississippi Literary Festival's 1st place in poetry and has also published poems in "character i" and "The Drum."

When he's not writing, he enjoys re-reading Nabokov's fiction in chronological order, eating very hot salsa, and dreaming up inventions with neither the capital nor the initiative to see them through.

25719965R00183

Printed in Poland
by Amazon Fulfillment
Poland Sp. z o.o., Wrocław